Praise for Julia Buckley

"Julia Buckley's delightful new series debut . . . includes three generations of strong, intelligent women, craving-inducing discussions of food, and a fascinating background of Hungarian culture along with a dandy mystery."

—Miranda James, *New York Times* bestselling
author of the Cat in the Stacks Mysteries

"Buckley's pleasantly old-fashioned fourth is filled with credible suspects and a creeping sense of menace."

—*Kirkus Reviews*

"Awesome. . . . It is never a surprise that author Julia Buckley writes a winner." —*Suspense Magazine*

"With her Writer's Apprentice mysteries, Buckley both delivers a solid new amateur sleuthing series and pays homage to marvelous old gothic and romantic suspense novels by Mary Stewart, Phyllis A. Whitney, and Elizabeth Peters."

—The Booklist Reader

DEATH OF A
WANDERING WOLF

A Hungarian
Tea House Mystery

JULIA BUCKLEY

BERKLEY PRIME CRIME
New York

BERKLEY PRIME CRIME
Published by Berkley
An imprint of Penguin Random House LLC
penguinrandomhouse.com

Copyright © 2020 by Julia Buckley

ISBN: 9781984804846

First Edition: June 2020

Printed in the United States of America
1 3 5 7 9 10 8 6 4 2

Cover art by Sara Mulvanny
Cover design by Vikki Chu
Book design by Laura K. Corless

This is a work of fiction. Names, characters, places, and incidents either are the product
of the author's imagination or are used fictitiously, and any resemblance to actual persons,
living or dead, business establishments, events, or locales is entirely coincidental.

PUBLISHER'S NOTE: The recipes contained in this book are to be followed exactly
as written. The publisher is not responsible for your specific health or allergy needs that
may require medical supervision. The publisher is not responsible for any adverse
reactions to the recipes contained in this book.

To all the Rohalys

All stories are about wolves.

—MARGARET ATWOOD

Wither'd Murder
Alarum'd by his sentinel, the wolf, whose
howl's his watch . . .
Moves like a ghost.

—WILLIAM SHAKESPEARE,
MACBETH, ACT 2, SCENE 1

Chapter 1

....

THE WOLF

My friend Katie called to me over several tables laden with wares at a Riverwood garage sale; we were there, at my insistence, at eight on a Saturday morning, when one might still find treasure. Since the October wind was blustery and held specks of ice, the sale's host was displaying his wares in his basement, which made me feel that I was in some eccentric antique shop; and indeed the dim, white-walled room was bulging with items and with possibility. "Hana, look at this! What a gorgeous sweater! Come here. This would look amazing on your hunky boyfriend."

I strolled toward her, my eyes scanning dishware and linens. One wall that I had not investigated yet held un-framed canvases adorned with original paintings, signed by the artist. Even at a glance I could tell they were very good—the work of a professional. I reached Katie, and she thrust the sweater into my face. "Look at this! It's an Ulveflokk. I'm dying to visit their store. It's right down the street from where I work, but I never have time. They were just featured on the Channel Seven news. Did you see them?"

"No. What's that weird name?"

"Ulveflokk! They're Scandinavian or something. But look at this!" The sweater was indeed lovely, a pale wheat color with a bright blue fleur-de-lis around the turtleneck, an elaborate dotted design in a lighter blue beneath that, and finally a solid wheat at the bottom. "Cotton yarn, very soft," she said.

"Why don't you get it for Eduardo?"

She looked away. "I don't know if we're dating right now. It's not his color, anyway."

"What do you *mean*, you're not—"

"Hey, Hana!" she cried, thrusting the sweater into my hands and lunging toward something a few tables away. "Oh my gosh, I'm finding everything that you're not today. You trained me well." She jogged to a shadowy corner and said, "You are going to owe me a *million* dollars!"

If people were punctuation, Katie would be an exclamation point. She came back, grinning from ear to ear. "I just found one of your Hungarian things. The company with the diamonds."

"What?"

"You know." She was hiding something behind her back; her eyes were wide with the joy of discovery. "That net covering."

"The fishnet design? Do you mean a *Herend* piece?" The Herend porcelain company in Hungary had a distinctive technique that set their figurines apart. Dating back to the 1800s, the method was inspired by a Chinese technique using a "fishnet" painted design meant to simulate the scales of fish. It ended up becoming a Herend signature look, and, of course, it made their figurines stand out.

"Yes," Katie said. "Tell me I'm the best friend." Her dark ponytail fell forward over her left shoulder as she leaned toward me, her brown eyes alight.

"You are, but first let me see what you have."

She revealed the figurine with a flourish: a small statue of a wolf, about seven inches long, covered with a chocolate-brown fishnet design.

"Oh my God," I breathed. "Katie, you are an amazing goddess of victory."

"Oooh, that's better than what I said to call me."

I took the figurine to study it more closely. "It's a Herend." I checked the maker's mark to be sure. "This is one of their wolves—they come in several colors, and this is the chocolate fishnet finish. God, it's beautiful! I've never seen one in person, just in the catalog. Look at the detail!"

Katie jumped around, eager as a child. "You have to buy it."

I hadn't even paid attention to the tag. What would he want for this? Brand-new it was worth more than five hundred dollars, sometimes even more, depending on the source. I looked at the porcelain belly of the beast, where the tag said five dollars. "Oh no," I said. "This would be like stealing. I have to tell him." An unhappy feeling rose in me, threatened to engulf me, and then receded.

"No, you don't," Katie whispered. "Finders keepers. Give him the five bucks and put it on your treasure shelf."

"I can't. I have to be honest with him." Katie murmured some protests as I walked up the aisle, past a few other browsers, and approached the man who sat in a lawn chair at the foot of the basement stairs, sketching in a book. I was momentarily distracted by the sketch—it seemed to be some kind of fairy, and the drawing was outrageously good for something he had tossed off in a dim basement.

"Hello," I said. "I'd like to buy some things. This sweater"—it would, in fact, look very good on my blond boyfriend—"and this." I held up the wolf. "But I have to tell you something. You're only asking five dollars, and it's worth much, much more. It wouldn't be fair of me to under-pay that way. Can I make you an offer?"

He looked to be somewhere between forty-five and fifty; his wavy brown hair tinged with gray made him look vaguely like a Romantic poet. When I spoke, his face, ruggedly hand-some but sort of tired-looking and grizzled, didn't change at all. No gleam of hope at the thought of a bigger sale. "Guess what, hon? It's worth no more than five dollars to me. So if you want it, that's all you have to pay. Frankly, it's got bad associations. You ever dislike a person who gave you a pres-ent? Maybe even wanted a restraining order?" He made the last thing sound like a joke.

"Oh, uh—"

He smiled. "No, you're not the type. You have that sweet little face. And hair like fire at twilight. You'd be a great subject for a portrait." His expression showed the first glim-mer of animation.

"Oh, you're the artist? Of all those paintings on the wall? I'd like to look at them, too. I'll just set these down on your windowsill. Don't let anyone else take them."

"Scout's honor," he said with a smoky laugh.

I went back to Katie. "He doesn't *care!* He's going to give me the wolf for five dollars." The joy of the collector surged within me, and for a moment I felt ready to jump along with my peppy friend. "But let's look at these paintings. He's the artist, and these are originals. I'm going to text Falken, let him know about this treasure trove."

Falken Trisch ran an antique shop called Timeless Treasures; it was one of the most distinctive shops in Riverwood. He and I had become friends over the last couple of years, and I regularly haunted the aisles of his lovely, whimsical store. I texted him: Just found a Herend wolf and a bunch of really good original paintings at a garage sale on Harrison. You should check it out! I think the ad said he's here until two.

Katie and I moved to the back wall, where the canvases were lined up thematically: on the left were landscapes; in the middle, still lifes; and on the right, portraits.

"These are crazy good," Katie said, moving toward the portraits. "Look at this old man's face. He looks like some ancient prophet. How did the guy get this effect, with all the fine wrinkles? That's amazing."

I nodded, then studied the landscapes on the other wall. They, too, were special, distinctive, with a subtle yet masterful use of color. I couldn't recall seeing forests that looked so grand or mysterious. One of the pieces, a street scene, caught my eye. It was whimsical and nostalgic, yet also sad; the houses seemed to lean against the wind that blew down the street, their colorful rooftops shining bright against a heavy gray sky. It was the painting of a memory. At the bottom he had scrawled "Keszthely, Hungary," and then his name: "William Kodaly."

"He's Hungarian," I murmured. I checked the back of the painting and saw that he was asking twenty-five dollars. Again, an undervaluing of what was clearly a valuable piece. Katie was gazing at a portrait of a man on a horse.

"I don't know why I love this, but I love it. I'm getting it, and this still life of roses. How do you pronounce his name, Hana?" she asked, quietly enough that he wouldn't hear.

"It's pronounced KO-dye," I said. "Like the composer."

"Oh, right. Well, I want to be able to mention him to visitors. These paintings are real conversation pieces."

I couldn't fault her taste. I floated toward her, drawn by the magic of the things around us, to look at the faces on the canvases in front of Katie. Men, women, children, couples—faces made beautiful beneath the artist's careful hand. One of them, a painting of a woman leaning against a fence in front of a summer sky, was particularly lovely. My gaze lingered on it for a moment, appreciating the rich use of color in the shading of her hair and in the flowers dotting the landscape behind her.

My eyes returned to the street scene in Keszthely, and I felt a burst of emotion so strong I had to put out a hand to steady myself.

"What was that?" Katie asked. Then, studying me more closely, she said, "Is this—are you having one of those insight moments? You said you might have some sort of hereditary ability, right?"

"I—maybe. But this painting . . . it's having a visceral effect on me. I can barely feel my body right now."

"Is that good or bad?" Katie asked, looking concerned.

I didn't know. What was I feeling? Was I being transported to a higher plane with the pleasure of seeing truly great art? Or was I sensing something?

I tore my eyes away from the painting and looked at my watch. "Anyway, I have to go. Mom and Grandma are expecting me—we have a ladies' luncheon tea at noon, and I'm supposed to meet Erik for a quick breakfast."

"Wow, how fun! I want to come to your tea house someday. I want to be a lady who has luncheon." Katie stacked up her canvases, ready to haul them to the front, and added, "How are things going with you and handsome, anyway?"

I sighed a little love sigh, and Katie laughed.

"They're going very well. We have—an undeniable attraction to each other. But we're holding back on the physical stuff a little so we can get to know each other. I told him I want regular meals out during which we ask each other questions and get real information. All I know right now is that he's a cop and his dad is full-blooded Norwegian."

"Well, that's fine. Get to know each other, but keep on kissing each other, obviously."

"No way to avoid it. We can barely keep our hands off each other."

"Then why do you look bummed out?"

I pulled out my wallet. "I don't. I mean, if I do, it's just for something stupid."

"What is it?"

I shrugged. "You know how my mom and my grandma both have sort of—a second sense? My grandma especially, but my mom is coming around to the idea that maybe there's something in her, as well."

"Yeah! And in you. Like with the painting back there."

I shrugged again. "The thing is—when my grandmother met my grandfather, she said she saw a gold light around him. That's how she knew he was the one."

"Oooh, how romantic!"

"My mom had a similar experience with my dad. She sort of—saw his aura or something."

"So?"

"So, I haven't seen anything around Erik. I would like to know that he's the one."

Katie had been examining some embroidered handkerchiefs on a table, but now she set one down and put her hands on her hips. "Wait. You wouldn't actually let this mess up your relationship, would you?"

I shook my head. "I'm not saying I would break up with him. I just—I wish I could have that—you know. Verification."

She snorted. "Well, wouldn't we all? But we have to find out the old-fashioned way. Or at least the non-magical way. By getting to know someone."

"Yes, okay, fine. You asked, so I told you. Now what's going on with Eduardo?"

Now she shrugged at me. "Nothing. We just decided to go our separate ways, see other people for a while."

The last time I had seen Eduardo he had looked pretty hung up on Katie. "Eduardo wanted that, too?"

"He was okay with it." She wasn't meeting my gaze.

"So what you're saying is that *you* broke up with him. Why?"

She bit her lip for a moment, then said, "He's a nice guy, but he does not have one romantic bone in his body. You know? The whole time we were dating—no presents, no surprises, no poems written to me, no endless comments about my beauty." She saw my look and said, "No, I didn't expect all those things, but one or two of them would have been nice. So I'm thinking maybe I should hold out for someone who's more naturally a romantic."

I studied her and said, "Look at us. Making problems where problems don't exist."

She sighed. "I don't know. We did get along, I'll say that. But so do brothers and sisters, right? Shouldn't I want something more?"

I thought about Erik Wolf, and the way his green eyes darkened when he saw me enter a room. The way he moved swiftly toward me, eager to make contact if only to touch my fingertips with his or to place his lips lightly on my hair. I recalled that when I sat in my apartment, I always knew when he was arriving for an unexpected visit. I didn't need to look out the window to see his car pulling into a visitor spot; the air changed somehow when Erik was near me, and I felt happier, the way one does when a spring breeze blows unexpectedly through the window.

"You should definitely want more," I said. And yet didn't Katie and Eduardo have something Erik and I did not? A month ago, Erik had sought my help to solve a mystery. This allowed us to speak freely, inspired by a challenge, by the puzzle of human behavior. Now that the case had ended, our conversation was more labored, and this concerned me. Why did we have nothing to talk about?

"Well, I do want more," Katie said. Then she made a rueful face at me. "But I kind of miss him. And he keeps texting me, even though we agreed we wouldn't do that."

"He misses you, too. Isn't that romantic?"

She shrugged. "I don't know." Then she looked at her watch. "I have to get going, too. My mom is expecting me at nine. We're cleaning out some of her closets because I have decided she's a hoarder."

I laughed. "She is not. She's sentimental. It's not like she's sitting on a giant pile of newspapers."

"Not yet," Katie said. "But today the dumpster will be our friend. I'm going to take this stuff up and buy it."

"Okay." My eyes went back to the Hungarian street scene. Something about it kept drawing my attention. I went to the wall and picked it up, along with the woman at the fence, and brought them to the front. I felt a little bit wealthy; my mother (and boss) had just given me a bonus after my work on a huge event that had made the tea house several thousand dollars. I had stowed the money in the bank, but some of it had gone into an account that I called "collections." I drew from this to fund my artistic purchases.

I walked to the stairs, where Katie was putting away her wallet. She pointed at me. "I'm going to put this stuff in my car. I'll meet you out there." She lifted her canvases and ascended the stairs, thumping into the wall now and then with her bulky purchases.

The man smiled after her and said, "Nice girl."

"Yeah. She's my best friend," I said.

He began taking tags off the items I set before him: the sweater, the wolf, the two canvases. He flipped over the first painting to see what I had chosen and contemplated the melancholy street scene. He said, "Keszthely. The place of my heart. Beautiful place, beautiful people." He stared at the painting while he said it. He seemed to be appreciating not his own talent but some memory elicited by the visual.

"You're Hungarian?"

He nodded. "Born there, but came here thirty years ago."

"I'm Hungarian, too. On my mother's side. Her maiden name is Magdalena Horvath."

His eyes lifted, met mine with sudden interest. "I know Magda. And Juliana. The tea house ladies, right? We Hungarians always seem to meet each other here and there."

"Yes, that's us."

He was still looking at me. "Your eyes have the shape of your mother's, but the color is more like your grandmother's. Do you have other things in common with her?"

I shrugged. "People say we're both hardheaded. I don't agree, though."

He smiled. "People like to apply their labels. It's difficult to really know a person, isn't it?"

"Yes."

He smiled again, with that pleasant crinkling around the

eyes, and he reached out to shake my hand. "And your name is?"

"Hana." I shook his hand; something opened up in my mind, a large space, full of light, but only for a second, and then it was gone.

"I'm Will Kodaly. We should have coffee sometime; I am fascinated by your family."

"Well, that would make you the first," I joked.

"I doubt it," he said, his face inscrutable. "In any case, let's finish ringing you up here." He turned over the other painting and paused briefly, his hand arrested in midair. He looked at the woman in front of the fence, the woman he had painted, and his gaze softened. Then his face showed regret, and the smile he flashed at me was grim around the edges. "Good choice," he said. "One of my favorites."

"Why are you selling them?" I said. "I would think you could get a gallery showing and—"

"I've got plenty more. These sales just help pay for art supplies, expenses." He had all the tags now; he added up the total and said, "Seventy-five dollars."

I got out my checkbook; I couldn't believe what I was getting for that price. A new-looking sweater that probably cost a hundred or more in the store, two original paintings by a professional artist, and a Herend wolf. I handed him the check.

He chuckled. "You have the look of a woman who got what she wanted."

"Oh, more than I wanted! Thank you so much."

He reached under his little table and produced some bubble wrap. "In case you want to wrap that," he said, pointing at the wolf. It was clear that he didn't even want to touch it.

"Oh yes. Thanks." I wrapped it carefully and stowed it in my purse. He put the sweater in a plastic bag.

"I don't have any way to wrap the canvases. Do you want me to walk them to your car?"

"I've got them, thanks. I hope you make a lot of money, Will. You're very talented, and those paintings shouldn't be hidden in a basement."

"Thank you." He bowed his head at me. "Neither should you, Hana."

I blushed, not sure what he meant. I thanked him again and climbed his stairs, relieved to be out of the rather dark space which had become more and more redolent of sadness.

On the street outside, Katie had finished packing her canvases away and was adjusting her silky ponytail. I gave her a hug and told her to call me soon.

"I will," she said. "Have a nice breakfast with your boy-friend. Stop looking for some magical light and just focus on how handsome he is."

She waved and climbed into her car. I went to my car and stowed the paintings along with the sweater behind the driver's seat. The wolf, safe in my bag, accompanied me to the driver's door. "You stay with me, my precious," I said. Luckily, Katie was no longer there, or she would have mocked me.

I pulled away from the curb and saw a gray car pull into the spot I had vacated. A man emerged from it almost im-mediately, and he seemed to be looking after my car in confusion. I studied him in the rearview mirror; he stood in the street, scratching his head, as though puzzled by my departure.

"Can't believe his good luck at finding a space," I said to myself, but I wasn't entirely convinced.

With a shrug, I focused on the road that would bring me to Amelia's Breakfast Nook, and Erik Wolf.

The freezing drizzle was still falling as I darted into the warm little waffle shop that Erik and I had made our place for stolen morning meetings. It was located midway between the police station and the tea house, and we tried to make time for each other every day, even when schedules were tight.

Today I found him already seated, looking adorably rumpled and undeniably sexy as he studied the fine print on a sugar packet with his Wolf-like scrutiny. I stomped on the entrance mat a few times, and Erik looked up and caught my eye. Something in his face relaxed, and he smiled slightly and stood up at his seat, like some old-fashioned gentleman at a dance. I moved swiftly and tucked into his arms. "Hey," he said, kissing my ear.

"Hey." I slid my hands over his shoulders and played with the hair that grew over his collar. "I brought you a present."

"Yeah? Besides you?"

"Mmm." I touched my nose to his neck, inhaling his sandalwood scent. "Something you have to try on. I left it in the car. You can give me a fashion show later."

He laughed. "Sounds good." A waitress walked past us with a mumbled "excuse me," and I realized we were blocking the aisle.

"I guess we should sit."

"Yeah." Erik stole a quick kiss, warm and soft, and I sat down with a slightly dizzy feeling.

Then we faced each other across the table and a familiar chasm opened. Erik's face took on a closed, shuttered look that said he resented being interrogated about his life, and I'm sure I looked assertive at best, leaning forward, ready to begin a new assault of "getting to know you" questions. "I know you hate this," I said, "but we agreed that we'd share personal stuff. How can we be together without knowing anything?"

He shrugged. "It's worked for a month. Are you happy?"

My lips curled upward of their own volition. "Yes."

"Me, too. Maybe the other stuff should just come when it comes."

"Just a few questions."

He took a sip of his coffee. "Fine. What are your questions, Hana?"

I loved the way he said my name. It distracted me briefly, and then I shook my head. "Where were you born?"

He scratched his cheekbone. "Chicago. My parents still live there."

"Okay, great." A worry surged to the surface. Why had he not asked me to meet his parents?

"Where were *you* born?" Erik asked, setting down his mug.

"Riverwood. I haven't left town much since then."

"Maybe I'll have to whisk you away somewhere." Again, his expression distracted me from my intentions.

"Stop being sexy all the time. I'm trying to learn things about you."

He held up his hands. "I had no *sexy* intentions. Please proceed." He was making fun of me.

I ignored his grin and said, "You know more about my family than I do about yours. You know I have a brother. You've met him, you've eaten meals with him. You've met my parents and my grandparents. How many Wolfs have I met? Or Wolves? What's the plural?"

Erik Wolf shrugged. "I don't even see them that much. They're all busy, so it's hard to coordinate schedules."

"And you have three sisters? Is that right?"

"Two sisters and a brother."

I sighed. That was all he was going to offer. "That's it? You're a cop! Can't you provide some detail? Pretend they're suspects."

He pondered this, looking into his coffee. Then he said, "Mom and Dad run a camping equipment store. They've always been outdoorsy types. They keep very busy with the store, both the physical store and the online one. It's called Trekker."

"I've heard of Trekker! I ordered a thermos from them once! I ordered a thermos from your parents!"

He nodded, unimpressed.

I sighed. "Fine. And your siblings?"

"My sisters also live in Chicago. My brother lives in Washington. He went to school there and kind of never came back. We visit twice a year."

"Who's the oldest of the kids?"

"My brother. Felix."

"That's a cool name."

Erik shrugged.

"And your sisters?"

"Runa and Thyra."

I sighed. "Like pulling teeth. I hope not every Wolf is as reticent as you—Oh! Guess what."

He looked relieved. "What?"

"I found treasure. Real treasure. Look." I lifted my purse just as a waitress appeared.

"What can I get you?" she asked.

Erik and I both ordered omelets, then she collected our menus and went on her way with a cheery promise to return.

I carefully removed the beautiful Herend wolf from the bubble wrap and handed it to my boyfriend. "Remember the beautiful blue rose you gave me? That was Herend; so is this. Their fishnet design. Isn't he gorgeous?"

Erik nodded. "Very cool. The eyes are amazing." He turned it over in his hands; I knew he was showing interest partly because he wanted to please me, and a little blossom of love bloomed within me. "I wonder how long it takes to—" Suddenly he froze. "Hana." He looked up at me with wide eyes: alert, cop eyes.

"What? What's going on?"

Wolf swept the room with his gaze, taking five seconds to assess everyone in it. "This is disturbing. Where did you get this wolf?"

"At a garage sale. The guy was really nice; he let me have it for only five dollars, and it's worth way—"

"Have you been home? Have you gone to your apartment since you left there?" His eyes had the laser focus that I had only seen in early September, almost two months ago, when he had been investigating a crime.

"What? No, I came straight here. What's going on? What's the problem?"

He thrust my ceramic treasure at me, holding it belly up. "Look, Hana!"

"What? At that little silver thing? I wondered what that was. I thought it just got added in the factory. What am I supposed to be seeing?"

"It's a tracker," he said. "If you're holding this wolf, someone can track your location. You're telling me this guy sold it to you cheap?"

"Yeah, but he was being nice. He said he didn't want it—"

"What's it really worth?"

"Five hundred, at least."

Erik's face was grim, even angry. "We're paying this guy a visit right now."

"What about breakfast?"

He stood up and looked taller than I remembered. "We'll take it to go."

Before I knew it, we were back in the cold, with a container of food and my Herend treasure once again wrapped up in my bag. The treasure had not lost its luster for me; I was sure that Erik would find it had all been a misunderstanding.

A glance at his face, his clenched jaw, told me that he did not agree, and that he considered my lovely wolf a source of mystery and danger.

Chapter 2

·························

THE MAN IN THE CAFÉ

The house looked somehow different when we pulled up in front of it. The day had grown darker, and the mood of the street had changed from a happy fall avenue to a dark and brooding lane. Wolf turned to say something to me, but we were both distracted by the woman who burst out of the side door of the house that I had left not an hour earlier; she was pale, distressed, and crying.

"Wait here," Erik said. I opened my mouth to protest and he locked eyes with me; his green gaze was beseeching. "Please, Hana."

"Okay."

He nodded and got out of the car; he crossed the lawn in a few strides and showed his ID to the woman, who touched his arm with one hand while wiping at her eyes with the other. Then she pointed into the house. Erik Wolf drew his weapon and went through the door. I looked up and down the street. It felt quiet, like the eye of a hurricane. A black dog trotted down the sidewalk, trailing his leash behind him, and a small boy ran after him and scooped up the leash; even through my closed window I heard his little voice chiding, "No, Padfoot." A *Harry Potter* dog, I mused. But then shouldn't his name have been Sirius? I rubbed at my arms, then looked down to see that they were covered with goose bumps. "Oh no," I said, and I looked back up to see Wolf on the lawn, his phone in his hand, his face grim as he spoke into it.

A car pulled up and the distressed woman pointed to it, saying something to Erik. He put away his phone and spoke to her briefly, then waved her on. She walked unsteadily to the car and climbed inside. By the time Erik walked back toward me, I could already hear sirens. I rolled down the passenger window and he leaned on it, his mouth grim but his eyes gentle. "Hana—"

"He's dead, isn't he? The man from the garage sale."

"Yes. I'm sorry. He's been shot."

"Are—you sure he's dead?"

Wolf's jaw tightened. "Yes. Can somebody come and get you? Or can I pay for an Uber to take you back to your car?"

"Yes, all right. But—do you need information from me?"

He scratched his head; he took a moment to wave to his partner, Detective Greg Benton, who had arrived at the scene with some other officers. Erik pointed to the door. "Basement," he called, and Benton strode across the lawn and into the house. Then he looked at me. "How did you happen to come across the wolf that he sold you?"

"Katie found it. It was buried on some dusty table. He wasn't trying to force it on me at all. But he was glad to get rid of it. He said it had unpleasant associations."

Erik's eyebrows shot up. "What else did he say?"

"Just something about not liking a person who gave you

a gift. And how that made the gift have no value, or something like that. It's why he was willing to give up the wolf for five dollars."

Erik nodded. "It seems that whoever gave him this gift had ulterior motives. That in fact your wolf may have led someone here to kill this man."

I gasped. "There *was* a man, right behind me."

"What?"

"I mean, he pulled in behind me as I was leaving. He was looking at my car with a funny expression, like he was surprised I was leaving. He was staring after me when I drove away."

Erik's face grew pale. "Hana. Oh, God."

"What?"

"If he was following the wolf, that means he got there as the wolf was leaving. With you. What if someone told him to kill whoever possessed that thing?"

I stared at him, my mouth open. Had that man been a murderer? "I—I don't—"

He touched my arm with his big warm hand. "I'm sorry. You're fine, everything's fine. What did this man look like?"

"Oh—I only had a glimpse. He looked—sort of unkempt, with brownish hair. And a kind of parka. And his car was gray."

He nodded and stood up, looking around the street. "We might get lucky with some home security cameras."

"Erik."

He leaned back in and studied my face with his green eyes. "Yes?"

"He was a nice man. He was Hungarian! And an artist, a professional artist."

"You know his *name*?"

"Oh—yes. I'm sorry. His name is William Kodaly. Look

at the paintings in his basement. You'll see that he was so talented . . ." My regret threatened to overwhelm me. I had met him just that morning, exchanged words with him. He had told me that I would be a good subject for a painting. We had connected over our Hungarian heritage; he had looked healthy, sturdy, and good-natured. In the last half hour, someone had killed him.

Erik bent to hold my face in his warm hands. "I'm sorry, Hana. I know you can feel—vibrations and things. And that you met him and talked to him. I know it's hard."

"It is. I'm sad, and I'm angry."

"We'll deal with this. We'll find this person," he assured me.

"But that doesn't matter!" I said. "What matters is that poor William can't come back."

Detective Wolf didn't have an answer to that one; he patted my hand and kissed my cheek, but his eyes soon returned to the door, and to the stretcher that had just been carried into the house. A young officer was wrapping police tape all around the lawn, and neighbors were starting to gather on the sidewalk.

"Hey, I'll have Officer Tate there drive you back to your car, okay?"

"Okay. Hey, Erik—who was that lady?"

"She was here for the garage sale. She saw the sign on the door that said 'Come on Down,' so she went down and found him dead. She ran back up and we were there. She said she was there less than a minute. I have her information."

"You'd better go," I said. "And I suppose you need this." I lifted my purse and, with some reluctance, removed the bubble-wrapped wolf figurine.

Erik took it, handling it with care. "Sorry, Hana. You know I'll give it back to you."

He touched my cheek, then walked over to Officer Tate and spoke to him. The young man nodded at him, clearly pleased to have a job beyond putting up police tape.

Moments later, I climbed into the back of Tate's squad car and told him where to find my vehicle. We drove down the street and I saw a man emerging from a car that had just tucked into a spot at the curb; I realized at the last moment that it was my friend Falken Trisch, and that he had come, on my recommendation, to find treasures at a garage sale. His wide eyes met mine as I glided past in the police car. I pointed at my phone.

Tate sped up and turned at the intersection, and I sent Falken a text: The man I told you about was murdered. It's a long and terrible story. When I've recovered emotionally, you and I can have lunch.

I put away my phone and managed to smile at the young officer in the front seat. "Thank you for the ride," I said.

"Of course. It sounds like you had a rough morning." His eyes were sympathetic in the rearview mirror.

"No, it was fine. It's just hard to accept what happened. I don't know how you police officers handle such—darkness. The rest of us, well . . . I guess we would just rather not see."

His look of sympathy remained. "It's not always dark. Sometimes we make real connections with the people we serve. But days like today, yeah, those are tough. Is this the lot? This little diner here?"

"Yes. My car is the blue one on the left. Thank you for the ride."

He parked, then turned to look at me. "Are you sure you're okay to drive?"

I took a deep breath and realized that I was. "Yes, thank you. I'll be fine." I stepped out of the car and waved as Officer Tate drove away. Then I returned to my vehicle and climbed inside. I called Katie on her cell phone, and she picked up after two rings.

"Hey! What's up? Don't tell me: you went back and bought more stuff."

"No. But, Katie—I have bad news."

"What?" Her tone was sharper now, and nervous.

"The man—the artist that we spoke to, the garage sale man—"

"Yeah?"

"He's dead."

"*What?* We just left there! He was fine!"

"Someone killed him, Katie."

"Oh my God! Is your boyfriend there?"

"Yeah. The place is swarming with vehicles."

"Oh, wow. I'm sorry. For him, and for us. This sucks."

"Treasure those paintings. You were the last person to speak to the artist, to experience his warmth."

"Don't cry, Hana."

"I'm not." I wiped my eyes and glared out the windshield. "I'm angry now, not sad. I want Erik to find this guy and put him away forever."

"Yeah. It's unbelievable. But wait—how did you happen to find out? I mean, why did you go back there?"

I sighed. "Erik found a tracker on that Herend wolf. The one you discovered for me."

"A tracker?"

"Like a GPS kind of thing. Really tiny."

"That's crazy!"

"So he drove us over there, furious, thinking the guy was trying to follow me. It turns out someone might have been tracking *him*. Anyway, I just wanted you to know. Because you and I were—you know. We spoke to him last, I think."

A silence on the other end, while Katie thought about this. "I'll say a prayer. The good thing is, we were nice to him. We complimented him and exchanged positive words. It was like a sort of—blessing."

"I suppose so. I hope so. I'll talk to you later," I said.

"Yeah," Katie said. "Boy, I really feel like calling Eduardo now."

"Do it."

She didn't say anything.

"Katie, call him."

"I'll probably hold off. Gotta go," she said. "Hang in there. Talk to you soon."

She ended the call, and I started my engine. The icy rain had stopped falling, but the wind still buffeted my car, rocking it slightly, reminding me that the universe was a force outside human control.

ᑲ

At the tea house, despite the work that waited, my family pampered me. My mother gave me a hug and tucked me into a chair at one of our tables with starched white cloths. My grandmother brought me a glass of Pálinka, assuring me that it would make me feel better. I sniffed my amusement; Grandma thought Pálinka made everything better, although I'd never been a fan of the strong plum brandy. Grandma pushed it toward me. "Try," she said. "Is different from usual. Normally we drink *szatmári szilvapálinka*, the plum from Szatmár, but this is a gift from Laszlo, you remember him? Is *újfehértói meggypálinka*, the sour cherry, made in Újfehértó."

I blinked at her. Sometimes I picked up on bits and pieces of meaning, but today nothing was penetrating. "What? That's all just a bunch of Hungarian words to me, Grandma. It's Greek to me, as they say."

She shook her head. "Hungarians don't say that. Right, Magda?" She turned to my mother, who nodded.

"Yes, that's true. In Hungary they say *Ez nekem kínai*—'It's Chinese for me.'"

"Whatever. The point is, it's a foreign language. And also, the point is that I can't understand a word Grandma says sometimes."

My mother and grandmother exchanged a regretful glance. "We should have taught you Hungarian," my grandmother said with a sigh. "We thought it was better to let you and Domonkos be a part of your country, America. Our little Americans." She sighed again, with her special blend of melodrama and melancholy, and I laughed.

My mother sat down next to me and patted my hand. "I'm sorry you had to go through that this morning. And so soon after poor Ava died right here in the tea house." I didn't like to think of that event, although it had been not even two months since it happened.

I covered her hand with my other one. "At least I didn't— you know—find him. But just to know that he was there, alive and vibrant, and he had a future, and all this talent. Oh, I didn't tell you—he was an artist. And he was Hungarian!"

My grandmother, standing beside me and reading her Pálinka bottle, suddenly clutched my shoulder. "Vat?"

"Yes, he was a Hungarian. He said he knew you—he mentioned meeting Mom at some Hungarian event, so he probably knew you both."

Their eyes locked over my head; a look of pure dread. "Do you know his name?" my mother asked in an odd voice.

"Kodaly," I said. "William Kodaly."

"Oh, no!" my mother said. She pulled her hand from between mine and sat up straight. Then she clenched her hands in her lap. "Will Kodaly. Oh, Mama."

My grandmother nodded grimly. "Oh, the wolf, Magda. The wolf pays the price."

I frowned at them. "Now you're speaking English and I still don't know what the heck you're saying. Why is he a wolf?"

My mother shook her head. "He just had a reputation among the ladies. A sort of 'love 'em and leave 'em' kind of thing. I actually know several women who had relationships with him. He was a great boyfriend in many respects, but he didn't tend to stick around long."

I turned to my grandma, who still clutched her brandy bottle and stood stiffly at my side, like a statue of herself. "What's wrong? Did *you* date him?"

She shook her head. "Bad luck, bad luck. Another Hungarian, dying on a day of ice and cold." She muttered to herself in her native tongue for a while; I got goose bumps again.

"Mom, make her stop," I said. But a glance at my mother's forearm revealed that she had goose bumps, too. "Oh, great," I said, pointing. "You're as psychic as she is, apparently."

My mother shrugged. "It's nothing. We're all just shocked because a man is dead, and he was a man we knew, if only peripherally. I wonder how those women are taking the news, though—the ones he dated. If they even know yet." Her blue eyes met mine, holding a mixture of casualness and curiosity. "I suppose your boyfriend is there now?"

"You mean Detective Wolf?"

My mother smiled. "I mean Erik. Don't put on your formal air with us, Hana. The boy has had dinner at our house."

"He's not a *boy*, mother," I said, sounding like a girl. "And, yes, he's there. We—he—got there just minutes after it happened, I think. Maybe half an hour."

"How did you know to go back, if you had already left?" my mother asked. "You didn't have a—psychic moment, did you?"

My grandmother brightened at the thought and studied me with her canny eyes.

"No, no. It's a weird story. Sorry, Grandma, but it has the word 'wolf' in it."

She shrugged, dramatic again. "What doesn't, these days?" She plopped down in the chair on the other side of me. Grandma hated wolves with a superstition that probably went back to her childhood, but she had encouraged me to date Erik, despite his unfortunate name.

Our pastry chef, François, walked swiftly out of the kitchen at the back of the tea house, bearing a china plate with three little sandwiches and three little cakes, all of them like tiny works of art. He set it before us with a flourish and bent to look in my eyes. François was a handsome twenty-three-year-old man, and it was always a treat to receive his focused attention. I'm sure my mother and grandmother felt the same way—women of all ages responded to François's charms. "I am sorry to hear of your trauma," he said. "Please eat. Food heals the soul, so. *Mangez bien.*"

I smiled at him. "Thank you, François. That is really sweet of you. And these sandwiches look amazing, as always." I selected a sliced egg sandwich with red pepper shavings and a dot of paprika-sprinkled sour cream on top and popped it into my mouth. "Mmm. So good," I said. "Mom and Grandma, join me."

My mother shook her head. "I know it's been a rough morning, but we have a group arriving in two hours, and I have to make the tea. Hana, are you okay to do the table arrangements?"

"Of course. It will calm me down." It always soothed me, working with our decorations, trying to create the most artistic tableaus on both the buffet table and in the centerpieces. Today, despite the almost wintry weather, we were decorating with a European garden theme—a popular choice with our clients. I had created centerpieces for each table: baskets full of silk roses, along with real-looking violets, daisies, gerbera, and trailing ivy. I set this splash of color in the center of each crisp white tablecloth. Then I laid out pale blue place mats and selected one of our favorite tea sets: a Wedgwood Blue Hibiscus set that we had purchased from a restaurant that was going out of business. The cups, white with gold rims and blue and gold hibiscus flowers adorning the sides, looked striking on the tables and added elegance and old-world charm to the room.

Once the dining tables were finished, I turned my attention to the side table. This served sometimes as a gift table (for weddings and showers); other times as a buffet table; and, in the past, as a place where my grandmother could entertain guests by reading their tea leaves. Since a tragic death in our tea house in early September, Grandma had not chosen to read leaves, and she did not plan to do it today, either.

I scattered some loose silk flowers around the table, where I set up a variety of colorful teacups and various laminated maps of European cities. At one end I put a discreet pile of business cards—green and pink with a scalloped edge—which read "Maggie's Tea House—Celebrate Your Event in Grand European Style!"

My phone buzzed in my pocket. I lifted it to see a text from Erik Wolf: You okay?

I texted back that I was fine, then saw another text, this time from Falken: Are you all right? When can we meet? I'll treat you to some afternoon pastry at Eleanor's.

My mother hurried past and I said, "Mom, can I take off after I clean up the tables today? Falken wants to meet with me, I guess to ask about Mr. Kodaly."

She walked back toward me and touched my hair. As ever, she looked like a European doll in her tea house uniform: white blouse, black skirt, colorful embroidered apron. Her blonde hair was swept up in the elegant twist she wore to work. Only in the evening did she let it hang loose, probably because she knew that my father couldn't resist playing with it. Her blue eyes held affection and sadness. "Are you ready to talk about it? Why not tell him maybe another time?"

"No, it's okay. I feel bad because I told him to come out and see what Mr. Kodaly was selling. He got there in time to find all the police cars."

"Oh, my."

I studied her face. "Kodaly was your friend, wasn't he?"

She shrugged. "Not exactly. I liked him, though. We always got along, when we chatted at one event or another. I should have resented him, because he hurt more than one female friend of mine, but it was hard to feel angry with him. He had a sort of—whimsical quality. So it was like trying to be angry at the wind, or at a bird, or something."

"I bought two of his paintings. I'll show them to you."

"Oh, my. It's still so hard to believe."

"Who are the friends that he dated?"

She sighed, then pointed at me. "One was your teacher. Remember Ms. Derrien?"

"My high school English teacher?" I gaped at her.

"Yes. He was with her for more than a year. And then Cassandra Stone from the library."

"The lady who hosted that book-a-thon? She's sort of ethereal. I could see why he'd fall for her."

"Yes. And I believe he was linked to more than one woman in the local Hungarian crowd. Sofia Kálmar, for one. She's an artist, too."

"Oh wow. She's a friend of yours, isn't she? And gorgeous. He sure went for the good-looking women."

"Yes, well. He had an artist's eye. I'm sure he did portraits of them all." She paused and cleared her throat. "He painted me once."

"What?"

"Our heritage group was raising money for a local food pantry. They wanted him to provide a painting for auction, and he asked if I would pose."

"I'll bet it was beautiful. Did Dad bid on it?"

She shook her head. "The bidding started at five hundred dollars. His paintings are in demand in the U.S. and even in Europe. He's quite famous."

My grandmother joined us at the table. "Looks good," she said, studying my carefully careless display.

I pointed at my mother but spoke to Grandma. "Did you know that William Kodaly painted her for some charity thing? And that some stranger bought the painting?" I turned back to my mother. "What did it sell for, anyway?"

She blushed slightly. "Six thousand dollars."

"Wow! Who bought it?"

"I don't know. It was an anonymous bid; they received it online. Alida Szabó was on the committee. She told me that someone's assistant came to pick it up."

"When was this?"

She shrugged. "About two years ago."

My grandmother looked up and nodded. "I remember. He was coming to their house every day, seating her in the backyard. Your daddy was always making excuses to go out. He had to weed the garden, he had to water the hedge, he had to spread mulch." Both women started laughing.

"He was jealous," my mother said. "But William was very professional. He never did anything inappropriate. It was actually quite fun sitting for the painting, and he completed it within a week."

"Did you like the finished product?" I asked.

Her face grew wistful; for a moment she looked eighteen years old. "It was lovely. Your father wanted it, but he wouldn't say so. And when he heard how much it earned, he realized we never could have afforded it."

"Luckily he has the real you," I joked.

"That's what I told him. He got over it quickly enough. But it was funny—your father is not the jealous type, but Will Kodaly brought that out in him. I think Will had that effect on a lot of men."

My grandmother stiffened slightly, then said, "I check on François." She moved away on her flat shoes, her skirt swishing as she walked.

My mother was still wistful. She touched my sleeve. "I would have liked to see a portrait of you, painted by Will. He was a genius, really."

"He told me I'd make a good subject."

Her eyebrows rose. "Did he?"

"Yes. He said something about my hair. He said—it was like fire at twilight." My eyes grew unexpectedly wet when I said these words.

"That is poetic." She took a lock of my hair in her hand and sifted it through her fingers. "And true."

My thoughts had wandered. "You don't happen to know who might have given him a Herend wolf, do you?"

"What? No. I haven't spoken to Will in more than a year.

I'm not even sure which woman he was pursuing these days."

"Huh. I got kind of a lonely feeling from him. Sad, even."

My mother opened her mouth to say something, but the phone rang in the kitchen. She jumped and went back into business mode. "I have to get moving. Tell Falken you can meet him. Cleanup shouldn't take too long today."

"All right, thanks."

She rapidly walked to the back room and disappeared.

I put the final touches on my table, arranging some blue roses around the map of Budapest; perhaps the color would prompt people to think of the Danube. As a finishing touch, I scattered some battery-powered tea lights to add a warm glow to the table. The result was lovely. The whole room, in fact, looked beautiful as the sun shone on the gleaming teacups and the colorful flower baskets.

Our guests were sure to experience what one had called, in a five-star online review, "the magic of Maggie's Tea House."

༄

Falken was waiting for me in the cozy dining room of Eleanor's Café, a restaurant where we'd shared the occasional pastry while discussing his latest antique finds. Falken knew that someday I'd like to have a shop like his, and I think he saw me as something of a protégé, someone with whom he could share his knowledge of antiques and business.

Today he clasped my hand with the solicitous expression of someone at a funeral. "How are you doing?" he asked, peering at me over the top of his glasses.

"Oh, fine. I didn't know the man before today, but it's still a shock. Katie and I had a nice conversation with him. I can't tell you how thrilling it was, finding the Herend wolf, and then discovering his paintings. I'm so sorry you won't get to see that treasure trove down there, Falken. He was charging twenty-five dollars per canvas, but my mother told me he painted her once for a charity event, and the painting sold for six thousand dollars!"

He nodded. "I looked up Kodaly after you texted me. He's a big deal. You're right in thinking you stumbled across treasure. In fact, the paintings you bought are probably worth thousands."

"Wow. I hadn't thought of that," I said. "I don't really know if I'd want to part with them."

"No, I'd hold on to them. Meanwhile, let's hope the police find this murderer. What a horrifying thing. A horrifying thing," he repeated, staring at his menu with a distracted expression. Then he looked up at me. "And you say you spoke with him? More than just to say hello?"

"Yes. We spoke about the wolf and various things. He knew my mother, but at first I assumed he meant my grandmother. I think every Hungarian in town has heard of Juliana Horvath."

I looked back down at my menu, and a figure appeared beside our table, casting a shadow over it. I looked up to ask the waitress a question and saw instead an older man, perhaps in his late sixties, hesitating at my table, smiling at me, his white mustache gleaming in the light. He had obviously been on his way out; his coat was draped over his arm. "Excuse me," he said. "I couldn't help but overhear you say the name Juliana Horvath. Are you related to her?"

I sent an ironic look to Falken, who grinned. It was true: everyone knew my grandmother. "Yes, that's my grandmother. Are you a friend of hers? Are you in one of the Hungarian societies?"

He shook his head, still smiling. "I've only been in town

for a short time. I knew she lived somewhere near Chicago, but I had sort of lost track of her."

"I'm sorry?" I said.

"Pardon me," he said. "My name is Henrik Sipos." He pronounced it the Hungarian way: SEE-pohsh. He held out his hand, and I shook it. "I am originally from Hungary, like your grandmother."

"Oh, so she knows you from the Old Country?" I asked.

"Not exactly." He shook his head as though to clear out cobwebs, and then beamed another smile at me. In fact, he seemed inordinately happy. "I knew her only indirectly, and her mother, Natalia Kedves. She was Juliana Kedves before her marriage, was she not?"

"Yes, that's right." I was becoming annoyed by all of his questions, and I know my face had stopped attempting friendliness. He seemed not to notice.

He set his coat down on a nearby empty table, took out his wallet, and retrieved a business card, which he presented to me with weird formality. "This is my card. Please—if you or your family ever need anything, anything at all, call me. I am in debt to you all, as is my mother."

"I'm sorry?" I said again, confused.

"It's been good to meet you, Miss—?"

"Hana. Hana Keller," I said. "And you are Henrik. I'll be sure to tell my grandmother that we met."

"She probably doesn't remember me," he said, still smiling joyfully. "And I don't really remember her. But she and her mother—they were much beloved in our household."

"Ah," I said. My mouth was open as I tried to formulate a new question, but he had already picked up his coat and started moving away. At the door he sent one final wave and smile, and then he was gone.

I looked at Falken, whose eyes twinkled with interest.

"Well, that was odd. This day has officially been weird from beginning to end."

Falken looked at his watch. "It's only four o'clock," he said. "You've still got time for some other strange occurrences." He grinned at me.

I slapped at his hand. "Stop that. I've had enough."

His face sobered. "You have. I'm sorry."

I studied my teacup. "Did you have any idea what our friend Henrik was talking about?"

"Not a clue. Interesting that he mentioned your great-grandmother, though. If she's the one he knows, then how did he recognize the name Horvath?"

"He said he knew them both, but—" Suddenly I was full of questions, and the elusive Henrik had gone. I looked at his card; it seemed for a moment to glow in my palm, and an image of my great-grandmother loomed up in my mind's eye: she was smiling and holding my hand. I shook my head and scrutinized the card. "It says here he works at the chamber of commerce. With an office in the Treadway Building."

"Hmm." Falken thought about this as the waitress appeared. He ordered coffee and I ordered hot chocolate. "And perhaps a croissant," I said.

"This seems like a chocolate pie sort of day," Falken said, wearing a paternal expression.

"François already gave me a pastry. I'll be fat if I eat every time I have stress in my life."

He was still studying me. "I'm sensing that you have stresses other than today's terrible event. Never mind, you don't have to tell me. But I can distract you briefly from the stressful world. I brought you a gift."

"Oh, Falken, you didn't need to—"

He held up a hand. "Just a little something. You know I like to keep my eyes open for things you like. But this one is not for sale. It's from Falken to Hana." He dug in the satchel that he carried around like a Pony Express rider and produced a small box. He handed it to me, and I took it, too curious and eager to refuse.

Inside the box, under tissue paper, was a small china sugar bowl. It looked like a Herend hand-painted piece; I flipped it over and saw the familiar maker's mark. "Oh, Falken, it's beautiful! The blue flowers, and this gorgeous bas-relief pink rose!"

"It's a little treasure. Not wildly expensive, but nice for your collection. I found it at an estate sale."

"You could make money from this. You should put it on your shelves."

He shook his head. "The size isn't practical. This is a piece with your name on it. You know I'm not reluctant to make a profit, but I never intended to sell this one."

I ran my finger along the smooth porcelain. I lifted the tiny lid, with its pale pink flower, and peeked inside the white bowl. "You're the best," I said.

"Yes, yes. Now." He leaned back. "If you're up to it, tell me about some of the treasures that I didn't get to see in the artist's basement."

༄

By the time I finished chatting with Falken, I felt better. It was five o'clock, and I knew my cats, Antony and Cleopatra, would be hungry and looking for some human company. I gave Falken a quick hug, thanked him again for the gift, and went to my car.

The icy rain of the morning had disappeared, but a bitter wind was blowing, and I huddled inside my coat as I fumbled for my key and climbed into my Escort. As I drove toward my house, I realized that the cold was a two-sided coin; I didn't like being buffeted by the bone-chilling wind, but I did think there was a certain poetry to a cold October night, especially because of the glowing jack-o'-lanterns and gold-eyed black cats that I spied in windows and on porches along my route. There was something pleasing, even hopeful, about lights in the darkness.

I reached my apartment complex and pulled into my spot, musing that cars always warmed up right when one reached one's destination.

I climbed out of the car; my purchases from the garage sale were still in my backseat, but I didn't have the energy, suddenly, to haul in the paintings. I locked them in my car and started walking toward the door. Erik Wolf's familiar gray car pulled into the lot as I reached the stoop; surprised, I waited for him to join me. I admired, as always, the long-legged stride that brought him to my side in record time.

He kissed my cheek. "Hana," he said.

"Are you finished already? Have you caught anyone?"

He shook his head. "No. I'm going back to the office soon, but I thought I'd take you somewhere for a quick dinner."

"You don't have time for that. Let me just feed you. I have *székely gulyás*."

"Oh, wow. That would be great," he said. "Do you have enough?"

That question meant he was hungry. "I have tons. In my family we always make large portions because of the Domo factor."

Wolf laughed. He had met my brother and knew of his predilection for simply showing up to demand food. "Well, now you have an Erik factor, too."

I opened the door and we climbed the stairs. "The cats are going to be mad at both of us. I haven't fed them since morning, and they'll just feel generally neglected."

"I'm on it," Erik said. "You make food, I'll make it up to the twins."

We went into my apartment and I turned on lights, bringing a happy glow to the space. I had my own Halloween decorations, including a string of orange lights on my fireplace, and I turned these on, as well. The cats mewed and circled our legs; Erik scooped them both up and talked to them as he moved toward the kitchen and their food bowls. He was already quite familiar with my apartment; it felt strange, all of a sudden, to see him looking so at home.

I shook my head and went to the refrigerator. I retrieved a pot of *székely gulyás*, still fragrant with onions and paprika and crunchy with sauerkraut. The tender pork always warmed up nicely as a leftover, and the sour cream sauce gave it a delicious flavor and aroma and muted the bright orange paprika to a gentle copper color. I put the pot on simmer and found some bread and salad, arranging things quickly on the table.

Erik petted the cats and murmured his apologies, then fed them. They crunched at their bowls, clearly in a forgiving frame of mind, and he came up behind me and touched my shoulders. "Need my help?"

"No, it's fine. Sit down. What would you like to drink?"

"Just some water. I'll get it." He went to the tap, found a glass in the cabinet, and filled it at the faucet. Then he came and folded himself into a chair, smiling up at me. I was briefly overwhelmed by the sight of him; he grew more and more handsome to me as I got to know him. I bent to kiss his mouth, lingering there for a moment before I scampered to the stove and stirred my food. Moments later I brought him a full plate. He kissed my hand and then dug in; *székely gulyás* was one of his favorite Hungarian dishes.

We didn't talk much as we ate; I was afraid to broach the subject of William Kodaly, partly because it made me sad and partly because I didn't want to put Erik in a difficult position. He finished his food and sipped his water, then looked at me with a smile and narrowed eyes. "So," he said. "I have to leave soon, but I figured we should talk."

"About what?"

He sighed. "The last few weeks—"

"Have been wonderful," I said, touching his hand.

"Yes, they have. But you—you've been giving me a lot of long looks. Studying me, I guess. And looking sad. Maybe you should tell me what you're thinking."

"What? I don't—"

He pursed his lips at me, and I deflated. There was no point in lying to Detective Wolf.

"Okay, fine. It's nothing, first of all. Just a silly thing. You know my family—my grandmother with her apparent psychic gift, and my mom with maybe the same ability, and so much superstition across the board—"

His green eyes assessed me. "What does that have to do with anything? Are you trying to read me?"

"No, no. I'm not interested in pursuing my—potential powers. Not right now, anyway. But—you'll laugh—I've been thinking, because I've been enjoying being with you so much—"

"Get to the point, Hana."

"Okay." I sighed. "Remember what my grandma told you last month at the tea house? About how she knew my grandfather was the man for her because he had a gold light around him?"

"Like a man emerging from the sunrise, she said."

"Yes. So romantic, right?"

"Yes." He smiled at me.

"And my mother—she had the same experience with my father, the night they met. An amber light, she said. Of course, it was Christmastime, and there were lights everywhere."

His eyes narrowed again. "So you've been looking at me, trying to see this light?"

"Uh—yeah, I guess so."

He pulled his hand away. "Does it really matter if you see it or not?"

I sat up straight. "Don't be offended. It's a good thing. It means that I like you so much, I was just thinking that I should see it, too, you know—if I've inherited what they have. And maybe I haven't. But it would be a beautiful sort of—validation of us."

His chair legs scraped the floor as he pushed away from the table. He stood up and brought his bowl to the sink, standing with his back to me. "And what happens if you never see that light, Hana?"

"Well—nothing. I mean, I still want to be with you."

"And suppose you see your magical light around another man? While you're with me?"

"Erik, don't be angry. And don't throw hypotheticals at me. You know how I feel about you. And you asked me to tell you this, so I did, because I always want to be honest with you."

He turned around, his face pale and unsmiling. "And in all honesty, you've told me that you're not quite sure about me because you don't see a gold aura around me."

"Erik." I held out my hands.

He walked to the living room and grabbed his coat; I followed him. "I have to go. Lots to do at the office." He went to the door, then turned to look at me. His face held more reproach than longing. "But I'll tell you this, Hana. I was sure about you the first time I kissed you. And I didn't need any supernatural sign to tell me that you were right for me."

He opened the door, slipped into the hall, and closed the door quietly behind him.

Chapter 3

....

OPENING THE INNER EYE

I wanted to text Erik immediately, but I held off because I wasn't sure what I wanted to say, and the wrong words at this point could only make things worse.

I brooded in my apartment, staring at Antony and Cleopatra while they took an elaborate post-dinner bath. Then, feeling restless, I ran back out to my car to retrieve the paintings by William Kodaly. I pulled them carefully from my backseat, locked the car, and ran back to the building. The air was frigid, and I had bolted down the stairs without a coat. Now I stood shivering at the door, fumbling for my keys and feeling cold in my bones.

When I finally reached my warm apartment, I put the heat on under the kettle and set the paintings on my couch, where they were high enough for me to study them and supported by the back cushions. The landscape, still lovely and now even sadder, had rich colors that immediately added a luster and sophistication to my little room. I stood on the couch and removed the generic framed landscape that hung above it; I replaced it with Kodaly's canvas, then stepped back to see the results. "Oh," I murmured. I needed to find the proper frame, but even without one, this canvas was striking. In viewing the art on my wall, I was getting the full effect of his talent and his vision. It was invigorating. His work was a piece of his life that had not been destroyed, a living, vibrant thing.

I put the poster in a corner; I decided I would offer it to my neighbor, Paige Gonzalez. If she didn't want it I would give it to Domo, whose apartment walls were rather barren.

Pleased with the painting and the newly splendid room, I turned my attention to the portrait of the woman at the fence. Her face, rendered with detail and emotion, was as delicate and lovely as the flowers in the field behind her. And now that I studied it more carefully, I realized her eyes looked familiar . . . On a whim, I grabbed my cell phone and snapped a picture. I sent it to my mother with the message, Does this woman look like someone you know? This is a portrait by Kodaly.

I waited a few moments, wondering what to do with this second painting, when I got an answering text from my mother: That's Cassandra! I wonder when he painted this.

I wrote back: Oh, wow. We can talk about this in the morning. See you then. I was trying to prevent a phone call. Like all slightly introverted people, I preferred texts to calls because texts were finite. You exchanged a sentence or two and then signaled you were ready to be finished with the conversation by tapering down to the ol' thumbs-up emoji, which I sent to my mother now.

I moved the painting of the woman to the same corner where I had put the poster. I took out my phone again and snapped a picture of the cats. Unable to resist contacting

Erik, but not wanting to mention anything regarding our previous conversation, I wrote, The cats miss you.

A few minutes went by; I feared he wouldn't respond, but finally my phone buzzed. I opened the text window to see a thumbs-up.

A *thumbs-up.*

I tossed the phone on the couch. "Fine," I said. The cats looked at me, surprised by my tone. "I guess he needs to sort things out. I'll give him all the time he needs."

Moodily, I went to my computer and clicked it on, checking my messages on Facebook, reading some crazy political posts on Twitter, scrolling through Instagram. Then, on a sudden whim, I Googled "William Kodaly, artist."

Pages full of hits came up, including some images of his face, both as I remembered it and then in much younger versions. I scanned a page of pictures in which he posed with other artists, or held an award, or stood beside a woman. Most of the photos seemed to be in the U.S., but there were a couple where he was clearly in Hungary, standing in front of the parliament building in Budapest and, in a second shot, laughing with a friend on a quaint dirt road where pecking chickens could be seen in the background. It looked like the road in my painting, actually. Sure enough, the caption said "Kodaly in Keszthely, Hungary." I looked back at the painting where he had written "Keszthely" in the caption. The mood, the place, the feeling was the same. Had he lived there once? Or had he merely visited? Something in his face in the photograph told me that this place, at one point, had been home to him.

With a sigh, I pushed the computer away. I went into my living room and flipped on the television. I didn't want to think; I wanted some mindless entertainment. I watched a silly romantic comedy on Netflix while my cats purred at my side. It was a nice experience, but when the warring couple finally came to terms and kissed each other at the end, I found myself missing Erik Wolf.

∼

At the tea house the next day we prepared for a Friends of the Library event. The staff from the Riverwood Public Library was honoring their patrons, and the room buzzed with the good humor of people who loved books.

I finished setting my final table; we had used orange cloths and a lovely black tea service with a silver fleur-de-lis pattern reminiscent of a spider's web. My grandmother had found it once at an estate auction; we didn't have a full set, but since today's group numbered only forty-five people, we found we had enough to make Halloween-inspired tables.

François had used his endless ingenuity to make cakes and sandwiches that reflected our theme. His little cakes were covered with cheerful spiders and grinning skulls, and the sandwiches were pierced with toothpicks that looked like bony fingers.

I trundled a cart to the back of the room, where I went through the kitchen doorway to find François at work, frosting the last of some cakes with eyeballs on top. I smoothed my Hungarian-patterned apron and moved to his side. "Can I help with anything?"

He shook his head. "*Non*. I am finished."

"It looks amazing, as always."

"*Oui*," he agreed. François was not one to hide his light under a bushel.

I observed him with some affection; I saw him as a vain, handsome, French little brother. "How's Claire? Everything okay in the love department?"

"Yes, yes." He straightened up and stretched. "She is devoted to me. I have given her a boyfriend ring."

"What's that?"

He smirked. "Just something that says you are exclusive with me. But we are not engaged, not yet. She has earned a job downtown at a fine restaurant, and we will both be quite busy."

"Oh, wow. Tell her I said congratulations."

He nodded, then focused in on me. "How is your Wolf? He has upset you?"

Wow. I thought my mother and grandmother were the ones with insight, but François had picked that up quickly. "No, not exactly. He and I—had a disagreement."

"Ah. And who must apologize?"

I shrugged. "I don't know. I didn't do anything wrong, but he's hurt anyway. And I understand why. So we're just kind of at an impasse."

"Hmm." He started putting little sandwiches on a tray. "How do you know you weren't wrong?"

"Well—because I just told the truth. It's a long story."

François looked at me with his startling blue eyes. Sky blue, and deep. "Imagine hearing what you said, as him. Pretend you are he, and that someone else is Hana."

"I'll do that," I said. "I'll be back for those trays in a minute." I walked swiftly out of the room and found myself face-to-face with my grandmother.

"What's wrong?" she asked. Another pair of eyes studying me, this time hazel-brown ones.

"What? Nothing. Why is everyone interrogating me?"

François appeared behind me. "Clearly she has said something to Wolf that has upset him."

My grandmother's gaze flicked from me to him to me again. "What did you say?"

I sighed noisily. "Geez! I said I wished that I could see that light you saw around Grandpa. And that Mom saw around Dad. How am I supposed to know—you know—if he's the one for me?"

She blinked. "Because of the way you feel."

"I know that, obviously. I wish you and Mom had never told me your stories."

"In any case, he is the one. You see nothing? No—what is it—aura?"

"No." I pouted at her. "How am I supposed to know? How do you even see something like that?"

François was still there, eavesdropping. My grandmother said, "You have the trays ready?"

"Almost," he said, and disappeared into the kitchen.

My grandmother led me to one of the tables, where my mother was going around with a bag of silver glitter and lightly sprinkling the orange cloths. The effect was sophisticated but also magical. Grandma sat me down and pointed at me. "You focus outward, expecting things. That's not what to do."

"What? How else should I see the world, if not by looking at it?"

My mother floated toward us, intrigued.

Grandma pointed at her. "Magda saw the light because she didn't expect. Yes? She only saw a boy, and his beauty, and allowed the inner feeling to come out. Even my Magdalena, who keeps things inside, had a freedom moment."

I glared. "No one knows what that means, Grandma."

She nodded. "You are upset because you like this boy."

I opened my mouth to complain, and my mother said, "Hana doesn't like it when we call him a boy, Mama. He is probably thirty years old at least."

"Fine, fine." She leaned in and pointed at my eyes. "There

is the outer eye. You see with this always. Now you must try the inner eye."

"Maybe I don't have one."

"You do, Haniska. Everyone does. But for some people, that eye is always blind. Yours can see—but it is closed. Open your inner eye."

I stared at her, then at my mother. "Sure, okay. And just how do I do that?"

My grandmother sniffed, dismissing this concern. "The same way you do these two." She pointed at my eyes again. "You concentrate, you find your blindness, you open your eye."

I stood up. "This has been *super* helpful, but I need to get going on the buffet table. Those skulls aren't going to decorate themselves."

My mother put a gentle hand on my arm. "Give it time, Hana. And do some meditating."

"Right." I wasn't angry, exactly, but I had experienced just about enough of my family's supposed psychic gifts. I didn't want them or need them. "By the way," I said, "some guy approached me yesterday when I was out with Falken. He works at the Riverwood Chamber of Commerce. He said he knew you both and that he loved our family. He said if we ever needed anything, to call him."

"What's his name?" my mother asked.

"Sipos. Henrik Sipos."

She and my grandmother exchanged a glance. "Never heard of him," Grandma said, shaking her head.

"Me, neither," my mother said. "Must have mistaken us for someone else. There are other Horvaths in town. Maybe other Kellers."

I shook my head. "No, he knew you both. He was very pleased to make the connection."

Grandma shrugged. "He has probably read about the tea house in the paper."

My mother agreed and moved off with her glitter bag. Grandma marched off to the little stage to set up the microphone.

I walked to the side table where I would adorn grinning skulls with lovely black leaves and silver-orange fringe.

Hungarians didn't celebrate Halloween; they focused far more on All Saints' Day and All Souls' Day, but my mother and her mother had taken to the American Halloween tradition with surprising enthusiasm. Our dark and ghoulish holiday was festive and exciting for them, and they loved the decor of the season.

I had set up my iPad on the table and selected a Halloween playlist from Spotify. "Monster Mash" came on, and once the laboratory sounds ended and the beat began, out of the corner of my eye I saw my grandmother dancing. She loved to dance, and everything was music to her. I had once seen her dancing to the *thwick-thwack* of windshield wipers in her car, bobbing in place with the joy of rhythm. Now she half strutted around the microphone stand and I smiled, despite my bad mood.

~

The library bash was in full swing, and we three tea house ladies scuttled back and forth with carafes of hot tea, replenishments of sandwich trays, and cloths for wiping the occasional spills. The group was in high spirits, buoyed partly by our Halloween soundtrack and then by the awards that were presented from the dais (at which point we turned down the music). At one point I stole outside to take a deep breath of autumn air; the icy cold had gone and we had been treated to a sunny day with temperatures in the sixties. I gazed at the view across the road—the lovely wheat-colored grasses, swaying gently in the fall breeze. The porch of the house across the way was dotted with bright orange pumpkins, and I thought I spied a cornstalk and bale of hay, as well.

I had wanted to take my Wolf away somewhere on one of his free days, off to some country inn or happy pumpkin patch so that we could enjoy autumn together before it was gone. Now I wasn't sure when I'd see him again. Had I been wrong to tell him about the light? Was it a crazy thing to wonder about? I had told him the truth—I felt strongly about him one way or another.

I thought of what François had said, and I looked at it from Erik's point of view. What if he had come to me and said he wished he could see a light around me, the way other men in his family had done? Would that offend me? Would I feel slighted? Rejected?

"Oh shoot," I said. With a burst of remorse I realized what I had done, and that I was in fact the one who needed to apologize. I would go after the event was over and we had finished cleaning up.

I turned and went back into the building; Cassandra Stone was just emerging from the ladies' room. She had been a librarian in Riverwood for about four years; before that she'd been somewhere in Chicago. "Hi, Cassandra," I said.

She had swept her long reddish-brown hair up into a twist, but two artful strands hung over her ears. She tucked one of these behind her left ear as she walked toward me. "Hey, Hana. I haven't seen you at the library for a while."

"Yeah, things got pretty busy the last couple of months. I'll be back soon."

"Great."

We started walking back toward the main hall, but I put a hand on her arm. "Cassandra, I just wanted to say I'm sorry. About William Kodaly."

Her eyes widened. "You know about him?"

"I was one of the last people to see him. I just happened to be at his garage sale."

"Ah." Her eyes were sad. "Will was such a good guy. So talented, and so romantic. In many ways he was the perfect boyfriend."

"When did you break up?"

She shrugged. "About two years ago. We stayed friends. I'm happy about that. He would sometimes be a resource for the library when we needed an artist's advice, or he would agree to be on panels we had during Arts Festival Week."

"He sounds great," I said.

She wiped moisture out of one eye. "He was a restless soul. Ultimately, I wanted stability, but it didn't stop me from missing him sometimes, you know?"

I did know, and I was missing Erik Wolf right now. "Are you—seeing anyone these days?"

She sighed. "Yeah. And it's going well. But this news about Will has a lot of memories flowing back. It's just hard to believe. I talked to him last week."

"There's something you should know. I bought a painting from him, of a woman in front of a field of flowers. I think the woman is you."

Her eyes widened. "Oh? We did go out to Michigan once on a spring vacation, and I posed for a picture on the side of the road, by a fence."

"That's the scene in the painting."

"Really? Will *painted* me. Well, it's not entirely surprising. He was a genius, and he worked so rapidly. He was always looking for new subjects, and sometimes he did go to his photographs."

"If you'd like it—" I said.

She smiled at me. "You're sweet, Hana. But that's a valuable painting. You keep it. I'd love to at least look at it sometime, though, if I could."

"Of course. We can set up a time, or I can bring it to the library."

"Thank you. That's very kind."

We moved back into the banquet area. I noticed that she moved very gracefully, like a dancer. She waved to someone at her table. I said, "Before you go, do you happen to know of anyone who might have given Will Kodaly a little wolf figurine? Made of Hungarian porcelain, so maybe a Hungarian connection of his?"

She gave me a quizzical look, but then considered my question. "Will wasn't much of a collector. He made art, but he didn't accumulate the art of others. He didn't really have the time, I guess. But a little figurine? No, that doesn't sound like him at all."

"And when you talked to him last, did he say anything about a conflict? Someone who was an enemy?"

She folded her arms so that she was hugging herself, as though she needed comfort. "Will had flaws, like anyone, but people didn't tend to dislike him. He was a likable person."

"Huh."

"I mean, I guess the one area where he had some bad feeling was in the romance department. I suppose there might be women who hold grudges, although none that I know. But the men—sometimes they were a problem. Ex-boyfriends, or maybe current boyfriends, if the women were playing the field. At one point there was word he had an affair with a married woman. In any case, I think guys felt really threatened by Will. It doesn't seem like a motive for murder though, does it?"

I shrugged. "Well, thanks for talking to me, Cassandra."

She moved away, and my mother appeared at my side. "François says there are only two more trays of petit fours. So we might have to bring them out on smaller plates. This group has energy, and somehow that seems to make them eat more."

"Got it," I said. I went to the back to help François transfer cakes onto tinier trays; this way I could still make several trips to tables and spread them over the remaining half hour of the event.

"How does Claire like her new job?" I asked.

He shrugged. "She is pleased to have been chosen. But the hours are hard, and we miss each other."

"I get that."

He pursed his lips at me. "Are you going to apologize, to your Wolf?"

I wiped my hands on a napkin and studied him. "Is it a French thing, that look of disapproval? Because you're really good at it."

"*Oui*, I think." Now he looked smug.

I picked up one of the small trays. "And, yes, I'm going to apologize. Right after I leave this place. But he'll be busy at work, so I'm going to leave a note at his house. That's more personal than a text."

"Just wait there for him, apologize in person," he said.

I shrugged. "I'm feeling kind of cowardly. I think I'll

start with a note. Maybe leave him some *paprikás*. The way to a man's heart is through his tummy, right?"

François thought about this. "Yes and no. But better than nothing, Hana."

I sent him my own disapproving look and marched out with the food.

Chapter 4

....

ULVEFLOKK

Before I went to Erik's place, I stopped at my house and fed my cats. Then I went to my room for an old book of Hungarian fairy stories; it was a volume Erik had seen before, while investigating a different murder. I looked up a story called "The Servant Girl and the Wolf," and turned to a spot three pages into the tale. On this page was a picture of a young woman in a plain dress standing in the forest and looking up at an enormous gray wolf who seemed about to devour her. The text said,

> *The servant girl knew she could not return home to her cruel master, and she sobbed out her fears to the wolf, who took pity on her and said that he would be her protector.*
>
> *"The woods are full of devils," the wolf said. "But even the devils fear me. At my side you will be safer than anywhere else. In return I ask only for your devotion."*

The servant girl hugged the wolf around the neck and promised to serve him for her whole life. The sun was setting, and she could see the devils accumulating in the trees. "I'm afraid," she told him.

"Climb on my back," said the wolf.

The girl climbed on his back, and the wolf moved boldly through the woods.

I took a picture of the page and then sent it to my printer. I took the printed sheet to my counter. Beneath the story and the picture, I wrote, "You are my wolf protector. And I am devoted to you." I signed my name and put the paper in a file folder so it wouldn't get wrinkled. I grabbed an un-opened bottle of Pálinka that my grandparents had given me for Christmas, packed one Tupperware container full of *kiflis* and another with the last of the *székely gulyás* that he had enjoyed the night before. I tucked it all into a bag and headed for the door. "I'll be back soon," I told my cats.

The phone rang. With a sigh, I put my things down and snatched up my landline.

"Hello?"

"Hi—Hana? It's Eduardo Cavallero."

"I'm sorry? I think you have the wrong number."

"It's *Eduardo*. From Katie and Eduardo."

I dropped into one of my kitchen chairs. "Oh, Eduardo. Sorry about that. I just—you never call me." I made sure that my tone indicated that he would have no reason to do so.

"Yeah, and I'm sorry to bother you. I just—if you have a minute—I wanted to get your advice."

Oh no. "Oh?"

"Yeah. I suppose you know that Katie and I broke up. At least, she broke up with me. And in all honesty, I can't figure out why. We were having a good time, we were a good fit, you know? And I still can't figure out what I did wrong."

His voice was suddenly so vulnerable that I felt a burst of pity. "Oh, Ed, you didn't do anything wrong!"

"What?"

"Katie just—she probably just needs to see other people. She needs a basis for comparison. That's why all people are supposed to date around before they settle down, right?"

"Yeah, I suppose, but, the thing is, I think she was happy with me. And now when I see her at work, she doesn't look happy. I don't like seeing her face that way. Katie should always be smiling."

He earned huge points with me for putting the focus on Katie. I wondered for a moment if Katie had made a mistake. "Listen, Ed. I'm not sure what sort of advice you want, but—"

"Well, obviously I want to know what I can do to win her back. She must have said something to you. Was I boring? Did she think I was lazy or impolite?"

"No, no, listen. It's not about you so much. It's about Katie. She's a romantic. She wants—romance."

His tone was aggrieved. "I *was* romantic! I always pulled out her chair for her at restaurants, and I sent her flowers on her birthday."

Blech. "Ed, this is none of my business."

"I want you to make it your business. Just for one minute. Do you think I'm good for Katie?"

"You seemed to be."

"Do you think she misses me?"

"Yes. But maybe just as a friend."

"What? Why?"

I sighed. "Listen. I'm just giving you my perspective now, not Katie's, okay? I cannot speak for Katie."

"Okay."

"But if a man aspires to be my lover, and not just my friend, then I want to know that he wants me. That he feels passionate about me, not just friendly. I don't need a brother; I already have one. Katie has three. You know what I'm saying?"

I heard a scratching sound. *He was writing it down.* "So what would you want a lover to do?"

Erik Wolf's face appeared in my mind's eye. I longed, in that instant, for things to be as they were. "I would want him to look at me like he doesn't see anyone else, because he actually doesn't see them when I walk in the room. I would want him to have trouble keeping his hands off me—not in an aggressive way, but in subtle ways. Touching my hair, my elbow, my fingers. Always keeping contact with me, keeping our connection. I would want him to think of me when he was away from me, and to let me know he was thinking of me. With texts, or calls, or little poems he writes about me in the margins of books. I would want him to show up to visit me unexpectedly because he said he missed me. To tell me that my dark eyes haunt him. I would want thoughtful gifts—not expensive ones! Just little things. A perfect orange from the store, because he knows I love them. Or a little pad and pen for my telephone table because he noticed I didn't have one, and on the first page he's scrawled my name a hundred times."

"You're talking about *your* boyfriend," he said accusingly.

"Just a couple of those were real examples. But he is very romantic. And he doesn't have to try, Eduardo. He's romantic because he is *into* me. So it's effortless. He's following his inclinations. You see what I'm saying? Katie wants something authentic, not something forced. If you're not passionate about her, well—let her find someone who is."

"I get that."

"Do you? Because the problem now is that she asked for space. So you can't be obvious about any of those things. My best advice would be to go super subtle. Compliment her without expecting a response. Give her a little gift, but then leave. Don't hang around waiting for her to love you. It would be best at this point if she came to you, right? But you have to leave that little trail of bread crumbs."

"Hana."

"Yes?"

"This has been very helpful. Thank you."

"You're welcome." I felt a rush of trepidation, regretting now that I'd talked to Eduardo at all. But what was I to do? End the call without speaking to him? I had socialized with him on numerous occasions, and he was a nice person. I couldn't be that rude to him. Still, I didn't want him to think that I was somehow conspiring with him behind Katie's back. "Listen, Ed. Like I said, this was just general advice. I'm not speaking for Katie."

"I know. And I'm not going to be obnoxious, or stalk her, or do some other idiot thing. I just needed some perspective, and you have provided that."

"You work at an ad agency. You make a living creating pleasing words. You should be able to come up with the perfect campaign to win a woman's heart. But here's some more advice: less is more. She will not be impressed with an orchestra or a mariachi band or something outside her window."

"Like I said, I won't be an idiot."

"Okay, great. I hope it works out for both of you."

"Me, too. Thanks, Hana."

I said good-bye and ended the call, then caught Cleopatra's eyes. She sat in front of me on the floor like a gray cloud, her eyes disapproving.

"What? I didn't do anything. He called *me*, Cleopatra."

She twitched an ear and began licking a paw with an indifferent air. Her brother roamed in and butted his head into her side. I laughed. "You two keep each other company; I'm going to go. But I'll be back soon." I gave them both kisses on top of their fuzzy heads. Then I grabbed my things, locked the cats safely inside my place, jogged down to the car, and began my journey to Erik's apartment.

He lived about ten minutes away from me in North Riverwood. Once, when he had thought I was in danger, he had driven to my house in six minutes. I still marveled at this, especially when I noted once again how many traffic lights there were. Had he run them all? I felt a blend of pleasure and horror at the idea that Wolf the policeman might have risked his life for me.

I flicked on the radio and sang mindlessly with Adele, watching the autumn color flash past my window. Adele finished singing, and the Beatles started up with some sad ballad. Kelly Clarkson had sung almost all of "Breakaway" when I pulled into the parking lot of Erik's building. He lived in a tall dark-brick structure with shuttered windows. I had only been here a few times, since normally he came to me and I made him dinner. The first time he had brought me home I'd been thrilled by my admission into the personal space of the very private Wolf. I had investigated his bookshelves and the knickknacks on them, the art on his walls, but soon enough he pulled me to his couch, and that was where we remained for the entire evening.

He had eventually given me a key; he said I should have it in case he ever locked himself out, or if I ever left something at his house and needed to retrieve it while he was at work. Basically, it had been a gesture of trust. I hadn't used the key. Until now.

I grabbed my bag and marched up to the front door. Surely he would forgive me, when he came home and found my homemade card and gifts of food and brandy? I let myself into his little foyer, past the mailboxes where the name "Wolf" was on the very last box, and to the elevator at the end of the room. I took it to the third floor and walked down to number 304, feeling suddenly shy. With a burst of courage, I thrust the key into the lock and turned it, then eased in with my bag.

Wolf's place looked as I had remembered it. He had left a couple of lights on; did he do that for security reasons? I moved toward his kitchen and set down my card on the island in the center of the room. I knew that he tended to stand there and drink his coffee while scrolling through his messages. He would certainly find it soon.

I turned to his stainless steel refrigerator and looked at the two magnets on the door—one from Brookfield Zoo and another, a figure of a little man wearing a backpack that said "Trekker." Of course—the family business. A third magnet, a *Tyrannosaurus rex*, held a small piece of paper on which were scrawled the words "Meeting on Friday, 9 a.m."

I wondered if the note were old or new. I peeked into his refrigerator and found it mostly empty, although it held some cans of Diet Coke, a pack of string cheese, some yogurt, and a dish covered in tin foil. I slipped the *székely gulyás* inside, but left the Pálinka and *kiflis* on the counter, along with my note. I wanted to scrawl an additional comment at the bottom of the card, and I scanned Wolf's countertops for any sign of a pen.

It was at this point that a person came around the corner, and I yelped in surprise. We stared at each other, wide-eyed and shocked. It wasn't just any person: it was a beautiful

woman—a ridiculously beautiful woman—with a tall, wil-
lowy frame, long ice-blonde hair in a casual-yet-elegant
braid, cool blue eyes, and carefully sculpted brows. My
brain whispered, "Wolf's revenge."

But what my mouth said out loud was "ahhhh," the same
sort of sound I might have made if she had punched me in
the stomach.

She recovered more quickly than I did. Her mouth curved
into a smile—a beautiful smile, of course—and she said,
"Well, who have we here?"

"I'm Hana," I said. "Do you—are you a friend of Erik's?"

She laughed. And then, somehow, she walked into the
kitchen again. Or that was how it seemed for an instant,
when a woman who looked just like her came around the
corner and stood at her side. "We have a visitor," said the
first blonde woman.

"I have a key," I said, in an attempt to justify my presence.

"A *key*," they said in unison, and then exchanged a
glance. "Well, this one must be serious, then."

"I'm sorry?" I asked. My fear and shock were slowly
being replaced by annoyance. I had introduced myself.
Who *were* these rude women? Why did Erik have beautiful
blonde twins in his house? "I didn't catch your name," I
said to the first woman.

"I know who you are!" she said, her face suddenly
animated. "You're the Hungarian girl!" Her smile was
broad; she was almost laughing. I was being mocked.

"I didn't catch your *name*," I repeated, my voice cold.

Now both of them were laughing. "Oh, my—such spirit."
The first one stuck out her hand. "I'm Runa. This is Thyra."

I had just heard those names somewhere . . . Oh God.
Erik's sisters.

I shook the hand she offered. "He never told me you

were twins," I stammered. "I only just found out yesterday that he had sisters."

Thyra sniffed. "Figures. He keeps the family at a distance. But that's nothing new. He keeps everyone at a distance. That's why you are quite a surprise, standing here in the kitchen like a little apparition."

"I—brought him some food and a card. Normally I would just text him, but he's—upset with me."

Runa flipped her thick braid over her shoulder and patted my arm. "He's sensitive, our little brother. When he was a kid, we would tease him, and it would drive him into his various hiding places. He still loves being solitary." She studied me for a moment with her amazing eyes. "How did you two meet? He mentioned you when we had breakfast a couple of weeks ago, but all we could get out of him was that he liked someone and she was Hungarian."

"Hungarian American," I said. "My mom was born there; I was born here."

"Okay," Runa said. Her eyes had traveled to my hair. "Thyra, look at this." She leaned forward to lift some auburn strands. "Look at it in the light. The color is amazing. Couldn't you just see it, with the Høst line?"

Thyra stepped forward; they both towered over me and displayed a bizarre interest in my hair. "Oh yes! Can you imagine, under the studio light?" Her gaze left her sister's face and landed on mine. "Have you ever done modeling?"

I had not expected that question. "Modeling? Like—clothing? No." I let out a short laugh. "I work at a tea house."

This distracted Runa. "A tea house? That place on Wild Heather Road?"

"Yes. You know it?"

She nodded. "You have those monthly book events. I've gone to two of them. They're very fun. And the food was delicious. Remember, Tee? I asked you to come with me, but you wouldn't read the book." The blonde sisters mock-glared at each other.

"Yes, that's one of our most popular events. How funny that you've been there. You probably met my mother and grandmother, then. They run it with me. Or I run it with them, I guess."

Runa leaned in. "Your grandma! She's the one who tells fortunes? I wanted her to do mine, but the line was too long after my last event and I had to leave. Now that I have a connection, I'll ask her to do it sometime. My new friend Hana will let me in."

Thyra was still assessing me with her cool blue eyes. "Now, back to the modeling. Would you be willing to do a photo shoot? You have a good look. Pretty but relatable. And that hair would be perfect for every single one of the pieces in our winter line. It would complete them. Just some additions for our website and Instagram advertising."

I shook my head and folded my arms. "Who are you? I mean, what do you do?"

They blinked at me. "Wow, he really has told you nothing, huh?"

"Not a thing."

Runa put her arm around her sister. They looked like some beautiful two-headed goddess. "We own a company in the city. Norwegian woolens, the best in the U.S.A."

I must have looked uncertain, because Thyra said, "We're called Ulveflokk."

"What? Oh my gosh, my friend was just talking about you yesterday! She's a huge fan. You two run that company?"

Runa nodded. "Our baby. This is why we have no real babies. We're always at work."

"Except when you're here?" I asked.

They shook their heads, dismissive. Runa said, "We wanted to look at our brother's clothes. See what needs replenishing. We're nosy big sisters. Erik's private, and we rebel against his privacy." They grinned twin grins at me.

"I bought him one of your sweaters just yesterday. Did you see it in there?"

Thyra's eyebrows rose. "From the winter wheat collection. You got him that? A very good choice."

"I thought—my friend and I—that it would look good on him. We found it at a garage sale."

She frowned. "It was in someone's garage?"

"No, his house. And it was an elegant sale. He was an artist, and he was selling paintings and things. He's famous."

Runa looked interested. "I collect art. What's his name?"

"William Kodaly."

She clapped her hands once, like a teacher telling the class to settle down. "I have a Kodaly!" She turned to her sister. "The *True Love* painting! That's by him." She returned her attention to me. "I'm jealous. You met him?"

"Yes."

Thyra laughed. "Why do you look so sad about it?"

"It's a long story," I murmured.

"Does someone die in the end?" Thyra asked, still half laughing.

"Yes."

I'm not sure how it happened—perhaps it was because I hadn't yet processed Will Kodaly's death, or perhaps being grilled by Erik's sisters made me nervous, or perhaps I was sad that Erik was being distant from me. But with that one word, I began to cry.

Suddenly the blonde, sophisticated Wolf sisters were transformed into motherly souls, ushering me to Erik's table, turning on the heat under Erik's little red teakettle, and dabbing at my tears with tissues out of a box they produced from the next room.

Slowly they got the story out of me, their faces compassionate but also nakedly curious. I told them about poor William Kodaly, and the fact that Erik was now investigating his death while the three of us sat in his house *uninvited*. I frowned at them, but they shrugged back at me, unconcerned.

Thyra stared me down with her uncanny eyes. "That's sad about the artist. I hope Erik catches the killer. But I think there's more getting you down. You said, before, that Erik was upset with you. Why is that? Is it making you sad?"

I sighed. Perhaps these two could offer the objective opinion I needed. So I told them even more. About my grandmother, and the fact that I had recently learned she had psychic abilities, and that my mother seemed to have inherited them, and that perhaps I had, too. I told them about the light around my grandfather and my father. About the light I didn't see around Erik. And the fact that I had told him so.

"Ah," said Runa with a wise expression. "Well, you've put him on precarious footing."

"I didn't mean to. I just—this is very confusing. It's like a curse. I wish I didn't have this new complication in my life."

Thyra covered my hand with hers. "Are you *kidding*? It's amazing! Rue and I *love* psychics. We watch all those fake ones on cable. Even though we know they're liars, we still love the idea of second sight." She leaned in. "But your grandma really has it, right?"

I sighed a jagged sigh. "I think so, yes."

"We *have* to meet her, Hana."

"If your brother breaks up with me, there probably won't be much opportunity."

Runa pursed her lips. "He's not going to break up with you. Do you know what he told us, when he said he was dating you? He said that we should butt out, because he didn't want to jinx this. You see? He valued your relationship so much he didn't even want to talk about it. Probably for fear we would meet you and be bossy, which is what just happened, right?" Her smile was almost friendly.

"I'm used to bossy people," I said.

"Good. Then you'll be a good girl and pose for our catalog," Thyra said. "We want to make some flyers for our winter line; we can debut you that way. I know just how I want him to light you."

"Him?"

"The photographer we work with. He'll love you," Runa said. They both observed me with a certain smugness. Then Runa pointed at the Pálinka. "What's that? Some kind of booze?"

"It's Hungarian fruit brandy. I brought it as a peace offering."

"Huh. That's cute."

"I'm sorry I cried on both of you," I said.

Thyra stood up. "The water's boiling. You can tell us all about tea, and how your grandma reads the leaves." She prepared some tea in mugs that she took from Erik's cupboard and brought them to the table. "I'll bet it's fascinating, watching her work."

I nodded. "She hasn't actually done it since last month. You might have read that there was a murder at our tea house. That's how I met Erik, actually."

Runa clapped again. "You met him while he was on a case? Oh, that is perfect. Of course he didn't meet you in a bar or somewhere. He doesn't do that scene. So he came to solve your crime, and you fell in love with him?"

"Pretty much."

They looked at each other with some secret expression, then looked back at me with wry smiles. "We like you, Hana."

I managed a smile. Then a thought occurred to me. "Hey—what's Ulveflokk? Does that mean something?"

"Of course," Thyra said. "We are the Wolf family, right? Rue and I wanted to name our business after our family, so we called it Ulveflokk. That means 'wolf pack.' That's us."

"Wolf pack," I said. "I like that. I have to tell Katie. She won't believe this. She loves your clothes."

"We'll give you some things for her," Runa said airily. "Okay, we taught you something Norwegian. Now you teach us something Hungarian."

"Um. I don't know. The brandy over there is called Pá-linka."

"Something better," Thyra said. "Tell us something your grandma says."

I sipped my tea, then set it down. "I was upset today. I felt like I ruined things. When I left work, my grandma said, 'Lónak négy a lába, mégis megbotlik.'"

"Wow. Hungarian sounds cool. What does that mean?" Runa said.

"'The horse has four legs and still stumbles.' Meaning, we all make mistakes."

"That's great!" Runa said. "I'm going to take Hungarian lessons."

Thyra smirked and ticked things off on her fingers. "You said that about Spanish, Italian, and Mandarin."

"And I might still learn those," Runa said lightly.

I took one last sip of my tea. "I should go. I'll wash this out."

Thyra stood up. "I'll do it. Give me yours, Runa. Do you feel better, Hana?"

"I think so. Thanks. It was nice to meet both of you."

Runa held out her hand. "Do you have a phone? We'll put our info in there."

"Uh—okay." I handed her my phone and she typed with expert fingers. "Okay, now you have Thyra's number and mine. And I have your number, as well. We'll contact you about the photo shoot."

"Uh—"

They swept around the room, putting away dishes, then left briefly and returned wearing stylish coats. Thyra said, "Don't worry. Erik doesn't hold grudges. He has a soft heart."

Runa nodded and said, "And remember, Hana: I want to meet your grandmother. And I'll find some treats for your friend Katie. Oh, and you should come to my apartment sometime to see my Kodaly. I won't look at it the same, now that I know he—well, anyway."

"Okay, we have to run," Thyra said, looking at her watch. "Lock the door when you leave, Hana."

They waved and swept out of Erik's apartment; the room felt eerily quiet.

I stood and gathered my things. I found a pad in Erik's kitchen drawer, along with a pen. I wrote another note. This one just said, "Good night," and I signed my name. I went down the hall to Erik's bedroom. I hadn't spent any time in this room; we had stayed in his living room the few times I'd come over, and then left to go to dinner or a movie.

His room was large; his bed sat in the center, covered in a gray and red quilt. His headboard held a few necessities: earphones, a stack of books, some framed photos. I crept closer and set my note on his pillow. My eyes lifted to the headboard and a picture of Wolf's whole family: his parents, his brother, his sisters, and him, taken perhaps ten years earlier. They all looked young and handsome. In the

other frame was a picture of me that I had never seen. I
remembered when he took it outside the tea house. I was
wearing my uniform with the Hungarian apron over a white
blouse and black skirt. I looked like a tour guide at some
European museum. It was a nice picture, though. I was
smiling at Erik Wolf; it was clear, even in the photo, how I
felt about him. And he looked at it every day.

This final thought buoyed my spirits. I left the room,
went down the hall, and claimed my purse. My gifts remained on the counter; I hoped that they would have the
desired effect.

Chapter 5

....

THE HUNGER

When I got home I decided to busy myself in my kitchen. The cats jumped on dining room chairs so that they could watch me work. The sun had disappeared again, and the room was gray with twilight. I lit some candles to brighten my mood, put on a Spotify playlist that I had titled "Variety," and listened to songs that spanned fifty years. Meanwhile, I started chopping an onion and preparing a beef mixture for *töltött káposzta*. I put a head of cabbage in boiling water and went into my living room to flip on some lights. The Kodaly hung on the wall, warming my room with its beauty. I was glad I had purchased it, for many reasons.

I went back to the kitchen and poured some food for the cats. When my cabbage was soft, I removed it from the water and let it cool on a paper towel. Slowly, carefully I pulled off leaves and began wrapping them around spoonsful of my meat mixture, tucking each cabbage leaf carefully around the filling. While I worked, I thought of Kodaly. Who could have been his enemies?

He was a talented man, and Cassandra had suggested he had many friends within the artistic community. But three women—my mother, my grandmother, and Cassandra—suggested that Kodaly had been a wolf around the ladies. Could this really have gotten him killed? Did men kill out of jealousy? Did women kill because they were rejected? I supposed they did, but it seemed like a stretch. Plenty of people had reputations as romantic manipulators and lived to tell the tale.

What else could be a motive for murder? If the tracking device on the bottom of the wolf was really meant for Kodaly, then that ruled out the possibility of a random assailant or a surprised burglar. It meant the crime was personal.

I finished folding my cabbage squares—fragrant with beef, rice, paprika, and onions—and tucked them into a large pot, covering them with my special Hana tomato sauce. I put them on simmer and turned to the cats. "What now?" I said.

As if in answer, the phone rang, and I snatched it up. "Hello?"

"Hana, it's me," said my mother.

I struggled with my disappointment for a moment, then said, "Hey, Mom. What's up?"

"I just spoke with Sofia on the phone."

"Your artist friend?"

"Yes. She's very upset about Will Kodaly."

"So was Cassandra. I spoke to her at the tea today."

"Yes. Really it is so sad, even to me. I can't imagine how much sadder it would be if you had been in a relationship with a person."

"Did Sofia have—any ideas?"

My mother sighed. "I don't think so. She hadn't been in touch with Will for a while. They had been an item once; I'm not quite sure when they broke up. But I get the impression that when Sofia married her husband a couple years ago, she had been trying to decide between two men. It's sad, because she and her husband divorced. Now she's dating some new man."

"Wow. Love is hard, isn't it?"

"Not always," my mother said, her voice placid and soothing.

Easy for her to say. She had married her first love.

"Anyway. Did you get any other information out of her?"

"Just that she's going to this autumn ball that the chamber of commerce throws every year, and I guess she's persuaded them to do a short tribute to Will at the event this Saturday. He was well-known in Riverwood. Sofia hinted that a lot of his former lovers would be present."

"*Really.*"

"Your boyfriend might want to know that."

"Yes. I think I should tell him," I said.

"You do that. I don't know that he can get in, unless he flashes his badge. The event is sold out, apparently. Anyway, I have to go. Your dad says hi."

"Hi to Dad, and good night to you both. I made stuffed cabbage, and my house smells great."

"Grandma would be proud."

I agreed with her, said a fond farewell, and hung up.

I paced around my house for a while. Did I want to call Erik? Or did I want him to call me? After all, I had made the first gesture. I had driven to his house, left peace offerings and two heartfelt notes. His silence, after that, seemed a bit churlish.

But perhaps he was working late, as he often did. If so,

then it would be wrong to let resentment build up inside me. Perhaps even now he was pursuing some lead about Will Kodaly or the Herend wolf, and his police brain didn't have time to think about his love life.

I glanced at my watch. It was almost eight o'clock.

With a sigh, I went to my television and stared at a mindless comedy for half an hour, then got up and checked on my cabbage rolls. I lifted the lid and smelled something divine; the aroma went through me like a bolt of pleasure, more powerful than usual, and I realized that I was experiencing something else, some other feeling, an intense mixture of pleasure and pain. It wasn't about the food; something was happening.

I turned off the flame under the pot, replaced the lid, and walked to my apartment door. I opened it to find Erik Wolf standing there, looking hungry, his hand lifted and about to knock.

"Hello," I said. "Did Iris buzz you in?"

He nodded. "We have an arrangement."

Iris was five and lived on the first floor. She was better than any hired security guard; she kept watch on the building, and she knew friend from foe.

Uncertain, not smiling, I said, "Erik—" and he lunged forward, pulled me against him, and spoke into my hair.

"I'm sorry. I overreacted," he said. "I don't know why. Of course you're curious about your ability. Anyone would be. And I understand why you would want—to see something that the others saw."

I leaned back and pulled his face down to my level. I kissed his stubbly cheek and the bridge of his nose and his mouth. "I don't care. I don't care if I ever see it. I know you're the man for me."

He kissed me back for a while, then pulled away and said, "Yeah?"

"Yes, of course. You knew that already. We both did."

He sighed, a man reprieved. "I've been feeling kind of sick for a day. It feels bad, not being on the right footing with you."

"I know. I felt it, too. But I have just the remedy." Relief flowed through my veins, practically sedating me. I took his hand and pulled him into my apartment, and he stopped short.

"God, it smells good in here. What is that, cookery witch?"

I laughed. "*Töltött káposzta.* Hana's version of Grandma's recipe. She says it's even better than hers, but of course she's lying."

"I'm salivating. And I've barely eaten today, for a lot of reasons."

I pushed him into the kitchen, and then into a chair. Antony appeared and began playing with Erik's shoelace. Slowly my boyfriend was starting to look like himself again. My grandmother would say that the fairies had freed him from a spell.

I got him a Diet Coke out of my refrigerator when he said he was too tired for wine. I began to prepare him a plate. "You got my notes, I take it?"

"What? Where did you leave notes?"

I spun around. "At your apartment. I went there and left you things. You didn't find them?"

He rubbed his eyes. "I haven't been home. I got caught up at work, and then I came here." His green eyes locked on to mine. "I always come here."

I smiled and turned back to his plate. "Well, you'll find some gifts from Hana when you get there." I brought the

plate and some silverware to the table. I made a quick blessing over Erik—a family tradition—and he began to eat.

And then he began to moan. "Oh God," he said. "Do
you have any of that bread left from the other day?"

I nodded and went to my pantry, where I got out some
beer bread and cut a large slice. I brought it back to him.
"The perks of having a Hungarian girlfriend."

He nodded. "But only one of about a million reasons I'm
glad you're my girlfriend." ·

The room felt good now, with happy waves surround-
ing us.

I couldn't resist saying, "That thumbs-up text was a
nasty little touch."

His eyes were remorseful. "I was hurt."

"I know. You know who explained that to me? François.
He took your side."

He tore off a piece of bread. "I was the talk of the tea
house?"

"No, I was. My failure to understand the 'inner eye,' as
my grandma calls it. Your sisters were fascinated by that."

He sat up straight. "What? *My* sisters?"

"Oh yeah, I forgot to tell you. I went to your apartment
to leave you apology presents, and they were there, both of
them, and they studied me like I was a little bug under a
microscope."

"Oh, Hana, I'm sorry! I was going to expose you to them
in small doses."

I laughed. "No, it's fine. I liked them. They're fun. I
think they liked me."

He had devoured two cabbage rolls and was sending
longing glances toward the stove.

"Would you like more?" I asked, laughing.

"Is there any?"

"Of course—remember what I told you?"

"Right. The Domo factor. I'm going to give him a run for his money. I'll get it, though." He went to the stove, and I admired his tall form, his lean body, strong without the bulging muscles that I tended to find unattractive.

"Your sisters told me what Ulveflokk means. I'm learning so many new things."

"Yeah. You have your Hungarian clan of psychics, and I have the Wolf Pack."

"We'll wait to tell Grandma. One wolf is enough for her."

He grinned and returned with his food. "Next time you go shopping, I'm going with you, so I can pay for your groceries. I'm always eating up your stock."

He sat down, looking at ease. Cleopatra strolled in, seemingly unconcerned that we had all been talking without her. Antony climbed onto Erik's feet and closed his eyes, making Erik laugh.

"We should go shopping together anyway. It's romantic."

"Yeah."

"So I'm afraid to ask: do you have any leads about Will?"

"Will? When did he become Will?"

"That's what my mom calls him. He was an acquaintance, I guess. She says he was friends with a lot of people."

He nodded. "Yeah, I'm trying to go through his network and make sense of it all. Do you have anything more you can tell me?"

"Well, yes. Do you have your sexy notebook?"

He chewed and swallowed some food while smiling at me. Then he said, "My notebook is sexy?"

"Very."

"I did not know that." He pushed his plate away and took his notebook from his pocket. "And, yes, I do have it."

"Good."

We sat at the quiet table for a moment. He reached out and touched my fingers. Something curled inside me, twined around my core. I sighed.

Then I leaned back. "Okay, here goes. My mother knows of three different women who were involved with Kodaly over the years."

Detective Wolf's pen moved rapidly. "Names?"

"Sofia Kálmar. She's an artist, like him. Then Cassandra Stone. You might know her if you've ever gone to the library. She's that really pretty lady with the office by the check-in counter. And then there's Amber Derrien. She taught me in high school. She still does teach at Riverwood High."

"Good, good. I didn't learn any of this today. I should just go to you first when someone Hungarian is involved."

"Hmm. Okay, then you should know that both my grandma and my mother said that Kodaly was a wolf."

"Meaning?"

"You know—always hunting the ladies. But I spoke with Cassandra at a tea event today, and she said that Will kept good relationships with his ex-lovers. That he was charismatic. But I think she was hinting that men didn't like him . . ."

"Okay. Helpful." He scrawled away, turning a page and writing more. "And what was this Cassandra's relationship with him now?"

"She's in a new relationship; she was done with Will a couple years ago, I guess, but she said there was a rumor that he dated a married woman, or something like that— some sort of scandal. I don't know. With stuff like this, you have to sift through the gossip and determine what's just falsehood."

"Sure."

"Oh, and another thing. Sofia told my mom that there's

going to be some sort of autumn ball on Saturday, sponsored by the chamber of commerce, and she thinks a lot of Will's old girlfriends will be there because he was well-known in the business and arts community."

"Huh."

"She says it's all sold out, but I think I can get tickets."

His eyes twinkled at me. "You have connections?"

"No, not exactly, but here's another weird thing that happened. I was at a restaurant with Falken—you remember him?"

Erik nodded. Falken had helped him buy a very special gift for me once.

"Anyway, this man came up to us because he heard me say my grandma's name. He said something about how he loved my grandma and our whole family, and he was in our debt, or something. I told Grandma and my mom, but they'd never heard of him."

"Huh. So?"

"Well, he gave me his card. Said if he could ever do anything, blah-blah. And he works at the chamber of commerce."

Erik grinned. "Hana, my little ace in the hole. Can I be your date?"

"First I'll see if I can get tickets. If so, I wouldn't want any other date."

This pleased him.

"There's something else," I said. "Come with me."

I stood up and held out my hand. He took it, and I led him into the living room and pointed at the wall. "Will Kodaly painted that."

"Wow."

"If you look at the caption, it says it's a town in Hungary. When I Googled him, I found a picture of him in this same town. I don't know if this has any meaning, but I wanted you to see his art. Oh, and this," I said, going to the wall and holding up the painting of Cassandra. "He painted it." I pointed at the woman at the fence. "That's Cassandra, one of the women I just mentioned."

"Ah. And did he always paint the women he dated?"

"Cassandra suggested he did. She said he was able to work rapidly and he was always looking for subjects. I told her she could have this if she wants it."

His eyes left the painting and rested on me. "You're a nice person."

I set the painting down. "It's been such a long day. I'd love to rest my feet here for a minute." I pointed at the couch, one of our favorite places. "Did you have any other questions?"

He looked at his notebook. "This is good for now." He tossed it onto my coffee table and lunged forward, tackling me against the pillows.

I screamed with laughter, but soon, under the intensity of Erik Wolf's kissing, I felt very, very serious.

And the thing that grew within me twined another tendril around my heart.

Chapter 6

....

THE BABY IN BÉKÉSCSABA

A giant inflatable witch floated on a plastic broom in front of the Riverwood Chamber of Commerce. I paused to contemplate her cheerful face; apparently Halloween decoration designers wanted to present a dichotomy of cheerful fun contrasted with a traditional symbol of evil. I had experienced my fill of witch tales in the last month; I shivered slightly and marched up the pumpkin-lined steps.

Henrik Sipos had been very glad to hear from me; he assured me that he could meet with me this morning for whatever I might wish to discuss. He had been so accommodating, in fact, that I had started to suspect his motives; however, since he could also have rightly suspected mine, I decided to give him the benefit of the doubt.

A sign in the lobby told me that "H. Sipos, Director" could be found on the second floor, so I climbed the white stone stairway and sought room 204. I didn't have to look for the number; the first door I passed was wide open, and the man I recalled as Henrik Sipos sat behind the desk, peering over his glasses at a computer monitor.

In the moment before he saw me I was able to study him, unobserved. Even though he was sitting, it was clear that he was a relatively tall man, and a thin one. I hadn't paid much attention to that in the restaurant, confused as I had been by his presence. He smoothed his well-trimmed white mustache with one finger while he read something on his screen. His desk was filled with papers, but they were neatly arranged, and the radiator behind him had been turned into a sort of table that held framed photographs. His gray suit looked well-worn but elegant. On his lapel was a pumpkin pin that flashed an orange light every other second.

He sensed my presence and glanced at the door. His face lit up with happiness and he stood behind his desk, then moved swiftly around it to approach me, his hand held out in welcome. "Miss Keller! How wonderful to see you! I am so glad you came to pay me a visit."

"Yes, well—thank you. Yes."

He ushered me to a seat across from his desk and sat back down himself. "Things are rather busy here around the holidays, as you can imagine," he said, still smiling. "All of our businesses try to increase foot traffic and we attempt to facilitate that in a variety of ways."

I didn't really want to hear his commercials for the chamber of commerce. "Mr. Sipos," I began.

"Henrik!" he shouted jovially. "Do call me Henrik."

"Um—okay. The other day, you sort of took me by surprise. You said you knew my grandmother?"

He nodded, then shook his head. "Yes, know her, but I also don't know her. Did you mention me to her?"

"Yes, I did."

"And she probably said she had never heard of me," he said, beaming.

"She did, yes."

Nothing got this guy down. He continued to grin at me. "The fact is, your grandmother last saw me when she was four years old. I myself was just a little boy. A toddle."

"Toddler," I corrected.

"Ah, yes! A toddler." He lifted his hands and put them out before him, then listed from side to side to simulate the uncertain walking of a baby. "But you see, your grandmother was much beloved in my family always, because she was the daughter of *Natalia*."

He said the name of my great-grandmother with such reverence that I got the chills, and again the face of Natalia rose up before me, gentle and smiling, almost as though she were in the room. "How did you know her?" I asked.

He sat back in his chair and sighed. "There is a story. Do you have time to hear it?"

As if I would leave without hearing it! "Yes, sure," I said.

He nodded. "My mother is still living. She is ninety years old; her name is Stefania Sipos. In 1960, she lived in Békéscsaba, Hungary."

"My grandmother was born in Békéscsaba," I said.

"Yes." His eyes twinkled at me. "The only child of Natalia, yes?"

I nodded. "My great-grandfather was killed in the revolution. In 1960, he had already been dead for four years." For some reason this made me want to cry.

Henrik Sipos nodded. His smile disappeared with my mention of the revolution, and he looked like a different man.

I looked at my hands for a moment, and I thought of my

great-grandmother's hands, veined and gnarled but always somehow beautiful, and possessing a very strong grip when they held on to mine. I looked back up. "But back to Békéscsaba."

Sipos's smile was gentle now. "I was the first child in my family; at that time, an only child. A pamper baby."

I didn't correct him this time. I was hanging on each word, waiting for clarity.

"My mother doted on me. She would walk me around town in a little carriage, and everyone knew me. I often feel that I have a vague memory of those days, of all the friendly faces that would peer at me in my comfortable buggy. But perhaps I manufactured those memories, ya? From the many times my mother told me the story."

I nodded.

"Everyone in town knew me, whose baby I was. There was no danger in our little town, no real conflict, except hurt feelings from town gossip or little fights about whose food was better, or whose horse was faster, or whose child was smarter."

I managed a smile, but a misery grew in me. Something was going to happen to that baby in the past. To little Henrik Sipos.

Big Henrik Sipos cracked his knuckles with an absent expression. "One sunny day in May my mother walked me down a street full of shops, peering into one after another to say hello to the proprietors, or to dart in for a quick purchase. She left my buggy on the sidewalk because it was large and hard to get through the doorways. She would tuck her little bags in a basket behind the carriage.

"At the end of the block was a candy store, and my mother had a sweet tooth. She pushed my stroller just past the doorway—just past, she said—because she wanted me to be in the shade. It was a rather warm day, and my eyes were watering from the sun. She regrets it now, regrets every choice that she was forced to recall, again and again."

I gasped. I knew what was coming. Poor Stefania.

"My mother went in to get her candy. She liked a chocolate called Macskanyelv—means 'cat's tongue,' because it was thin and shaped that way, like a tongue. She got a box of them that day, but never bought them again, couldn't look at them. She didn't even like cats afterward. Because she walked out of that little store and my carriage was gone. Simply gone. No one had seen a thing, heard a thing. The buggy hadn't blown anywhere because there was no wind."

He looked up at me, amazed by the memory and his own role at the center of the mystery. "Years later people told us they could hear my mother's scream in their memories—so chilling they thought that witches had come to their town."

"Oh, Henrik," I said.

"Oh, at first she wasn't afraid. She assumed a friend or shopkeeper had wheeled me into a store to pick me up or pet me or pass me around, as people sometimes did. They called me *Kis Henhen*."

Little Hen-hen.

"Did she call the police?" I whispered.

"Yes, yes. Everyone flowed around her; the police were there in no time. They were stern, serious. They took statements from everyone, drove everywhere, did all that they could do."

"But they didn't find you?"

"No." Henrik shook his head. "Two weeks went by. My mother became thin, frail. My father could not get her to eat."

In a burst of something like light, I felt her misery. Saw her refusal to look at her own face in the bathroom mirror.

Saw what she saw as she eyed her husband's razor on the edge of the sink . . .

"Oh, your poor mother."

"Why do we always blame ourselves?" he asked, shaking his head. "For accidents, for things out of our control? But we do."

"I'm so sorry," I said.

His face brightened. "But here I am before you! And my mother lives here in Riverwood, in a little in-law apartment in my home!"

"So—what happened?" I asked.

I knew the answer before he said, "Your great-grandmother happened!" and beamed at me, his hands folded together as if in prayer.

I sat up straight and stared at him. I don't think I blinked for the remainder of the story. Henrik smoothed his tie. "My father was greatly distressed. His son was gone, and his wife was dying of despair. He asked the people in town to help him, and one of the young mothers said that he should go to see Natalia."

A looming image: my great-grandmother's old, sweet face. She would have been twenty-seven or twenty-eight then. My age. "Natalia."

"Yes. She lived in town in a little apartment near her parents' house. Just her and her daughter Juliana, who was four, almost five years old."

"Yes."

My grandmother as a child. My chills increased, causing something between pleasure and pain.

"People said that Natalia could see things. That she had helped them find lost watering pails or stray chickens, or once even an old grandpa who had wandered away. She never claimed to be anything—they just went to her."

"Who went to Natalia? Your father?"

He shook his head. "For some reason my father wanted the police to go. He knew one of the investigators—a man named Joe Rohaly. They were about the same age. Rohaly took my absence personally. He couldn't sleep at night, wondering what he had missed—what all of them had missed. My father—Istvan was his name—convinced Joe to hear this woman out, this Natalia who worked as a seamstress and a sometime babysitter.

"So they go to her house one night. Natalia was reading to her daughter, Joe told me, the little girl in her lap." He paused in his reverie and looked at me. "I got the accounts from my mother and father, but also from Joe, who is an old man today. Still alive, yes! These old Hungarians never die."

"Does Joe live here in Riverwood?"

"No, no. He is in Budapest these days. He sits by the Danube and paints watercolors. A very strong old man, and kind." He seemed to be assessing my mood. Then he added, "I also got the account from Natalia. She was alive, too, when I came to America. I talked to her once, over coffee at a Chicago diner. It was an emotional reunion. She hugged me and called me *kis* Henrik, and *csoda baba*. Means 'miracle baby,'" he said.

I nodded. My great-grandmother. Alive again, her feet striking the pavement as she walked to a meeting with the boy she saved. "Go on," I said.

He scratched his head. His phone rang, and I jumped. He picked it up and said hello, then, "Oh yes, Celia. Absolutely. I'm in a meeting right now, but I can do that around noon. Does that work for you? Splendid! See you then." He hung up the phone and jotted a note on his calendar, then looked back at me.

"Where were we?"

"Joe went to Natalia's house."

"Yes. Natalia told me that Joe had brought her a bear, a stuffed bear that belonged to me. She held it in her hands and she felt things right away, but she didn't want to tell the policeman what she felt."

"What was it?"

"That a boy had died. That he lay unblessed in a box."

"Oh God."

"Yes. She feared the boy was me. But then her little daughter took the bear and smiled at its face and told her mother that Henrik missed it."

"What? Did my grandmother know you?"

He shook his head. "No, not then. She had never heard my name." He cleared his throat. "So Natalia looked in her daughter's eyes, and then she looked at the bear. And she kissed it. She put her lips on the bear's fuzzy face, where the child would have put his lips."

My eyes filled with tears, and Henrik handed me a box of tissues.

He said, "Then she knew that I was still alive, as her daughter had suggested."

"So why did she see a boy in a box?"

Henrik sighed. "He was the boy I was meant to replace."

Chapter 7

....

THE WOMAN WITH MAGIC FINGERS

Henrik Sipos looked at his watch. "It's a long and complicated story, isn't it? Let me hurry and finish." He pushed some files out of the way and set his elbows on his desk. "There was a girl in a nearby farm town. Her name was Hajna. Her husband had died, and she had only her baby. She had been nursing the child through a terrible flu, and the baby died."

I took another tissue.

He nodded wisely at me. "They say that something in her died then, too. That she became a ghost walking around. All she knew was that she could not live without her child—exactly how my mother felt a few days later. Hajna's mind offered her a solution the night her poor boy died. He lay still on the bed and she prayed over him, alone. But then she was convinced that the angels told her to find another boy, and to tell the world that he was her son. No one yet knew that her boy was gone."

"The poor girl," I said.

"She had no coffin, but she had a wood box of her husband's. She tore an old dress with a satin skirt and lay her child on the satin bed. She closed the box and put it in her backyard, under an awning. Then she went to start her husband's ancient car, and she drove two towns over, to Békéscsaba, to find her new son."

"Oh, Henrik!"

"No one ever saw her because she strode up to my carriage with confidence, and anyone glancing at the scene would think she was the mother of the child. It was as if she were invisible."

"How did Natalia see that?"

He shrugged. "She told Joe that she saw the baby, fat and happy, while another boy lay dead. She said she felt that one boy was meant to fill the chasm of grief left by the other."

"Joe said he leaned in and studied Natalia's eyes, which were wise and calm. He said, 'Where?' She didn't know, but she told him what she saw: chickens pecking, a rusty car, a blue barn."

"My god."

"Joe went back to the station. Whatever he said convinced them, and they looked up every woman in the region who had given birth in the last two years. Then they sent cars around, looking for a blue barn. It took only one day."

I leaned forward. "What happened to that poor girl?"

He nodded. "Joe said when they saw the barn, they called for backup. Then the cars pulled into the sad little driveway. She lived in poverty. She came to the door holding me. Joe said he recognized me right away. He felt great relief to see me alive. I was drinking a bottle and smiling at him. Then he turned his attention to the girl, who was not healthy. She was thin and pale and her eyes were unfocused."

"Were they gentle with her?"

"They were. All of the police were kind. They went inside with her and praised her house and helped her make some lunch, and asked where was the baby that they saw in the pictures all around the room?"

"Oh, my."

"Hajna never hesitated. She said he had died, and she made him a satin bed and kept him close to her; she pointed at the back door. One officer went outside and found the sad little box."

We sat in silence for a moment.

"They took Hajna to her family. When my mother and father heard the truth, they said they would not prosecute. The girl was eventually brought to some kind of sanatorium. My mother kept track of her; she worried over her. She—understood the loss, she said. She told me, when I was about fifteen, that Hajna had married again, a late-in-life marriage, and that she was well and happy. She had a child, too, I think—a little girl."

I wiped at my eyes and half glared at him. "That is a crazy story, Henrik."

"Yes. Do you know, I really do think I remember the moment that I was reunited with my mother? Because I can see her face now: never have I seen such joy. Never again in my life."

"Stop making me cry."

He laughed softly, handing me another tissue. "My parents met your great-grandmother about a week after I was returned. Joe went to my parents and said he thought they should know the role she played. That she had given them the blue barn, and without it I might never have been found, and Hajna might have descended into madness."

"And so the women met? The two mothers?"

Henrik smoothed his mustache. "My mother says that she held your great-grandma very tightly, for a very long time. That she had felt all sorts of things on that day she met her, leftover feelings that she didn't know how to process—joy, grief, worry, regret, guilt, sadness—and that Natalia, in her embrace, touched my mother's hair with her fingers; stroking, stroking her hair. Suddenly my mother felt peace—such peace, like she had never known even before I disappeared. And it stayed with her. They had coffee and *palacsinta*, and they talked and laughed together, and Natalia held me in her lap, and her daughter, Juliana, petted me and said that she knew I had missed my bear."

"Wow."

"Yes. You can see why your family is beloved by mine. My mother kept track of your family always. When Natalia's daughter grew up and got married, my mother sent a wedding card. When Natalia moved to America with her daughter and her husband and their children, she made sure that they left a forwarding address. I think my mother wrote to Natalia until the day Natalia died. And my mother and I were at her funeral. We were in America by then."

Natalia's funeral. I had been fifteen years old; it was hazy to me now, but I recalled a church full of people and my surprise that she would know so many in a country that was not her homeland.

"Thank you for telling me this, Henrik."

"You are very welcome. Do you know, you look very much like young Natalia. I suppose you know this."

"I don't have a ton of pictures of her from when she was young."

"My mother has one; someone took it of the two of them together, not long after I was returned to her. I'll ask her for it. Truly, you resemble her."

Something like joy, warm and glowing, moved inside me.

Henrik said, "In Békéscsaba, people jokingly called your great-grandmother the woman with magic fingers, because of her gift for sewing. But after this event, the name took on other connotations. They heard Natalia had touched the bear with her magic fingers and told young Joe where he would find that child. After that, she was revered. *Revered*. She wanted for nothing in that town."

"That's amazing," I said.

Henrik's eyes narrowed; he was looking back into a time that he barely remembered. "I remember something Joe Rohaly told me when I met him for lunch once in Budapest, long after I grew up. We talked about the case, and about Natalia's role in it. Joe said, 'I asked her after the baby was back home and all was well, how did she do it? How was she able to summon those details out of the air?'"

"Yes? What did she tell him?"

Henrik shook his head. "I've always remembered it. She said, 'The mind is a forest with many paths. Sometimes, when you are lost and need to see the way, one of those paths will be illuminated. You just have to wait for the light.'"

I took one last tissue and dabbed at my eyes. "There's a lot to process in that story. Thank you for taking the time to tell it to me. I should let you get back to your job."

"But is that all? You came only to hear the story? I thought you mentioned a favor on the phone. For reasons you now know, I would love to grant it." He smiled at me with a benevolent expression.

"Oh—well, it seems silly and unimportant now. But I heard that there's a dance this Saturday and that the tickets have all been sold. I also heard there will be a special tribute to a man named William Kodaly—"

"Oh yes, Will Kodaly. My friend."

"What? You knew him?"

He smiled. "All the Hungarians know one another—doesn't your grandma tell you this? Will and I had much in common. I was very sad to hear of this crime that took his life."

"Yes. For a variety of reasons, I'd like to go to the dance, and I wondered if you'd be able to get tickets for me."

Henrik Sipos stood up behind his desk. He walked around and reached out his hands. I stood and took them, and he pulled me into a gentle hug. "I embrace you as I once embraced your great-grandmother Natalia Kedves, who saved my father from sadness, my mother from despair, and me from a life not meant to be. In her name I am happy to grant you this wish, and any others you bring to me in my lifetime, if it is in my power to provide."

⤸

Henrik escorted me to the first floor, where he introduced me to a woman named Bailey, who looked slightly harried but managed a smile when she said, "How many?"

I asked for four, and Henrik said, "Make it six. She might recall some friends she'd like to invite." Bailey disappeared into her office and came back with the tickets. I thanked her, and Henrik escorted me to a little easel by a window at the end of the main hallway. On it was a picture of Will Kodaly, circled by a wreath someone had made out of roses and greenery. A little placard read "In memory of Will Kodaly, friend to the Riverwood community."

I looked at Henrik. "I had no idea Mr. Kodaly was so popular."

Henrik shrugged. "Not so much; he was a quiet man, liked to keep to himself. But he came here often because he knew us, and he, like all of us, supported small businesses. He *was* a small business, after all. And we know him here because he painted our mural."

"Which mural?"

"Oh, you haven't seen it? Come with me." Once again he led me, this time to a room at the back of the building that said "Community Room" on the door. "We have meetings here with the public, so this was where we wanted Will to create something for us. It's very popular."

We turned the corner and I saw that one entire wall had been dedicated to Kodaly's vision of community: a rescue. In his scenario, an entire town had gathered below a building where a child was about to fall from a window, her little fingers digging precariously into the ledge. Below her, people were climbing onto each other's shoulders with determined expressions, and they were calling to the child. Her face was not terrified but hopeful. It was a melodramatic painting but surprisingly moving.

"I have to get out of this building," I murmured.

Henrik understood. "Lots of emotion. And do you know what? Will knew my story, too, about Békéscsaba. A few weeks ago, we shared a beer after my work, and he told me he painted it."

"Painted what?"

"The reunion of mother and son. The way he imagined it. He said the story had stayed with him, and he had painted it, but it had sold from a gallery; otherwise he would have showed it to me. He said he had a digital picture of it somewhere and he would bring it next time." He looked at the mural and said, "Often life is unfair. But I cannot complain. Can you?"

"No," I said fervently. "And thank you, Henrik. For making time for me and getting me these tickets. I'll let you get back to your busy day."

He bowed to me, formal as an ambassador, and kissed my hand.

Chapter 8

....

DARK INTENTIONS

I sat in my car for a while with my eyes closed, trying to process everything that I had heard.

My great-grandmother had been psychic—not just intuitive, but psychic.

I had talked with a man who had been kidnapped as a baby.

My grandmother Juliana, at age four almost five, had known that the lost child was alive.

My great-grandmother, at twenty-seven, had looked like me.

The last idea had me feeling emotional, and I shook my head, not sure what I wanted to do next or if I wanted to talk to anyone.

Fate solved that problem by making my phone ring. I dug in my purse and took it out. "Hello?"

"Hana? It's Mom."

My mother's voice was concerned, almost agitated.

"What's up, Mom? I'll be at the tea house in a few minutes."

"I just—I got the sense that something was wrong. Are you okay?"

"Oh, for gosh sakes. It really is all of us."

"What?"

I let out a slow breath. "I'm fine. Thank you for caring. I'll be at the tea house in a few, and, boy, do I have a story for you."

"Oh—all right. As long as you're okay."

I had a sudden memory of my mother's face, twenty-some years in the past, when I was six or so and I'd decided it would be funny to hide in a rack of clothing at the department store. I was pleased with myself, feeling independent and figuring my mother would congratulate me on disappearing so effectively. Instead, I heard her voice, near tears, asking the saleswoman if she had seen a little girl in a red dress. "She was right here, and she's not the type to wander off!" my mother said. Her voice had grown louder as her fears grew, and I slunk out of the clothing to reveal myself to her.

The saleswoman pointed at me; my mother swung around; and her face, red with fear and impending tears, grew soft with relief and love. "Oh, *Hana*!" she cried. "You should never, never do that to Mommy! I thought someone took you *away* from me!"

I had started to cry, shocked by her emotion, and she bundled me into her arms. "Oh, my baby," she whispered. "Never leave me."

Now I felt her relief over the phone.

"Hey, Mom? I love you," I said.

At the tea house my mother and grandmother were already bustling around, getting ready for an evening event with the Riverwood Youth Symphony. The conductor treated her musicians once a year to a high tea in keeping with their elegant music.

I ordered them both to sit down, and they did so, surprised. My grandmother still clutched a teapot, and my mother held a bottle of Windex and a cloth; she had been polishing mirrors. "You need to put that stuff down so you don't drop it," I said.

They did so, sitting at a round table which was already set for the visitors.

"You both said you never heard of Henrik Sipos."

They nodded.

"But he knows us. I went to him to ask for tickets to that dance sponsored by the chamber of commerce. Long story. And I asked him how he knew you."

They looked at me, expectant and intrigued.

"He knew you because when he was a baby he was kidnapped in Békéscsaba."

"What!" my mother cried.

My grandmother sat up straighter; her eyes grew wide and luminous.

"That's not all. Great-grandma Natalia and her four-year-old daughter, Juliana, helped the police find him. They never would have found him without you, Grandma."

My grandmother closed her eyes for a moment, then opened them. "He had a bear," she said.

"Yes! And you helped your mother. Grandma," I said, pulling her into a hug, "what a special little girl you were."

Grandma was remembering. "She got gifts, from every-one in town. *Kolbász* and jellies and a chicken that became my pet. A pretty fan made of feathers, I think. And a comb with rhinestones. Was like Christmas."

My mother leaned close. "What exactly are we talking about?"

I sat down across from them and told them the whole tale: the disappearance, the police, the lack of clues, the suggestion that they talk to Natalia. And then the bear and the blue barn.

My mother's blue eyes were compassionate. "What a sad, sad story." Then it seemed to dawn on her, our very real connection to the tale. She turned to her companion in surprise. "I can't believe that little girl was you!" She slung an affectionate arm around her mother and said, "And that the town seer was my *grandmother*. My sweet Natalia."

I waited until my grandmother looked at me. "Henrik said that I looked like Natalia when she was young."

She nodded. "Oh yes. You do. Even the lovely color of your hair. And your big brown eyes. Yes, anyone looking at you would know you were related to her."

We sat together in the quiet tea house, quiet except for the occasional gust of wind that slammed against the windows. I'm sure we were all thinking about Natalia, the fourth woman in our little circle of insight.

My mother suddenly looked at me and said, "Why did you say you needed to see Henrik? You spoke to him about the chamber of commerce dance?"

"Yes. That's related to a different mystery—Will Kodaly. They're doing a special tribute to him at the dance, as you said, and since you told me many of his friends and acquaintances would be there, I figured I'd try to get tickets, and Henrik gave me six of them."

Grandma's eyes were like laser beams. "You had a talk with your detective?"

"Yes. We're okay."

"Good, good." She smiled.

"So do you guys want to go to a dance?"

My mother shook her head. "Take Domo and Margie and some other young people. You'll have fun. Sofia told me the dance is always quite lovely."

"Okay." I looked around the tea house. "So I guess we should actually do our job, rather than chatting about our fascinating family history."

My grandmother stood up. "I fix the microphone and select the classical playlist."

My mother stretched. "We're doing the navy blue and white service—is that right, Hana?"

"Yes. I think that service says elegant, and so does the symphony. I'll go get the bags with the mini musical instruments."

We Horvath-Kellers loved our decorative decor, and we had plastic bags with all sorts of thematic decorations. I walked to the back and into the kitchen where a cubby sat against the south wall—something my father had appropriated when Riverwood High replaced the storage unit in their in-school daycare. The kindergarten cubby unit was perfect for alphabetized decorations. I went to the *M* square and rifled through the bags until I found "music." I took this to the main room, where my mother had already put white cloths on every table and was currently putting a navy blue runner down the center of each one, then touching up any bent corners with her travel iron.

I went to each table that already had a blue runner and put together a quick centerpiece of a bouquet of white silk roses and a silver and black ceramic cello, about six inches high. Against this I leaned a crisp white card that said "Welcome, Riverwood Youth Symphony." I stood back and looked at the table—yes, that would do.

The front door opened, and François slouched in, wearing a bomber jacket and carrying a leather messenger bag. He looked like a handsome postman from a 1940s movie. He tossed a newspaper on one of the tables. "This was outside," he said.

We got two papers delivered to the tea house: the Riverwood *Review* and the *Chicago Tribune*. My grandmother liked to read them in the kitchen/break room while she ate her lunch, and we liked to have them on hand in case any of our patrons wanted to borrow one for the ride home; this latter happened often when a bus full of retirees came for an event.

"Thanks. I'll tell Grandma."

He looked past me at the table decorations. "The Youth Symphony?"

"Yes—I told you that yesterday. And it was on your schedule."

"Yes, *oui*. I don't always remember—just what food I am to make."

"Fair enough. But make sure you do that thing where you paint musical notes on the petit fours. They were surprisingly excited by that last time."

He shrugged. "Yes, all right."

He made his way into his lair, his kitchen domain, a paradoxical cross between excited and disinterested.

I laughed and went to the table with the newspapers. I picked up the *Review* and glanced at the front cover, then looked more closely. The headline read "Riverwood Artist Slain During Home Invasion." Beside it was a picture of Will Kodaly, smiling into someone's camera and making a peace sign. The background, a blur of milling people and helium balloons, made it clear that he had been at some sort of party. Despite the work I still needed to do, I sat down and read the story.

Riverwood resident and renowned artist William Kodaly was slain in his home on Saturday morning. Kodaly was holding a garage sale in his basement; a potential buyer found him there at approximately nine thirty a.m., according to a police source. A Riverwood detective was already at the premises, and he was able to secure the scene.

Kodaly had lived in Riverwood for twelve years; he had previously lived in New York, where he taught at the renowned Pratt Institute. He emigrated from Hungary in 1995, and most of his family still lives there. His sister Juli Kodaly, who lives in Budapest, said that her brother would be interred in Riverwood, but that they would also have a memorial stone erected in Keszthely, where he had been born, and where, his sister said, he had spent his happiest years. "He grew up there; he began to paint there; and, later in his life, he even fell in love there. He loved the town, and the town loved him."

Kodaly began his art career in Hungary and was invited to be a visiting lecturer at Columbia University in New York in 1995; he stayed on and later took the position at Pratt. Kodaly's paintings hang in a number of art museums, including the Art Institute of Chicago and the Museum of Fine Arts in Boston. His most famous work, according to Pratt colleague Arthur Ringold, is called Light Touches the Valley, *which Ringold says "explores the nuances of morning light as it illu-*

minates all living things in a Hungarian meadow." The painting sold at auction in 2006 for $124,000.

Kodaly made the news just two months ago when one of his paintings was stolen from a display at the River-wood Public Library. Kodaly had agreed to a gallery showing for the library's Arts Festival Week events. The painting, titled Dark Intentions, *depicted a predatory man looking at a woman through her window. In an interview about the library event, Kodaly had referenced* Dark Intentions *while talking about his art. "Most of my work is focused on positivity—on the bounty of nature or the beauty of women or the power of love. Sometimes, though, my darker soul rises.* Dark Intentions *was a warning to all women: don't trust men."*

I put the paper down, thinking. Had I read something about that painting being stolen? I had been busy the past month, but I must have seen it somewhere. Riverwood wasn't a town that normally had *art theft* as a headline. I had already been planning a visit to Cassandra at the library; this seemed like a good thing to discuss with her then.

I tucked the papers under my arm and walked them to the back room, where I set them on top of the storage cubby for my grandmother. While I was there I took out my phone and texted Wolf: Make sure you read the article about Kodaly in the Riverwood Review. Then I dialed my brother at work.

"Hey, Han Solo," Domo's voice said in my ear. As usual, he sounded cheerful and completely unstressed. That care-free nature was a quality I greatly envied.

"Hey. What are you and Margie doing this Saturday night?"

"Why? Do you have something good to offer?"

"I do. Riverwood is having a fancy autumn ball. I guess they have it every year."

My brother snorted. "And you thought I would care about that *why*?"

"Because you have a girlfriend who loves dressing up, and because that girlfriend loves those movies where everyone is waltzing around in circles. This would be an opportunity to take Margie somewhere formal and nice for *free*, and it would be a way to get her out of the house."

"Huh. That's true," he said grudgingly. "She is doing pretty well with the going out lately. You helped a lot, taking her here and there."

Margie was an introvert that my extrovert brother wanted to draw out of her shell. "It should be a nice event. I'm bringing Erik, and I'll probably invite Katie."

"Okay, you convinced me. So—I have to wear a tuxedo or something?"

"A nice suit would be fine. You look good in a suit. Margie will swoon."

"Yeah." He sounded distracted. "So is this like prom, where I have to buy Marguerite flowers?"

I laughed. "No. But there are so many opportunities to impress your woman at an event like this. Soft lighting, romantic music, dancing in the gazebo . . . You could totally sweep Margie off her feet."

"Hmm. You'll have to be my romantic guide. My Sherpa of Love Mountain."

"I'll put aside a pair of tickets for you. Go design computer programs."

"Okay," Domo said. "I'm going to text you some pictures of suits. Tell me which one to wear."

"Margie can do that, but okay."

"Thanks, Han." Domo ended the call and I dialed Katie.

"Hello?"

"It's Hana. What are you doing this Saturday night?"

"Sadly, nothing." She did sound sad, too.

"Well, come out with me and Erik and Domo. And Domo's girlfriend. We're going to the Autumn Ball in Riverwood; I've got an extra ticket."

She sighed. "I don't know. It sounds like I'd be a fifth wheel."

"You can bring someone if you want. I actually have two extra tickets."

"I don't know," she said again. This did not sound at all like my ebullient Katie.

"What's going on?"

"I sound like Eeyore, don't I?"

"No—just kind of bummed out. Are you—have you been fighting with Eduardo?"

"Fighting? No. He's perfectly nice and respectful at work. He's been a real gentleman. In fact, I would say he's been more awesome to me in the last couple days than he was when we were dating."

Good boy, Eduardo. "Well, that's good, right? It means you're still friends."

"Yeah." Her voice was distant, moody. "It's weird—he's been smiling at me at work, catching my eye, like we have some secret joke, but then he looks away, or even leaves the room. Yesterday I was working late and he brought me a sandwich from this shop that's a mile away. He said he was there and he thought I'd like it. And then he just left."

"So? That was nice."

"I don't know. He's confusing me. He was talking to me, and he kind of absently touched his fingers to mine, and then he left. He's got this new haircut; it makes him look different."

"What does any of this have to do with you being sad?"

"It doesn't. I'm just saying. I went to tell him something this morning, something that reminded me of a joke he told me once, and he was in his office with Sharon."

That wasn't good. Sharon was the office flirt, according to Katie. "So they were probably just working on a project."

"I told myself that, but then at lunch Sharon asked me if he was back on the market."

"I don't like that expression, *on the market*. People aren't beef." I paused. "What did you tell her?"

"It's complicated."

"Not really."

"No, that's what I told her. I said it was complicated, like I was a Facebook status. She just sniffed at me and walked away."

"Well, why does any of this matter? You don't care if he dates Sharon, right?"

"I don't know. Maybe I do." She sighed. "When I left, this guy who's always in front of our building was kind of harassing me. I mean, he's harmless, but he was telling me that I'd better watch out for the alien waves, or something, and I didn't know what to say, and Ed just appeared out of nowhere and said something to the guy and steered him away from me. It was—gallant."

"'Gallant'! What a fancy word."

"I'm confused. I wanted to break up. I should probably just stay with that, but—he's got me all muddled."

"Fine. Here's the plan. Invite Eduardo to the dance Saturday. You can wear a sexy dress and be alluring. Or you can just use the time to figure out how you feel. You can ask him real casually, say I needed a sixth person for my table."

"This is—a formal thing?"

"Yeah. Really fancy."

"Okay. *Okay!*" she said, sounding happier. "I will. I'll let you know what he says."

"Hey, guess what?"

"What?"

"I met the women who own Ulveflokk."

"You met the—what do you mean, you *met* them? How do you just meet famous businesspeople?"

"They're Erik's sisters. His *twin* sisters. In Norwegian, *ulveflokk* means 'wolf pack.'"

"Get *out!* That is so weird! We were just talking about them at that garage sale, and—"

"I know! Everything is connected, like we're in some giant puzzle. It turns out Kodaly knew my mother and grandmother. And then Falken was coming to the sale, so he and I had pastries, and a guy overheard me talking, and he said he knew my grandma, too, and that he would love to do a favor for my family."

"Why?"

"Long story. So he's the one who gave me these tickets; he works at the chamber of commerce, where they also knew the artist Kodaly. And it turns out the woman in the painting I bought is the town librarian. Which reminds me—I need to go there."

"And I need to get back to my cubicle. I'm in the break room right now, but I have work to do."

"Okay. Go ask Eduardo. Play it cool, like you have a hundred other guys you can ask."

"Right. Thanks, Hana." She ended the call. I looked up to see my grandmother in the doorway.

"You finished with your chatty friends? Some tables still need work."

"Yes, ma'am," I said, standing up. "And I was telling

Domo I had tickets for him and Margie, and then I told Katie the same thing. But I'll get to work now."

She nodded. My phone buzzed in my pocket. I looked at the screen to see that I had a text message from Runa Wolf. "What the—?" I said, and clicked on it.

Thyra told me you're taking Erik to a dance on Saturday. Don't worry—Thyra is going to be sure he looks good. And if you need a dress, text me your size. I have something in mind for you that will look perfect with that hair.

My mother peeked around the corner. "Hana, are you coming?"

François, who had been working silently in the room the whole time, looked up with a smirk. "And she says I am too much on the phone. Look at her, calling, texting. A regular teen."

I made a face at him and marched out into the dining room, still distracted by the text. I wasn't sure how to feel. On the one hand, it was neat to have the attention of a famous person who wanted to plan my attire as though I were an actress going to the Oscars. On the other hand, I wondered if Runa and Thyra were going to want to boss me around for the foreseeable future.

I sent a quick text back. I'm usually a size 8. Thanks for thinking of us.

Then I surveyed the room, found a spot that needed work, and made a beeline for the iron.

Chapter 9

SUMMONING SZÉPASSZONY

When I got home that evening I had two texts from Erik: Busy tonight, but I'll miss you. He added about ten heart emojis, and I grinned like a fool. Then I read his second text: Send me whatever you hear about Kodaly.

I thought about this as I made my solitary dinner—nothing Hungarian this time, just a burger on a pretzel bun—and ate it with a certain solemnity in the quiet room, lighting an orange taper in a Zsolnay vintage ivory candle-holder that Falken had found for me in a jaunt to Iowa. I traced the twenty-four-karat gold edging and felt the special glow that beautiful things always gave me. With a sigh, I returned to the idea of helping the police.

A month ago, I had been very helpful to a murder investigation by being observant. Feeling wide-awake and invigorated by a slight chill that crept into my room from the arctic winds outside, I got into flannel pajamas and warm socks, grabbed a legal pad and a pen, and jotted down everything I could think of.

- Went to Kodaly's sale. He was friendly but distracted. Seemed to have something on his mind.

- I bought a Herend wolf, a sweater, and two paintings. Both paintings felt significant.

- The owner told me he didn't want more than five dollars for the Herend wolf. He said it had bad associations, asked me if I had ever disliked a gift giver. He mentioned a restraining order!

This last idea had just come back to me; I would need to send this whole list to Erik.

- Had the gift giver been harassing Kodaly? If so, about what?

- He reacted to the painting of Cassandra but even more to the landscape, and he called Keszthely the place of his heart.

- Mom and Grandma both said he was a wolf, but I didn't get that vibe from him. He just seemed tired and sad.

- Why would he sell his paintings at a garage sale? They are in demand and he can name his price!

- Henrik Sipos said that Kodaly had many friends— that Kodaly was *his* friend.

- Kodaly painted a mural at the chamber of commerce, and now a small shrine stands near it.

- Sipos said Kodaly was well-liked, but a loner.

- Sipos said Kodaly had painted the reunion of mother and son at Békéscsaba.

- Cassandra said Kodaly had flaws, but that he tended to stay on good terms with his exes.

- Cassandra suggested that Kodaly was not popular with men.

- My mom said that Kodaly supported charity events and painted her once to help raise money for the food pantry.

I thought for a moment, then wrote:

- Try to find these Kodaly paintings, or images of them:
  - *Dark Intentions* (stolen)
  - *Light Touches the Valley*
  - The one he painted of the reunion between Henrik Sipos and his mother
  - The one he painted of Maggie Keller

- Runa Wolf said she owns a Kodaly.

I got up from my bed and took a picture of my list. I sent it to Erik. Then I wandered into my living room and found the Old Hollywood channel, one of my favorites. I had learned, over a year or so, about old-time actresses and actors who had died before I was born but who had once been young, beautiful, and vibrant, and that vitality had been captured onscreen. Just as I was fascinated by tales of my own Natalia, I was intrigued by these stars of the early twentieth century. In the last few weeks I had discovered both Joan Fontaine and Lana Turner, along with Laurence

Olivier and Clark Gable. Tonight's movie was called *Suspicion*, and it starred Joan Fontaine and Cary Grant. A Hitchcock film. "Oh, nice," I said to Cleopatra, who was chewing the toe of my sock.

My phone buzzed; I had a text from Erik.

I have a lot of questions. I'll catch up with you tomorrow.

I sent a heart emoji and the words "Good night."

He sent a GIF of a bear blowing kisses.

I laughed and returned to my movie.

When it was over, I felt a bit chilled in my drafty living room. I got up and brushed my teeth. My cats were on the bed, waiting for me; they did not look pleased about my tardiness. I threw back the covers and climbed in, glad for their warmth, and of the two feline bed warmers, as well. I plumped my pillows and sat against the wall. "Okay, guys, I'm going to open my inner eye," I said.

Snug in flannel sheets and using the sound of purring as my mantra, I focused on a photograph on my sprawling bookshelf. It was Natalia, already old, smiling at a family graduation. I squinted until she was just a blur, then closed my eyes and tried to retain her image. This worked momentarily, but she faded. I kept my lids closed, but pictured a giant eye in my center, a closed eyelid floating in my psyche. "Open," I whispered, and I imagined the giant lid lifting.

My eyes flew open. I looked rather nervously around the room, half fearful that I'd unleashed some sort of uncontrollable psychic power and that objects would start careening against the wall. But no: a glance at the window showed the same gentle droplets and occasional flecks of ice that had sporadically returned throughout October. A look at the bed revealed my cats as they always were: fuzzy, relaxed, on the verge of slumber. I studied my hands; they did not glow, and they had not grown some sort of magical extensions that would allow me to cast spells. If my inner eye had opened, there was no physical evidence.

I sighed with relief and decided to try something different. I lay back against my pillows and stared at the white wall, pretending it was a wall of snow. From this whiteness I tried to make out the form of Szépasszony, the fairy lady. Centuries ago in Hungary she had been viewed as a goddess of love, but she evolved into an angry witch spirit who sought revenge. She was fascinating in any fairy tale, and I pretended now that I could see her emerging, her silver-white hair and her white, white skin. I imagined that I absorbed some of her power. I stared until I was convinced I could see her pale eyes emerging from the whiteness, eyes filled with vitality, intention. "Open, open," I said softly. Her eyes, her eyes, becoming more real as I projected my image on the wall.

For an instant they were visible in my lamplit room.

Then the cats stood up and meowed at me, indignant or afraid.

"What?" I said, caressing them. "Was I making a noise? Did I squeeze you? I'm sorry. I'll stop now. I'm trying to flex a muscle, guys, and I don't know where it's located. You see my dilemma?"

They did not. They seemed to forgive me, though, and they nestled back against my side.

I reached over and flicked off the light. Now the room was illuminated only by the streetlight beyond my parking lot. I tucked myself more deeply into my covers and said a Hungarian prayer my grandmother had taught me once, translating loosely to "Lord, let me lie down in peace and wake up in peace."

Then every eye in the room was closed, including mine.

But the image of Szépasszony, as I had imagined her, hovered in a silvery light that I could see without opening my eyes.

Chapter 10

························

THE EYES OF MAGDALENA

I was at the tea house by seven the next morning; we were hosting a breakfast tea for another ladies' group. A half-dead-looking François served tiny croissants with egg and cucumber, butter and jam, cheese and pickle.

The ladies ate every morsel and downed a great deal of hot tea; the weather was good for business. The women were initially loud and excited, but their meeting ended with a "guided reflection" from a self-help guru named Sonata Terry. She asked the ladies gathered to center themselves and to "find a place of contentment" while they relaxed in their chairs. I hovered in the doorway, holding a dishrag and eavesdropping. Ms. Terry had a soothing voice, and I found myself responding to it.

"Go ahead and close your eyes," she said. "It helps with the centering exercise. Now imagine a little carousel, going around and around. Everyone you care about is on the carousel. Watch them as they go around."

I closed my eyes and focused on the faces that bobbed up and down. My mother and father. Grandma. Domo and Margie. Katie. Erik Wolf, looking embarrassed to be on a carousel. A wave of feeling rose in me and my eyes flew open. François was walking past, still zombie-like, and he smirked. "You don't like the meditation? It is too intense for you?"

I shrugged, then went on the offensive. "You should get some sleep at night. I'm afraid I'm going to find you back here with your face in the frosting."

He looked wounded. "Normally we are not this early. It is an adjustment."

"Just half an hour more, and you can go back to bed."

"*Oui*," he said hoarsely. He trudged past me, headed toward his workstation.

I took my rag back into the main room and began to wipe off the buffet tables. The speaker was telling the relaxed congregation to breathe. "I can't stress how important breathing is," she said softly. "Breathe in deeply through the nose; exhale gently through the mouth. Become conscious of your own rhythm, and imagine it's the rhythm of the universe: the winds, the tides, ebbing and flowing . . ."

"Wow," I said under my breath. And yet it was impossible to deny the calming effect of her voice.

My grandmother appeared at my side. "You know who was on my carousel?" she whispered. So she had been doing the visualization, as well.

"Who?"

"You, Domo, Maggie, Mama. Your daddy and grandpa, of course. But then who bobs up?"

"Who? François? Mr. Kalmar, the landscaping man?"

"No." She scowled at me. "Your boyfriend. And his partner."

"What?" I whispered, making sure the women at the tables couldn't hear us. I grinned. "Wolf and Benton?"

Her mouth was a grim line. "I put them both on one horse. No room for them."

This image brought me dangerously close to explosive laughter. I leaned close and spoke into her ear. "I know there's room for Erik, Grandma. I know you like him. I can't explain the Benton thing, unless you're secretly excited by his mustache."

She sent me a scandalized look, and I scampered away, bubbling with mirth.

My mother pointed at a tea cart and pantomimed that I should start loading cups. This was our subtle sign to the visitors that their event was almost over.

I rolled my cart to the first table and began to unobtrusively pick up china. The women were obediently breathing along with Sonata. "In—and out. In—and out," she said in her mellifluous voice. "Get in touch with your breathing, and you get in touch with yourself."

◦◦◦

After the contemplative morning event I drove to the library. It was one of my favorite Riverwood locations, tucked into an old, rambling Victorian house. Each genre was located in a different room, adding a touch of whimsy to the most mundane of research tasks. Today I had a multitiered agenda, and, since Cassandra happened to be standing at the circulation desk when I arrived, I figured I would ask her to be my guide.

She waved and greeted me. "You look determined," she said with a smile.

"I am. I wonder if you could help me with a few different searches?"

"Of course."

"First, in regard to Will Kodaly—"

Her face took on a shuttered look, a slight flicker in the eyes, but she nodded. "Sure, what do you need?"

I leaned on the desk. "Well, clearly he was a prolific painter, and I'm looking for images of some of his works, starting with the one that was stolen a couple months ago from this very place."

She frowned. "Oh God. Testament to our negligence."

"How did it happen, anyway?"

She shrugged. "We still don't have that figured out. Of course, the event has convinced the library board that we need security cameras, but"—she looked around and lowered her voice—"we had none. Will was philosophical about it, saying these things happen, but I think—he was disturbed."

"What do you mean, disturbed? Like, angry at you?"

"No, no. Wondering at the motive of the thief. To act with such desperation and to take such a dark piece. The room was full of more positive images and more valuable paintings."

"How do you walk out with a painting? Kodaly's paintings are huge."

She shook her head. "This one wasn't. The size of a legal document, maybe."

"Ohhhh. I see. Well, I'd love a printed image of it, along with one that might be harder to find."

Her face brightened. Lord, librarians loved a challenge. "Bring it on," she said.

"My mom recently informed me that Kodaly painted her. A piece that was to be auctioned off for a charity event."

She looked disappointed. Clearly this was not that hard a task. "Sure, I remember that. I even know what he titled it: *Magdalena's Eyes*. It was lovely. I actually bid on it, but it sold to some banker. I can find out his name, but I'm pretty sure I can upload the image from the program that day. No problem."

I stared at her. "Wow. You're a miracle worker. Okay, then three other things. I would love to get more information about Hungary, especially a couple of towns there. Keszthely and Békéscsaba."

She held up a hand. "Whoa. I do not know what you just said. You'll have to write those down."

"Of course. I'm also interested in newspaper coverage of a kidnapping that happened in Békéscsaba in the spring of 1960. A little boy was stolen from his mother." I didn't want to mention the name Sipos; perhaps Henrik did not want that story known to all and sundry.

Cassandra took my arm and started leading me to the research room. "Now you have me intrigued. Old American newspaper clippings, no problem. Old Hungarian ones, a bit more of a challenge. But that's half the fun."

We entered a quiet room lined floor to ceiling with reference manuals and periodicals. Two people sat hunched over individual desks, staring at monitors. One dusty-looking man sat in the corner, winding through a microfiche display screen.

"Find a station there," she said in a reference-room whisper. "You can play around online while I hunt in the library. Was there anything else?"

"Just—anything you have on psychic phenomena. Like—encouraging a psychic gift."

Her brows went up, and I shook my head. "Just something I'm looking into."

She nodded once. "Great. You got it." She waved and moved swiftly out of the room, apparently in quest of answers for me.

I sat down at a computer and logged in as a library guest. I went to the search bar and typed "Békéscsaba, Hungary newspapers 1960." Google made it clear moments later that in order to view an old Hungarian newspaper I would probably have to look at microfilm at the Library of Congress, or to request a copy of it. Since I had no idea which newspaper would hold my information, or even what information there was to be had, this seemed too risky and complicated an undertaking. I was able to see that there were newspapers with names like *Békés Megyei Népujság* ("Population of Békés County"), but I would probably need a Hungarian to help me negotiate the brambles of translation.

I stared at the screen, tapping my fingers on the table. Then I Googled the search term "Hungarian psychic woman in America" on the off chance that someone had caught wind of the tale here and put it in a Midwestern features section.

I got all sorts of weird articles, from tales of Gypsies to recipes for *paprikás*. I had just glimpsed a headline that read "Woman Grateful to Hungarian Immigrant" when Cassandra appeared at my shoulder.

"Hey," she said softly, her eyes scanning the other patrons in the room. "I've got your images. Here's the one that was stolen."

She set a color-printed copy of a painting in front of me and I studied it. The piece was rather impressionistic; a dark shape of a house, a white rectangle of a window with the vague figure of a woman behind it. Everything was in shadow, suggesting evening light. A man hovered outside in the bushes, watching her with narrowed eyes. What made the painting shocking, and oddly satisfying, was that the man lurking in the bushes was the only finely detailed part of the painting: his features were entirely visible. In addition, he was in a spotlight, as though a helicopter (or the Furies) had singled him out for exposure.

"Wow!" I said.

"Yeah. It was a very popular piece at the show. It could easily have been a fan who stole it."

"Can I keep this?" I asked.

"Yes. I made that for you. And here's your other one. Isn't it enchanting?"

She set down a second painting, and I gasped. It was a portrait of my mother, painted by an admiring man. She sat in a chair in front of a window, looking out. It was her kitchen window; I recognized it instantly. Kodaly had captured the quality of the light and the way it brought out an eerie loveliness in my mother's blue eyes, which were the central focus of the painting. I had always known my mother was a pretty woman, but Kodaly had made her beautiful. "This—is amazing," I whispered. "I'm going to make copies and then frame it."

"It is great. I knew I wouldn't get it when I bid, but I wanted to hang it in my foyer, which is painted blue. The blue of her eyes is just so compelling. Like two sapphires."

I nodded. What had my father thought, when he saw this beautiful image of his wife, painted by a man? I recalled what several women had suggested about men not liking Kodaly, perhaps because women did. Had my father liked him?

An image returned, unbidden, of Kodaly smiling at me, admiring my hair, telling me it was like "fire at twilight." Would he have wanted to paint me? Would Erik Wolf have been jealous if he did?

Cassandra tapped my shoulder. "Any luck with your other search?"

I shook my head.

The dusty man in front of the microfiche sent us a wounded

look. She lowered her voice to a whisper and said, "Come out in the main room so I can show you something."

"Sure!" Intrigued, I followed Cassandra out of the room.

At a table in the nonfiction room she had laid out several books about psychic phenomena. At a glance, I saw titles about ESP, about "skeptics" who changed their ways, about "proof" that heaven existed. "Oh, um—this isn't really what I was—"

"That's what I figured," she said, studying me. "I've heard the rumors, you know. About your grandma. About all the women in your family. The Hungarian grapevine has been busy with talk of the Horvaths."

"Oh—well—I don't really want this to get around."

"Of course not," she said, brushing a piece of lint off her sleeve.

She held up a volume called *Am I Psychic? How to Tap into Your Perceptive Potential.*

"Okay, that's closer," I said. "I'll take it."

"Great! I'll put it at the front counter. I might need more time to find your Hungarian newspapers. Can I call you with that information?"

"Sure. I have some stuff to start with here, so that's great. Thank you!"

I followed her to the front, where she handed me a file folder for the printed images, then checked out my book. I thanked her again, then walked briskly out of the library, down the pumpkin-strewn steps, and toward my car.

A face appeared before me so suddenly that I yelped and jumped backward; I shook my head and realized that no one was there. The face had appeared in my consciousness, a blot over my other thoughts, demanding attention. A man's face, with dark, angry eyes, narrowed against the light.

I reached my car and climbed inside, locking the doors after me.

I opened the file folder and stared again at the painting called *Dark Intentions*. There was the man, lurking outside the window, his dark intentions illuminated by some cosmic guardian.

This lurker, this man—his was the face that had loomed up just now, and I leaned my head back with a sudden terrible awareness: this image was based on a real man.

And Kodaly had been sending a message.

Chapter 11

....

INTERCONNECTEDNESS

The autumn ball was being held at the Riverwood Pavilion, a tubular building in a large field on the north edge
of Riverwood. I had gone to my senior prom there, so I
knew that it was actually a charming place, with an indoor
gazebo at one end so that dancers could float out to dance
under the stars, protected by a roof with a skylight.

Erik and I had met briefly with Domo and Margie to find
our table, at the center of which glowed a sparkling jack-o'-
lantern, then gone our separate ways to get drinks, greet
people we knew, and get the lay of the land. The room was
loud with merriment, and I was flushed with what felt like
the effects of wine but was really the result of the long exchanged looks between Erik Wolf and me.

He had picked me up at my apartment an hour earlier and
simply stared. "Where did you get that dress?" he asked.

"Your sisters dropped it off. Like Norwegian fairy god-
mothers."

"It's—you look—I can't even describe that color." He reached out to touch the delicate top in the palest cocoa, with soft rosettes against thin brown silk in a rather daring spaghetti-strapped bodice, a filmy thing that met with a full skirt made of tulle—an ethereal cloud of softness that made it look as though I were floating along the ground.

"Runa said it's called French Chocolate," I said. His mouth had been moving closer to mine and was now about an inch away.

"You certainly are delectable," said his lips.

I kissed him, luxuriating for a moment, and then said, "You look wonderful. I've never seen you so well-dressed. Your sisters are good at this."

His smile was rueful. "They made me their little mannequin all my life. It's probably why I don't care about clothes at all."

I stepped back to look at him: he wore a pale brown shirt with a dark brown silk tie underneath a dark blue suit. The tones were matched just right; he looked as though he had dressed to stand beside me, but he was a showstopper by himself, with his shock of blond hair above the elegant brown silk.

"We need a picture," I said. "Like prom."

He looked at his watch. "Maybe at the pavilion. I want to get going. Remember, I'm on duty tonight."

"Yes, yes." I reached out to smooth his suit jacket and came into contact with the shape of his gun. "Oh, yuck. Violence descends."

He kissed my hair. "You'll never see it."

I nodded and grabbed my little purse. Erik bent and said a soft good-bye to my cats, who stared unabashedly and occasionally tried to claw my skirt.

Then we were on our way. If Erik thought he would escape without being photographed, he had underestimated Iris and her mother, Paige. They peeked out their window and saw us in the parking lot, then ran out with a camera, which Paige balanced on her pregnant belly while she gave instructions. "Hold her against you. That's nice! Now look down at her, and you look up at him, Hana."

Iris said, "You look like a prince and princess! My Halloween costume is a pirate, but I only get to wear it tomorrow."

"Be sure you come and get candy from me, Iris," I said as Paige snapped another photo.

It really did feel like prom, and Erik looked uncomfortable. I held up a hand. "Thanks, Paige, but we have to go. Send me copies when you get a chance." I waved and tucked into the car while Erik held open my door.

Inside, I told him about my visit to the library and the image of *Dark Intentions*. "He's a real man, the guy in that picture. I feel it. So the question is, was Kodaly trying to send a message *about* this man? *To* this man? Did the man steal the painting, or did someone who recognized him do so? Or is it all a big coincidence?"

Erik thought about this. "Lots of other paintings on display that day. I don't think it's a coincidence."

"It was a small painting. Highly portable. I suppose you could say the thief was looking for something small. But I guess there were other small works, as well."

"I'd like a copy."

"You can have mine. His face is seared on my brain for some reason."

"I don't suppose you recognize him?"

"No. But he's important."

"Huh. Meanwhile, I found out that Kodaly has a son."

I swung toward him. "What?"

"A child he had with one of his first girlfriends, when he was quite young. She's American, and the boy is American. Well—not a boy, I guess. He's twenty. I'm hoping to go see him tomorrow. He's working at the pumpkin patch on Route 4, helping to earn college money, his mom said."

"Did Kodaly know about him?"

"Apparently so. But he hadn't been in the boy's life very much until recently. They connected in the last year and had been spending time together."

"I suppose the mom resented that?"

He shook his head. "She seemed relieved. Said she always felt bad that John had no father figure in his life."

"This is nuts. Not one woman has a grudge against Kodaly, even though he's supposedly a wolf. Does that ring true? Or are all the women conspiring to pretend they didn't hate him?"

He shot me a quick glance. "That sounds paranoid."

"Yeah, I guess." I looked at the dusky scenery. "Hey, you know what?"

"What?"

"This is our first fancy date."

His green eyes looked me up and down, then met mine. "*Te gyönyörű vagy*," he said.

"Oh, wow, did you practice that? Your attempts at Hungarian are getting better than mine. What did you just say?"

He smiled. "I'll tell you later."

∽

In a room that glittered with battery-powered candlelight and glimmering black and orange backdrops, I found Sofia pouring herself a glass of punch. I waved and greeted her. "I'm Maggie's daughter," I said.

"Yes, yes, I know you, Hana." Sofia looked like a poem

in a form-fitting orange dress that accentuated her dark hair. Her eyes were melancholy, but they always looked that way. My grandmother claimed that Sofia had the "eyes of the Old Country," and that they were imbued with the sadness of generations. Somehow her mournful eyes made her lovelier.

"Will you be the one doing a tribute to Will Kodaly tonight?"

Sofia touched her hair with a slightly shaking hand. "Yes, with some artists who worked with him. I am very nervous. Look at this crowd!"

"Yeah, the dance seems quite a success."

Erik drifted over, looking like a moody movie star, and I introduced him. "Erik, this is Sofia. She knew William Kodaly."

Based on the weird way that Detective Wolf's hands hung at his side, as though someone was about to challenge him to a gunfight, I assumed he was tempted to go for his notebook.

He said, "Are you from Hungary, Sofia?"

"No—my parents. But I've visited. A beautiful country, beautiful. And I speak the language. I have done since I was a child." I felt a pang of jealousy; my grandmother now wished that I was bilingual.

"You dated Mr. Kodaly?" he asked, aiming for a casual smile.

"Yes. We have a history, I would say. But we always somehow missed each other. I was dating, or he was, then I was married, then he was dating someone else. But I have very special memories of our time together. Treasured memories." She put her hand over her heart; some tiny beads on her dress clicked together.

"And when did you date him?"

Her lids came down and she studied the toes of her black shoes. "Uh—about two, three years ago. Since then he has dated other women in this town."

"Cassandra Stone?" I asked.

"Yes. But then Cassandra decided that he was unreliable. She went back to an old flame."

"And what about Ms. Derrien? Amber Derrien?"

She nodded. "I saw her here tonight. She's wearing blue." She scanned the room over our heads. "I don't see her now. She might be getting a drink at the bar. Cassandra is here, too. She looks like a Greek goddess."

"Any other women you can connect directly to Kodaly? Anyone else he dated?"

A look of consternation crossed her face; then she shrugged. "I suppose some artists. They all hung around together. In any case, that is all I know. I must go join Zane. I'll introduce you later—"

"Sofia," I said. She looked at me with her sad eyes. "I'm sorry for your loss."

The tears came so quickly that they surprised all three of us—silent, plentiful tears that streamed down her face and made the pain in her eyes, now magnified by the light reflected in her teardrops, one of the most heartbreaking things I'd ever seen.

"My goodness. My makeup," she said. "I'm sorry. Perhaps I'll see you later."

She rushed past us, leaving the scent of a floral perfume and a palpable, lingering sadness.

⌒

Domo appeared at my shoulder, looking dashing in a black suit and a royal blue shirt. He wore no tie, but he got away with this cheat because it made him look like a disheveled playboy. "Hey! Pretty cool party. Marguerite is having a great time."

"She looks like Grace Kelly tonight," I said.

"Who's Grace Kelly?" said Domo.

"Remember the movie we watched, *Rear Window*? With Jimmy Stewart as the photographer who breaks his leg? And he has that amazingly beautiful girlfriend who walks around in what look like Dior dresses?"

"Oh, *her*," he said. Then, making the connection, he said, "She does look like Grace Kelly." He wore a sort of dazed expression.

Erik said, "Hana tells me you've kept in touch with an English teacher you both had at Riverwood High. Ms. Derrien?"

Surprised, Domo nodded. "Yeah, sure. We send each other links and stuff. We're both big Dostoevsky fans. Why is that pertinent at all?"

Erik's face remained impassive. "I've been told she's here tonight. If you see her, could you introduce us?"

"Uh—okay. What's this about?"

I sent him a no-nonsense look. "Erik is investigating a murder. The man who was shot in his own home."

Domo's dark brows rose. "I saw that on the news. And then Grandma told me while she fed me dinner. About how he was Hungarian and an artist and stuff, right?"

"Yes. He also had—kind of a reputation with the ladies." I spoke softly, although the music and loud chatter effectively cloaked our conversation. "And he dated Ms. Derrien."

"Really? Wow. She was pretty hot back when we were in school. But that's not why she was popular," he added, shooting a glance at Erik.

"In any case, I'd like an excuse to speak to her at more length. So any help you can give me in that regard would be appreciated," Erik said.

Margie appeared at Domo's side, looking small and golden and lovely. Domo's arm slid around her, intimate without being overtly possessive. "I'm having fun," Margie said, offering a sweet smile. "Hello, Detective Wolf."

"Hello, Margie. It's nice to see you again."

Erik had spent an evening in Margie's apartment, back when he and I were investigating another crime. Margie had found him fascinating and handsome. I wondered what she thought of him tonight, in his beautiful suit.

"I'm ready to start dancing!" she enthused. "Domo didn't realize how much I love to dance. I was thrilled when he invited me to this. Let's go sit down—they're starting with hors d'oeuvres!" There was a slightly manic gleam in her eye as she tugged on Domo's arm. A natural introvert, Margie was probably going to need two full days of silence after tonight's event.

Domo rolled his eyes good-naturedly and went off with Margie. Erik Wolf's eyes were scanning the crowd. I was torn between feeling neglected and feeling excited by the chance to watch him at work. He had a certain focused intensity while working a case—admirable but also sexy.

Cassandra Stone floated past in a gold and white dress. "Cassandra!" I called. She turned, then smiled and walked up to me. "Cassandra, I wanted to introduce you to my boyfriend, Erik Wolf."

She smiled up at him as he shook her hand; she looked less like a Greek goddess (as Sofia had contended) than she did like a Renaissance painting. Her long reddish hair hung down in natural waves, and her green-blue eyes were striking in her pale face. "Nice to meet you, Erik. Are you both having a good time?"

"We just got here," Erik said, distracted by something

he saw across the room. Then, realizing how that sounded, he said, "But, yes. The place is quite elegant."

She nodded, pleased. "Yes, they always put on such a lovely event. I'll have to introduce you to Richard, my fiancé. He went to get us some wine, but then he disappeared." She laughed at this, and Wolf managed a smile. He became sort of a robot while he thought his way through a case. "Oh, here he comes," Cassandra said. "Richard!"

A brown-haired man, graying at the temples, approached us, carrying two glasses of white wine. He handed one to Cassandra, and she sipped it, then said, "Richard Crenshaw, this is Hana Keller—Maggie Keller's daughter. And this is her date, Erik Wolf."

Crenshaw stuck out a hand. He was a full head shorter than Wolf, and slightly thick in the middle, but he had a surprising, palpable charisma. "Erik, Hana, nice to meet you. Are you enjoying the dance?"

"Yes," I said. "Although so far it's just kind of networking, right?" I asked.

"Yeah. But in many ways, the best part of the evening. Later there's not as much of a chance to talk, and I like to say hi to friends, meet new people. By the time the dancing starts, I'll be focused on romancing my lady."

"How long have you two been together?" I asked.

Cassandra and Richard exchanged a look. "About a year," he said. "Cass jokingly calls us a 'recycled relationship.' Frankly, there are a lot of those in this town."

Wolf leaned in. "I'm sorry? What does that mean?"

Cassandra played with a tendril of her beautiful hair. "Richard and I were both with other people, and now we're together and those other people are with people we know. There's a lot of interconnectedness in the Riverwood dating scene."

My fingers tingled slightly. I leaned forward. "Was Will Kodaly a part of that interconnectedness?"

Richard laughed. "Will Kodaly was probably the hub. The guy had some mysterious chemistry that just drew women. Right, Cass?" He touched her shoulder and left his hand there.

"Oh yes. Will was very attractive. He said all the right things, and I think he meant them in the moment. But eventually he would get restless. He was a wanderer at heart." Her sad expression made her look fragile.

Wolf's blond brows furrowed. "I'm not following. Just because you both dated other people, what makes that 'interconnected'?"

Cassandra sighed and took another sip of wine: a dramatic moment that made her look beautiful. It seemed calculated to get her lover's attention, which it did. "Let's see," she said. "Here's a quick example. Three years ago, I dated Will Kodaly. We were pretty serious for a while. Richard here was married to Sofia Kálmar."

Richard winced. "She never did take to being Sofia Crenshaw. She said the name sounded like a crustacean."

Cassandra moved closer to him, perhaps in sympathy. She said, "Sofia told Rich she needed time away. When she came back, she had divorce papers."

"Ah," Erik said.

Cassandra nodded. "Will was in Hungary during that time. I'm pretty sure he cheated on me there. We had a fight, and he left. A couple months later he was dating Sofia."

"Okay," Erik said. He was clearly dying for his notebook. If I knew him, he would soon be escaping to a quiet corner to write down his notes. "So did Kodaly marry Sofia?"

She shook her head. "No. Something happened between them, and they broke up. Meanwhile, Amber Derrien had separated from her husband, Brad, and ended up having a fling with Will Kodaly. That lasted a few months; they didn't even hide the relationship, even though Amber was still officially married. Brad, whether out of revenge or I don't know what, started dating Sofia."

"Wow!" I said. "This is better than a soap opera."

Cassandra shrugged. "Richard and I found each other because we wanted someone who could commiserate. We agreed that we did not enjoy the drama. That we just wanted a quiet home, a simple life, someone to love."

She reached out her free hand, and he snatched it up. His eyes told me he was smitten with Cassandra. It looked like this relationship would last.

"That's quite a ring you have there," Wolf said.

Crenshaw and Cassandra both looked at the ring. He said, "I found it at an antique shop. It's Victorian-era. The color was perfect with her hair—that apricot-colored topaz—I knew I had to have it. And those are all-natural half pearls around the center stone."

The ring gleamed in the light, and my soul responded joyfully, as it did to all beautiful things. "It's stunning," I said.

I looked up to find Erik's eyes on me. I smiled, but he didn't. Something was wrong . . .

"Anyway, you can see why the Riverwood dating scene has a certain odd feel. Almost incestuous, somehow," Crenshaw said, still smiling at Cassandra's ring.

I patted Cassandra's hand. "I think your name sounds perfect with the name Crenshaw," I said.

She beamed. "So do I!"

They said farewell and wandered into the crowd. Erik said, "Would you like a drink?"

I shrugged. "I suppose."

"Why don't you go to the table, and I'll bring you one?"

"Okay."

He kissed the top of my head, and I moved toward table number twelve. I bumped into someone who turned out to be Eduardo. He looked dashing in a crimson suit. His dark brown hair was swooped back from his face with some kind of product, and he looked dangerously handsome.

"Eduardo! I was wondering where you guys were. Where's Katie?"

"She went to the ladies' room."

"Your suit is amazing."

He shrugged. I realized, in a burst of insight, that he was nervous. "I stole this from my father's closet. He wore it on special occasions when I was young, and we laughed at him and said he looked like a chocolate salesman."

This struck me as hilarious. "A *chocolate* salesman? Is that even a thing?"

His gaze was restless, scanning the room over my head. "I don't know. We thought so. But we also thought the suit was ugly, and now I think it is powerful. For romance."

"You're doing pretty well so far. You got this invitation, right?"

"Yes, yes. But I feel like I'm on eggshells. I don't want to blow it. I really like Katie. I want her in my life. And tonight—she's so beautiful, Hana."

"You'll do fine."

His eyes met mine; their gaze was intense. "Did you see the silent auction items, over on the side? There are some ruby earrings. Katie loves rubies."

I held up a hand. "Don't even think about it. There are rich people at this thing. They always win the silent auction stuff because they like to show off their wealth during the bidding. That's what my dad says, anyway."

Eduardo leaned closer. "I have an IRA from my last job. I can cash it in. I think I could get them for her."

"Eduardo, I know you want to make a romantic gesture, but those shouldn't cost you your IRA. You can sweep her off her feet just by whispering in her ear."

He looked toward the table, where expensive gift items glimmered in the light. "I think rubies would be better," he murmured.

I saw Katie making her way through the crowd; she wore a filmy pale-pink strapless number that was getting her some appreciative glances. Her chestnut-colored hair, like heavy silk, hung straight onto her shoulders, and her eyes were bright.

I said, "Eduardo, this is none of my business."

"Okay," he said.

"Except that you're making a mistake."

His eyes widened. "Why?"

"Because this is Katie we're talking about. She would be furious if she knew you cashed in your future to buy her earrings. She would never wear them, and she'd get angry every time she looked at them."

His face fell.

"You know I'm right, Eduardo."

He nodded.

"Just do this: tell her the truth. The truth is the most romantic thing to Katie. Tell her what you are thinking when you look at her in that dress. Tell her—"

"What's up?" said Katie, appearing next to us. "Hana, you look fantastic."

"Thanks! You, too."

Eduardo said, "I found our table."

"Sorry we're late," Katie said. "I had a passionate argument with my hair straightener."

I laughed. "Well, you obviously won. Your hair looks great. I forgot how silky it was. Eduardo was just reminding me."

"Really?" Her eyes moved to him, and he nodded.

"I'll go get some drinks," he said, and disappeared into the crowd.

Erik appeared with a glass of punch for me, and a Diet Coke for him. I took the frosty glass, and he said, "Hello, Katie."

"Hey, Erik." They had met only once before, when we all went out for pizza, and they were still a bit stiff around each other. "You look great," she said.

"Thanks. That is a lovely color on you."

She thanked him, and he said, "Well, I'm glad you're here, because now you can talk to Hana while I run to the lobby and make a few notes."

"Sure," I said, waving him on. "I know you've been dying to do it. But be back soon. It looks like people are sitting down now."

"Got it." He squeezed my arm and darted into the throng. Five minutes later I was seated at the table with Domo and Margie, Katie and Eduardo, and two other couples who were strangers to us. Both seemed to be in their mid-fifties. One of the men, who had introduced himself as Bob, was explaining how things worked at his meat-packing plant while we forked into our predinner salads.

Eduardo caught my eye and pretended, with subtle pantomimes, that he was dying of boredom. I grinned down at my salad. Bob paused for breath, and Domo said, "Hey, this building is pretty great. I never paid attention to it in high school, when we used to have proms here, but I wonder how long it's been around."

This distracted Bob, and by the time the main courses

came, in large family-style bowls, we had learned that the building was erected in 2000 and was initially called the Millennium Building before they changed it to the River-wood Pavilion. "That's interesting," Margie said with a sweet smile.

Bob's wife, Carol, leaned forward and pointed her fork at Margie. "Has anyone ever told you that you look like Grace Kelly?"

Margie blushed and said no.

"Well, you do," Carol insisted. "Here, would anyone like the bowl of mostaciolli?"

"I'll take it," Domo said. "I was *just saying* that Margie looked like Grace Kelly, wasn't I, Hana? I'm a fan of her movies. *Rear Window* is a favorite."

Domo was a smooth one. Soon Bob and Carol were his best friends, and they chatted while the rest of us listened and passed around large bowls of pasta, chicken, beef, mashed potatoes, and rolls.

Erik reappeared, bending to whisper an apology in my ear. "Did you get it all down?" I asked.

"I think so. I have follow-up questions, though."

"Eat some dinner first." I handed him the bowl of pota-toes, and he scooped some onto his plate. He started to say something, but someone on the dais at the front of the room tapped a microphone. A man in a tuxedo stood there, look-ing almost like the ringmaster at a circus.

"Good evening, everyone! I'm Trent Holloway, and I'm your master of ceremonies for this evening. I hope you're all enjoying our annual autumn ball!"

People clapped politely. Trent continued, "We worked hard this year, not only to make the room look this beautiful"—some more applause—"but also to pay special tribute to a friend of Riverwood who was taken from us too soon. So this evening's festivities are held in honor of William Kodaly. Will, we drink to you." He held up a glass, as did everyone in the suddenly quiet room. Then we all drank in honor of the man I had met only once.

Trent was talking again. "We'll have a special tribute to Will later tonight. He was a renowned artist, and he was generous to this town, sharing his time and talent with us on more than one occasion. His famous mural at the chamber of commerce is a testament to his talent. Several of his fellow artists are here to tell you a bit more about him, including Sofia Kálmar, another of Riverwood's artistic geniuses.

"But more about that later. Right now, while you're enjoying that delicious meal, I'll briefly tell you about all the goodies we have for you at the silent auction table. Proceeds benefit several local charities and help to support small business endeavors in Riverwood."

He launched into a description of gifts, from Eduardo's ruby earrings to time-shares in Colorado to season tickets to the Chicago Cubs. At first, when the bad feeling started, I thought that I just found Trent irritating. But the feeling grew, and the room seemed less in focus, and I realized that I was experiencing a phenomenon I'd known only once before, and which I'd dubbed "the misery." A general feeling of wrongness, of evil, had permeated either the room or me or both. I felt sick with it.

"Erik," I whispered.

"Hmm?" He was sawing away at a piece of beef, looking watchful but serene.

"Something's wrong. I feel it the way I felt it at the tea house last month, right before Ava was killed."

His eyes widened and his head swiveled, scanning the room. He set down his fork and said, "I'm going to have a look around. Maybe call Greg as backup, just in case. He trusts your instincts. He's fascinated by them, actually."

I managed a smile. Erik touched my hand and walked away. Domo looked up from his pasta. "Where's he going?"

"Just stretching his legs. He gets restless," I said, trying to sound lighthearted. To my own ears my voice had a dead quality. Only Katie seemed to notice; she studied me with a frown.

And then, as strangely as the feeling had emerged, it vanished, and the table glowed again with cheery Halloween light, the women glimmered anew in their soft and glittery dresses, and Katie's concern was something I could wave off with a casual hand. "Nothing," I said to her unspoken question. "I was feeling kind of sick, but it went away."

Her worried look remained for a while, but eventually Eduardo asked some question that drew her attention, and she grew animated again.

By the time they brought ice cream in little dishes shaped like skulls, we were a festive and merry table, and I was enjoying myself.

৹কেজ

Erik Wolf wasn't a particularly good dancer, nor was I, but we had fun on the dance floor, jumping around to some Beatles covers done by the live band. When they finished their Beatles trio with "And I Love Her," I was relieved to tuck against Erik's chest and move barely at all, just sort of shifting my weight from foot to foot.

"Any more feelings since dinner?" he murmured in my ear.

"No. I don't know what that was. It was weird, I'll tell you that. And it was real. But I can't trace it to anything."

"Greg is going to come by later, just sort of circle the building a few times. I want to have eyes outside."

"Okay. Nobody inside looks particularly threatening."

"No." His chin had been resting on my head, but now he lifted it and glanced around. I looked with him: some tipsy people, laughing in one corner. A huge cluster of bodies on the dance floor, and another crowd milling around the silent auction tables. Some people still at their tables, chatting or eating or looking at their phones. Many of the dancers were edging toward the gazebo.

"Before we leave, we have to dance in there," I said, tipping my head toward the gazebo.

"Oh? Why?"

"Because it's dimly lit and full of starlight, and it makes people fall in love."

"That was poetic, Hana. But I don't need the starlight room. I'm already in love with you."

I tripped and stepped on his toe, and he said, "Ow."

I stared up at him, reading his face.

"Did I say that too soon?" he said.

The band moved on to Elvis and a raucous "Jailhouse Rock."

Katie and Eduardo practically crashed into us. "Hey!" Katie said. "We just bid one hundred dollars on a weekend at a Colorado time-share. If we win, you guys are going with us."

I said, "That sounds great," and gave a thumbs-up, drowned out by the music.

Erik's phone must have buzzed in his pocket. He looked at it now with some concern, and then he put his mouth by my ear. "Greg's outside. I'll be right back."

He left the room and I floated back to our table, where Domo was clearly trying to scandalize Margie with whatever he was whispering to her. She was blushing and smiling like an innocent.

I sat down at the table and Domo said, "Hey, there's Ms. Derrien. Let me grab her." He jumped up and returned with my high school English teacher, who still looked pretty "hot" in a long black dress with a sequined bodice. She was probably in her mid-forties now, but she was one of those women who looked youthful and probably would do so well into old age.

"Hello, Hana," she said, reaching out to shake my hand. "How's my Shakespeare lover doing these days?"

"Not bad," I said. "I still love Shakespeare, and I still annoy people by quoting him to them."

She smiled, sitting down in the empty chair beside me. "And what quote would suit this noble assemblage?" She waved an ironic hand at the undulating dancers.

A burst of bad feeling made me say, "'Something is rotten in the state of Denmark.'"

She laughed. "Can't say that I disagree. No less than three men have implied ignoble intentions toward me this evening."

"I hope your husband put them in their place."

Her nose wrinkled in a rueful expression. "Sadly, he's at a conference in Indianapolis this weekend, so he cannot be my bold protector."

Erik returned and sat across from us.

Domo said, "Erik Wolf, this is Amber Derrien, our former teacher and current friend."

Erik stood up and reached across the table to shake her hand. "Nice to meet you."

"You, too. And you're here with—?"

"Hana," said Erik.

"And what do you do, Erik?"

"I'm a detective with the Riverwood Police."

Perhaps it was a trick of the light that Ms. Derrien's skin

seemed to grow pale at his words. Then she pointed at him. "You investigated that woman's death last month. I saw you on television."

"Yes. I'm investigating the death of William Kodaly, as well."

"Oh. Poor Will," she said with genuine regret. She tucked a strand of dark hair behind her ear. Her hair, with just a hint of gray, was swept up in an elegant bun that had been her preferred hairstyle even when I was in school.

"I understand you dated Will Kodaly," Erik said, his gaze directed at Ms. Derrien.

Her eyes widened. "Wow, word travels fast, huh? Yeah, I did. Brad and I had separated, and I met Will at an art fair last summer. We hit it off and started seeing each other. He was fun, really fun. And romantic." She shrugged. Her hands were in her lap, pulling at each other. "It didn't last. And I suppose I was just using Will as a way to avoid addressing the problems in my marriage. Brad had gotten involved with Sofia, I suppose you heard that, too?"

Erik nodded. "I had heard that. And how was it that you ended up back together?"

She shrugged. "Sofia was losing interest in Brad. She had met someone new, I think. You'll have to ask her. He was drowning his sorrows at the Hardigan Pub one night, and I had gone there to do the same thing." She laughed without mirth. "Relationships ebb and flow, that's all I can tell you. They ebb and flow. Will and I had ebbed, and that night Brad and I started to flow again. And now we're working things out."

A man loomed up behind her and put his hands over her eyes. "Guess who?" he asked.

I exchanged an irritated glance with Domo. What was this guy, in third grade?

Amber wasn't amused, either. "I have no idea," she said, not playing his stupid game.

He took his hands away; she turned and said, "Phil!" and suddenly his dumbness was forgiven as Amber hugged him. "Oh, everyone, this is Phil Drungill. We used to teach together at Arwell Academy, about a million years ago!" She turned back to him. "I can't believe you're here! I thought you lived in Chicago."

"Come over to the bar. I'll buy you a drink and tell you all about it."

"In a minute," she said. "I'll meet you there—I'm just finishing with my friends here."

Phil nodded, sent a vague wave to us, and sauntered off. Amber really did lure the men.

She turned back to us. "Sorry about that. It's just—unbelievable to see him, after all these years." She homed in on Erik. "So it must be a tough job, trying to catch a murderer."

Erik nodded.

Ms. Derrien pointed at my brother. "Domo and I share a favorite book: Dostoevsky's *Crime and Punishment*. Have you read it?"

Erik shook his head. "I can't say that I have."

"You've got to read it, man," Domo said in that annoying voice that men use when they're bonding. "It's intense."

Ms. Derrien went into English teacher mode. "It's a fascinating study, not just of the psychology of guilt but of the psychology of detection. There's this amazing police detective, Porfiry Petrovich, who solves the case mainly through psychological profiling. I just wonder how much of that you have to do."

"A fair amount," Erik said. "It's become a sophisticated process."

The band started singing "Dancing Queen." My feet tapped under the table.

Amber's eyes floated toward the bar. "Well, anyway. I hope you find him soon and poor Will can rest in peace. My dear friend Will."

Erik said, "Did you feel angry at him when he left?"

Her eyes, like those of Will's two other lovers, were sad. "He didn't leave, Detective Wolf." She sent a quick, glittering glance around the table. "I did."

Erik processed this while the female vocalist on the stage did a creditable Agnetha Fältskog.

Domo said, "I'm glad you and your husband have worked things out. Maybe you should text him and tell him that guys are hitting on you."

She let out a watery laugh. "I may just do that. But first I'll have a drink with Phil, to celebrate old times." She stood up and waved to everyone, touched me briefly on the arm, and glimmered away in her sequined gown.

On the stage the band said they were taking a break, and a group of people approached the microphone. Sofia stepped forward. "We hope you're all enjoying the dance and this festive prelude to Halloween. Earlier we paid tribute to Will Kodaly, our friend and mentor, and we artists especially can credit him as someone who shaped the way we see the world. This is one of two paintings I did of Will; I tried to capture his spirit, and I like to think I have done so."

A painting of Kodaly was projected on a big screen behind the stage: a powerful image of him laughing, head thrown back, captured in bold, minimalist strokes. It was simple and beautiful; Sofia had talent.

She spoke a bit more about Kodaly, about the first time she met him at an artists' retreat, about his gentle humor and his loyalty. "And now," she said, "several Riverwood artists will tell you what Will Kodaly taught them about art. While they share their stories, please look at the screen to see some of Will Kodaly's work. One of his pieces, called *Summer Wheat*, is available in today's silent auction." She stepped back, looking relieved, and another artist came to the microphone, a young man with a shock of dark hair. I tuned him out and focused on the images that flashed behind him. I stole a glance at Erik and saw that he, too, was looking carefully.

There were beautiful landscapes, detailed portraits, whimsical still lifes. There seemed to be nothing Kodaly couldn't do. I recognized one of the paintings Katie had bought, along with the one of Cassandra standing at the fence. *Magdalena's Eyes* came a few slides later; it was even more striking on a large screen: my mother's eyes, made luminous and beautiful by the hand of a talented man. The crowd let out a little "ahhh" and I felt a burst of pride in my mother. And then, shocking and surprising me, came an image called *Mother and Child Reunion*. A baby's head was visible from behind, held in someone's arms. Past the child was the focal point: the face of a woman running toward him, her mouth wide with joy, her hands reaching. It was a picture of euphoria and gladness. "Oh, Henrik," I whispered. The final image was Kodaly's masterwork, *Light Touches the Valley*, and the crowd burst into spontaneous applause even as my eyes filled with tears.

A thing of beauty is a joy forever, wrote Keats, and here was Kodaly, alive with us through his work. The painting's power lay in its magical use of light; in fact, it seemed to me that only someone with supernatural guidance could do the things Kodaly did on a canvas.

After the final artist spoke her words about Kodaly's influence, the band came back and sang "I Will Remember

You," and then everyone clapped, and some cried, and the screen went dark.

The band introduced their second set, and dancers swarmed the floor. Margie dragged Domo out to the gazebo, and Katie and Eduardo were nowhere to be found. Erik, still across the table, came to sit by my side. "Want to dance?"

I nodded. "Just a couple more, and then we can go, if you want. I know you have to check in with Greg."

"Right now, I'm all yours." He stood up and held out his hand. By the time we reached the gazebo, illuminated with wall sconces and starlight, the band had started to play "The Way You Look Tonight." Erik led me into the darkened room and pulled me against him, and we did our minimal slow dancing, our eyes locked on each other. The song was so romantic that I felt it wrapping around me, making me weak in a good way.

Erik put his mouth against my ear and sang some of the lyrics. I had never heard him sing, but he was good. "You should sing all the time," I said.

He lifted his head and looked down at me. "I know you heard what I said before," he said. "Should I be worried that you're pretending you didn't?"

I smiled. "I'm not pretending, I'm savoring." I tripped again, and this time I was the one who said "ow."

"What's wrong?"

"I hate high heels. I think I've about had enough of these. Let's go by the window. There are some little benches there, and I can take off these darn—shoot." My ankle twisted, and I lunged painfully forward. I felt a sudden pain on top of my left shoulder. "Oh no! I think I just burst a spaghetti strap," I moaned. "Or a bee stung me," I joked.

Erik bent to look at my dress. "It's not—" he said, and then everything went into slow motion.

I felt the misery rise up fast, like a floodwater, even as Erik's eyes widened with horror and his head whipped side-wise to study the window, where a spiderweb of cracks had appeared. Then he was dragging me, half carrying me, out of the room. My shoes fell off and my dress snagged on a nail; I felt rather than heard it tearing. He pushed me down against an inside wall and said, "Stay there. Stay there, Hana!"

Then he was holding his ID in the air and saying, "*Po-lice!* I need everyone to leave the gazebo *now*."

Someone screamed, and a stampede of feet ran by me as I sat, dazed, on the floor. I put a hand to my shoulder and my fingers came back covered in blood. Erik rushed past, his gun in one hand and pointed down, his phone in his other hand and pressed against his ear; he was talking rap-idly into the phone and alternately shouting instructions to the people in the room.

Finally, he went to the microphone and said, "Attention, please. I'm Detective Erik Wolf with the Riverwood PD. This building is on a soft lockdown until I can determine what is going on outside. Please do not leave the building or go into the gazebo until the police have determined the area is safe. Thank you."

He stepped down and spoke to Domo, who stood with Margie near the stage. Erik pointed at me and then disap-peared. Domo came running, grabbing a clean napkin from one of the tables on the way. He said that the sight of me terrified him because the bodice of my dress was covered in blood, as was my left cheek and the hand that I held out to him, but I was laughing, chortling like a madwoman, although no one could hear me in the chaos of that room.

How could I explain to him that even in that moment of horror I was happy, exhilarated, relieved at the opening of my inner eye?

And that Erik Wolf, charging around the room and giving orders, desperately trying to keep everyone safe, was bathed in a beautiful green-blue light, glimmering with overtones of gold.

Chapter 12

....

NIGHT OF REVELATIONS

Domo was putting pressure on my wound with the napkin. "How did this happen, Hana?"

I focused on my brother's concerned face and took a
deep, calming breath. "All right, don't freak out. Someone
shot me."

"What?" yelled Domo and Margie in unison.

"Look in the gazebo. There's this hole in the window
and lots of webbing around it. And I thought I had been
stung by a bee, or that my strap popped off and somehow
whipped me. But neither of those would explain the blood,"
I said, ruminating.

"How can you be so calm?" Margie cried, patting inef-
fectually at my stockinged feet.

I leaned my head against the wall. "Because he's gone."
It was true; I had felt the misery recede soon after the chaos
began.

Erik ran up with a woman I had never seen. The halo of

light was still around him; I squinted in its glare. "Hana, this is Dr. Angela Stevens. She's going to look at your injury."

I nodded, and the woman bent down and removed the towel. She poked me for a moment, one time painfully, and then said, "Well, good news. You're missing a divot of skin there, which is why it's bleeding so much, but it didn't penetrate you at all. A surface wound. The bullet skimmed across the top of your shoulder. You don't need the emergency room, but I do recommend disinfecting that area and using a good butterfly bandage to make sure it heals with minimal scarring. I might have something in my car I can give you." She looked up at Erik. "Can I go to my car?"

He shook his head. "Not yet. So she's okay?"

"She's A-okay. Just a surface wound and lots of bleeding."

"Thank God. I appreciate it, Doctor."

She stood and gazed down at me. "That dress, on the other hand, might be a casualty. What a terrible loss." She shook her head. "Let me know if you need anything else, Detective Wolf." She waved at me and moved back into the noisy crowd. Erik left too, with a promise to return shortly. The panic had lessened and now the hum of activity was more about curiosity and adrenaline.

I wondered what Runa and Thyra would say if they saw the dress. They had given it to me believing I would take good care of it . . . I sat up straight. What if it hadn't been a gift, but a loan? The dress was torn and covered in blood!

Katie and Eduardo appeared, looking worried. I saw them speaking to Erik, who was sort of yelling at them. Then, chastised, they came toward the wall where Domo, Margie, and I sat in a daze. Katie knelt down and stared at me. "What in the world happened here? Are you okay?" She gave me one of her Katie hugs, but made sure not to touch my left shoulder.

"Long story," I said. I was suddenly very, very tired. "And, yes, I'm okay. I wonder if there's any punch left?"

"I'll get some," Eduardo said, and he darted away.

"Where were you?" I asked Katie. "I was worried about you."

She looked at the three of us, wincing slightly. "Okay, I don't want to hear about how immature I am."

"No promises," Domo said as he studied the hand Margie had tucked into his.

"Eduardo and I were in the lobby, and then we went down that little hallway that leads to the bathrooms. There's a janitor's closet there. We peeked inside; it was actually kind of a big room. Anyway, Ed pulled me in there and started kissing me."

"So you were making out in a janitor's closet while the rest of us stampeded around like spooked horses?" I asked.

"Yes."

I turned my head to study her bright eyes. "Was it good?"

She smiled. "Yes. Very good. We're back together."

"Oh, I'm glad, Katie. I think we're going to see a whole new Eduardo."

She nodded. "Or maybe more dimensions of the same old Eduardo. Which is fine with me." She sighed, then looked back at me and my bloody dress. "This is really scary, Hana. Does Erik think this was a random crackpot?"

I shrugged. "I assume so." I glanced at the windows, where red and blue lights made the scene both surreal and safe. The crowd seemed to be edging toward the door. "I think they're letting people go."

They were. Within half an hour everyone had been allowed to leave after showing Erik or one of the police officers their IDs and jotting down their contact info. Dr. Stevens returned with a little medical bag and brought me to the washroom, where she painfully sanitized my wound and then carefully bandaged it. "There. That should minimize scarring. You can shower, but you'll have to leave this shoulder out of the spray. Don't get it wet for a week or so. Then you can take the bandage off. Come see me if you'd like. Here's a pain pill that should make you feel fine until morning. And I'll include a couple more for tomorrow. Here's my card, should you have any questions."

I took the pills and the card, thanked her, and trudged back to the nearly empty ballroom. Cassandra Stone stood with some of the artists near the dais, packing up the equipment from their Kodaly presentation. She looked at me with a haunted expression, but then someone claimed her attention and she turned away again.

Domo and Margie approached me. "Hana, do you want to stay at my place tonight?" Domo said. "You'll be safe there; it's a secure building."

"No, I'm okay. I need to feed my cats, and I have a pretty early event at the tea house."

My brother looked uncertain. "Is Erik going to stay with you? Because I don't want you to be alone, Han."

I patted his arm. "I'm sure he is. If not, I'll have him drop me at Mom and Dad's."

"All right. Call me if you need anything."

Margie had grown quiet; her burst of extroversion was at an end. "It was fun, Hana. Before all this. Thanks for inviting us," she said in her small voice.

They left, followed by Eduardo and Katie, who were holding hands.

Greg Benton appeared in the doorway, and Erik talked briefly to him. Then Erik, glowing with residual gold, walked to me where I stood leaning against a table. I moved into his chest and his arms wrapped around me. "Let's get you home," he said.

I nodded. We didn't say much in the car, although he reached for my hand. His hand was warm. I closed my eyes.

As we neared my apartment, he said, "Are you all right? Emotionally, I mean?"

"Yes. I'm very curious, though. I mean, I'm hoping I wasn't a particular target—"

I felt the tension in his palm, then turned to see it in his face. "What?" I asked.

He shrugged. "We can talk about it tomorrow."

"No, don't be silly. What's on your mind?"

He pulled into my lot and parked the car. Then he turned to me, his face solemn. "I've been going over this in my head. It's like a nightmare. I can see it still: something dawned on you, one of your moments of wisdom, and then your ankle twisted and you bent forward." He leaned toward me and lightly touched my bandage. "And the bullet grazed you here."

I nodded, remembering.

"But if you hadn't twisted, Hana, and your shoe hadn't given out, it would have struck you here." His finger moved down and pointed at my heart. "My fear is that he actually had excellent aim. That it was just you he wanted to shoot."

At first this struck me as almost funny, and a short laugh burst out of me. "What in the world would make me a target? I don't—*do* anything."

He knew what I meant, and he shook his head. "I don't know. And why at the dance? You were probably moving around on your own for much of the time these last few days."

"Yes. That is really scary in retrospect. I mean, yesterday I was driving in my car alone, and marching up the library steps—"

"Right, the library." He thought about this. "What were you doing there? I mean, besides getting those images of Kodaly?"

"I asked for information about Békéscsaba or Keszthely. Towns in Hungary."

"Why those?"

I let out a long sigh. "You'd better come in. This is a long story. Maybe we should have a midnight snack."

"Okay." He got out and came around to my side; he helped me out of the car and pulled me against him. "I'm not going to let anything happen to you, Hana. Not now that I've found you."

"Good. I don't want anything to happen to me," I joked. We walked hand in hand to the door; little Iris the gatekeeper had long since gone to bed and was probably dreaming of being a pirate the next day. Halloween.

Wolf unlocked my door and we mounted the stairs. Inside, he fed my complaining cats and I went into the bathroom to view the damage to my dress. As I had feared, it looked even worse under the bright lights. The bodice looked redder than delicate frothy chocolate, and the pretty skirt had a six-inch tear. I peeled it off and took a quick rinse in the shower, leaving my shoulder out of the spray as instructed. Then I put on some pajamas my mother had made me: cream-colored flannel, patterned with smiling cats. They felt particularly cozy on this cold night. I combed my hair, stepped into slippers, and went back out to Erik, who was looking at his phone.

"We don't have a man yet, but we do have his footprints," he said. "That's good."

I sat down beside him and he smiled at my outfit. "Very

cozy," he said. He sniffed near my neck and said, "And fragrant."

"Mm. Kiss me." He did, eagerly, and I slid my arms around him. For a time, it was just us, warming each other. Then I pulled away and said, "You need to know some things, I guess."

"Okay."

"First, we have to go back to 1960, when a little baby disappeared in the town of Békéscsaba. His mother was shopping; she left him in plain sight on the sidewalk, in his stroller, and he disappeared."

He stroked my hair. "And why do we need to go to 1960 Hungary and this little town?"

"Because the police couldn't find the baby. They had no leads. Someone sent them to my great-grandmother."

He sat up straight, his eyes wide. "Your little Natalia? From the picture?"

"She was twenty-seven then. Grandma was four."

His eyes remained wide as saucers. "Your Hungarian women found the baby."

I nodded. "Told the police where he was, at least. Natalia said she saw a blue barn and some other details."

"So you were asking about that in the library, along with—what other town?"

"Keszthely. Kodaly loved it; I think he was born there. Look at my painting." I pointed to the wall. "That's the Keszthely of his memory. Oh, and at the dance, remember all those Kodaly paintings? Remember the one of the happy mother, reaching for a baby?"

"Yes—I wondered why you were so moved by that one."

"That was Kodaly's vision of Henrik Sipos's reunion with his mother. Henrik is the baby from back then. He lives in Riverwood, and he loves my family, for obvious reasons."

"And Kodaly knew the story?"

"Yes. They met each other in some Hungarian circle or other, and Henrik ended up telling him about his town and his story."

"Okay. Were these the only things you looked for at the library?"

I hesitated. "Well, Kodaly's paintings."

"Yes."

"And I asked for books about psychic ability."

"What?"

"I just—I figured I should try to tap into what I have. Cassandra found a whole pile for me."

"Cassandra, huh? So she probably put two and two together. What if she told other people? There are already rumors about your family in the Hungarian community. That could easily spread. Now maybe the artists know, too. And some of their friends. It's out there."

"She did mention something—" I thought back to our conversation, trying to reclaim her words.

"What?"

"Something about how the Hungarian community had been buzzing about our family. About psychic ability."

"Oh, boy."

"Not ideal, but so what? Who cares? I'll never meet those people."

He pointed at my bandage. "Maybe you already did. What if the guilty person heard that you were researching Kodaly's birthplace? Asking to see a visual of Kodaly's stolen painting? And then insinuating, without intending to do so, that you had psychic ability? What if someone didn't want to take that chance?"

"Wow." I slumped back on the couch. Oddly, I felt more relieved than terrified. If the person had an actual motive for singling me out, that was better than someone just randomly stalking me. "This is good, Erik. It means that you catch him, and this is all over."

"But it also means that until I catch him, you are in danger. So you are not going anywhere alone. Do you understand?"

"Yes, sir." I sat for a moment, feeling safe but also constrained. How long would I have to worry about going outside?

I sighed. "Would you like some stuffed cabbage?"

Despite everything, I saw HFG in his eyes. This was Domo's acronym for a term he had coined: Hungarian food greed. I laughed and said, "I'll warm it up."

Soon we were snuggled on the couch, watching an old movie while we dug into my warmed-up *töltött káposzta* and some Hungarian bread.

When we finished eating, Erik took our plates to the kitchen, then came through the doorway. He had long since removed his jacket and tie, and he had rolled up the sleeves on his brown shirt. He looked wide-awake, despite his very long and intense evening. He paused a moment to text someone on his phone. Then he came back, plopping down beside me.

I leaned back on the couch. The pain pill had worked so well that I didn't feel my shoulder at all.

I flicked off the movie with my remote. "It was kind of boring," I said.

"It was really boring," he agreed. He waited until I looked into his green eyes. "So this book you took out—is it helping you at all? I mean, to come to terms with your—inner power?"

I reached up to stroke his cheek. "I haven't read much. But I did an inner eye exercise of my own invention, and I listened to some self-help guru at the tea house. Then I read a chapter of the book. None of those equals deep research, but, you know what? They did help me. A lot. I'm starting to get a better sense of my own instincts, and what they mean. At the dance, there was a moment that I felt terrible. Miserable. I couldn't find any happiness. Remember, I told you?"

"Yes. When was that, do you recall?"

"About an hour before the shooting. We were just all at the table. Maybe he was marching around outside."

"Maybe." He pondered this. "But the feeling didn't stay?"

"No. It faded. But it came back right before I felt the bullet."

He stiffened with the memory. "You said, 'Oh no.' I thought you meant your shoe."

"No—I think I was trying to tell you something."

"Huh." He sat back on the couch. "Then what were you laughing at?"

"What?"

"When I pointed you out to Domo, you were laughing. Like someone had just told you a hilarious joke or the best news."

"It was the best news. The best ever."

"What?" He looked genuinely confused.

I crept closer to him. "Everything was kind of in slow motion, from the time you knew something was wrong. I saw the realization dawn on your face. And then you were dragging me, and pushing me down, and lifting your badge and shouting to everyone. You were everywhere at once. You were magnificent."

He shook his head. "I was doing my job, Hana."

"But you didn't see what I saw: an amazing blue-green light, like the sea in the sunshine, surrounded by a glittering gold."

"What?" Awareness dawned, and his eyes widened. "In the room? Or around me?"

"Just around you, Erik Wolf. I still see the gold edges now, like someone cut you out of some magical paper."

We looked at each other for a long moment; at first it seemed he didn't believe me. I waited until he saw the truth.

Until he smiled.

He pulled me onto his lap. "What if you hadn't seen it? Were you not going to tell me that you loved me?"

"Don't be silly. I've known that I love you for weeks."

He stared at me, stunned. "So why not say it back to me?"

I smoothed his hair. "Because I wanted to say it here, where you first kissed me."

"Say it, then."

"I love you."

"Say it again," he said, lightly touching my mouth with his fingertips.

I slid off his lap. "I will, but I have another special place that I want to say it."

"Oh?" He smiled lazily.

"Yeah. Come with me."

I led him to my bedroom; the cats followed us, ready to cuddle up for the night.

I said, "Sorry guys, not right now," and I closed the door.

Chapter 13

....

SÁRKÁNY *THE DRAGON*

I woke up smiling. I wondered if in fact I had smiled in my sleep all night long. Erik Wolf was not beside me, but my cats were, staring at me with reproachful eyes that spoke of morning hunger. I donned a robe and went out into the hallway. Erik was on the phone, but his face lit up when he saw me, and I'm sure mine sent light back to him.

"Yeah," he was saying. "I can be there by ten."

My spirits drooped a little. He hung up and walked swiftly to me. "Good morning," he said, pulling me into a hug, but being careful not to touch my bandage.

"It's a very good morning. Except that you have to go."

"I do, in a while. But I've got security for you all day. You won't be alone, and I'll be back late this afternoon. I want to see Kodaly's son at that pumpkin patch, and I'll need you there to tell me if you pick up any vibes."

"All right."

"I have to call Greg real quick, and then we can have breakfast together."

"I'll take a shower, then."

He kissed my hair and went to dial his phone. I would have been offended by his divided attention except for two things: first, I knew he had a job to do, and it was difficult. Second, I could feel his immense relief every time he looked at me. He had wanted me to make things permanent, and now that we had a rock to build things on, he was happy.

I took a swift but fragrant shower, leaving my left shoulder out of the spray and softly singing "The Hokey Pokey." Then I donned a pair of jeans and a bright orange sweater and padded out into the kitchen. Erik was gone.

"Huh," I said.

There was a light tapping at the door. Perhaps he had brought something in from the car? I jogged across the room and flung it open, saying, "You disappeared on me," only to find it wasn't Erik Wolf who stood there but two other members of that family: Runa and Thyra.

"Uh—hi," I said. "What—how did you know where I live?"

"Nice welcome," said Runa with a smirk, brushing past me. She smelled like exotic perfume. They both wore casual clothing, but it looked expensive. Runa sported black leggings and a long blue sweater with a gold silhouette of the Eiffel Tower embroidered on its front; Thyra's attire featured a caramel-colored turtleneck and a long white vest, with a wide gold belt around them both. Runa's hair was swept up in an elegant ponytail, but Thyra's hung down almost to her waist. I realized that I could tell them apart, but I didn't know why.

Runa was poking at my shoulder. "You have a bandage, huh? Where you were shot?"

My mouth hung open. "How do you know about that?"

"We're psychic," Thyra said, grinning.

My temper kicked in a little. Katie would call it my "Zsa Zsa spirit."

"Seriously, though, what are you guys doing here?"

Runa laughed. "Calm down, passionate woman. We were summoned."

"What? By whom?"

Erik appeared behind them holding a dish of cinnamon rolls. I recognized the pan as one of Paige's; clearly, she had called him to the first floor to claim the sweets for our breakfast. Now he looked at me with an apology. "By me. These two are your morning security detail."

"What?" Now I was the one laughing. "Erik, I think I could just have Domo or someone, if you're looking for, like, civilian guards. I'm sure your sisters are super busy at the store . . ."

Thyra flipped her hair behind her shoulder and sat down on one of my kitchen chairs. "We're our own bosses. And our bosses gave us Sunday morning off. Fun how that works, right?"

I was sending Erik urgent glances that he managed to ignore. He said, "Hana, I couldn't get a police guard, but these two are the next best thing."

I stared at his glamorous sisters. Runa was contemplating her long blue-painted fingernails. Was I missing something?

Erik saw my face and smiled. "Listen. Runa and Thyra are both black belts. They are also licensed to carry concealed weapons, and they know how to use them."

"What?"

Runa put her hands on her hips and faced her sister. "Get up and attack me," she said. Thyra, graceful as a cat, slid out of the chair and advanced on Runa in three strides. Then they were sparring: hand against hand, in gestures almost too swift to see. At one point, Thyra squatted low, as if to take out Runa at the knees, and Runa flew over her.

Flew across my kitchen, her legs extended, like a cartoon action figure.

"I get the picture," I said breathlessly. "Your whole family is—fit and ready to defend."

"Sure thing," said Thyra, springing up from her squatting position as though she were made of rubber. "Can I have one of those rolls?"

Erik set them on the table. "The twins are going to go with you to the tea house and hang around there until I can pick you up. Okay?"

Runa had been prowling around the room; she peered out my front window, then returned and found my dress hanging over a chair. "Oh, my," she said, picking it up.

"Hey, I'm really sorry about that. There's a tear in the skirt, too. If it was on loan, I can pay you for it—"

Runa shook her head. "It was a gift." She held it up. "Thyra, we can probably salvage the skirt, give it a different bodice, donate it to the high school, maybe." She shrugged, then looked closer. "A lot of blood for a graze, surely?"

Erik said, "It hit her at a weird angle. Took a chunk of tissue and cut into a blood vessel." He walked over to her and looked at the dress. They said some things about blood spatter in low voices, and I gasped.

"Oh my God, you guys are so weird," I whispered.

Erik grinned at me. "Too late now. You're committed." He strode over and pulled me into another hug. "Come and have some breakfast with me. I'll make my sisters tone down their eccentric tendencies."

Thyra sniffed. "*Eccentric* got us where we are today. It got us Ulveflokk." She had torn off a cinnamon roll, and now she took a bite. "Mmm. Delicious."

I sat down at the table. Erik brought the pot of coffee and poured me a cup. I took a bracing sip. "I wanted to thank you for the dress," I said. "Before the shooting, it looked perfect. I can show you." I grabbed my phone from the sideboard and pulled up the pictures Paige had sent me. I handed it to Thyra, who scrolled through. "Mmm. Just right. We should have come to do your hair, but this is fine."

"She was *beautiful*," Erik said, pouring coffee into his own cup.

Thyra switched her focus to him. "And your tie was good—we wondered about the shading, but this works. Brown is a good color on you," his sister said. She handed the phone to Runa, who scrolled through, as well.

"Mmm," she said, looking at me. "Yes. I would try this shade again sometime, but maybe next time something crimson. Often looks surprisingly good with hair that color."

"Anyway," I said, "I really appreciate it. I thought you said you only made woolen things."

Runa shook her head. "We're expanding. We have a new prom and wedding line. It's called Ulveflokk Evening. The sales have been crazy good."

Erik took a sip of coffee and studied my face. I must have looked bereft, because he said, "Can you two do a perimeter check? I want to be sure everything's okay before Hana leaves this building."

Thyra smirked, wiping her fingers on a napkin. "Yes, we'll leave so you can make out with your little sweetheart. We should tell Andy what's happening, anyway."

"Who's Andy?" I asked.

Thyra pointed at Runa. "Her little puppy. He follows her everywhere, so we decided to make him chauffeur today."

Erik translated. "He's her boyfriend. For a year now, isn't it, Runa?"

I stared. "Why is he in the *car*?"

Runa dismissed this with a snap of her fingers. "He's fine. He listens to the radio; it calms him."

She may as well have been talking about a golden retriever.

Thyra became businesslike. "We'll be back in ten. Runa, grab a roll. They're really good."

Runa did so, lunging forward with her lithe body and snatching one out of Paige's pan. They left on a cloud of spicy perfume, their blonde hair flying.

Their absence created a vacuum; Erik seemed to be waiting for me to blast him with complaints. I took a sip of my coffee, then put my cup down. "So, that was something that never came up in our 'getting to know you' sessions."

"I'm sorry. Now that you've met my sisters, would you be able to prepare other people for them?"

"No."

"I figured sooner or later you'd just have to experience them. And since you already met them, I thought it was okay to hire them for security detail. They're good. They both went to the police academy, way back when. Ultimately, they decided that they loved fashion more, but they're cops at heart. And they have really fast reaction times. I used to spar with them, and I lost as often as they did."

I believed that, and I also realized, to my own amazement, that I was going to feel safe with them. They projected competence, whether about clothing or martial arts.

I actually sort of wanted to see someone threaten me to see what my tall Norwegian bodyguards would do.

I sighed. "I wanted us to have a quiet breakfast where we just gazed at each other until we went back to bed."

"Me, too." His eyes were regretful. "But I'll be back."

"You can help me feed the trick-or-treaters."

"I might have to work until late."

"I'll wait up."

He looked down at his plate. "I think I'll always love cinnamon rolls, Hana."

"Me, too." My smile was back in place.

He looked at his watch and stood up. "I want to see your bandage." He came close to me and moved my sweater carefully, tenderly, poking the flesh around my wound. "It looks good. No redness, no sign of infection."

"Great."

"In a minute I'll change the gauze, start you out fresh."

"Okay."

I tilted my head upward, and he kissed me, a kiss so deep I disappeared for a moment inside pure sensation. Then, slowly, I came back to my kitchen.

༄

The twins returned minutes later; Erik left with apologies and another stolen kiss, and I changed into my tea house uniform: black skirt, white blouse, apron with Hungarian embroidery.

I expected comments from my visitors, and I wasn't disappointed. They called me "cute" and "tiny dancer" and "Erik's Hungarian doll" and a bunch of other things that I managed to ignore while I tied back my hair.

Finally, they grew tired of teasing me. I sat on the couch

to slip on my shoes, and they sat across from me. Thyra said, "So, who's having tea at your tea house today?"

"I think it's a family reunion. They're having a lunch-time tea and then going off to some show downtown."

"How cute," Runa said. "I want to watch. And I want to meet this grandma of yours. Will she read my leaves?"

"We'll be busy," I said. "This is my *job*."

Thyra nodded. Professionalism, she understood. "We won't get in your way. We can help, if you want. Or we can be invisible."

"Invisible would be good," I murmured, looking at my shoes.

This had them laughing again. "Oh, you are a delight," Runa said.

༄

In the parking lot I met Andy. He stepped out of the driver's seat of a Cadillac to shake my hand; he was a quietly hand-some man somewhere in his mid-thirties; he wore a sur-prisingly dowdy corduroy jacket with his jeans, but the queens of fashion made no comment at all. "Andrew Bell," he said with a charming smile.

"Nice to meet you. I'm Hana Keller. I'm so sorry to dis-rupt your day this way."

He shook his head. "Life with Runa is always chaos. This is actually rather peaceful, sitting here in your lot and watching those grasses blow in the wind. And I saw a little pirate walk by. Super tiny but very spirited."

"Yes, that's Iris. If she were a real pirate, she would rule the seas."

He laughed. Runa slid behind him and whispered some-thing in his ear. His smile stayed in place, but his skin reddened with something that looked like desire. "Let's get going, then." Thyra got in the backseat, and Runa instructed me to get in beside her, whereupon Runa climbed in on my other side.

"Why are we all in back? Don't you want to sit with Andy?" I asked.

Runa said, "We're flanking you. We are protecting our brother's little chick, the way the eagle does. By covering you."

I sighed. When we sat side by side like this I realized how tall they were and how short I was. I leaned back on the seat and said, "Okay, great."

Andy caught my gaze in the rearview mirror. He smiled at me, and I realized that his eyes were a beautiful shade of brown. They crinkled at me now in solidarity. What must it be like to date one of these women? Did Thyra resent it that Runa had a boyfriend?

"So—what do you do, Andy?"

He flipped on his blinker. "I teach math at Columbia College."

"Ah. My dad's a teacher."

"Our noble profession," Andy said.

Runa leaned forward. "Left up here, babe. Then take that to Wild Heather Road."

My phone buzzed in my pocket. I saw that I had a text from Falken: Call me when you can.

"Excuse me, I have to make a quick phone call," I said.

I pressed Falken's name on my speed dial and he said, "Timeless Treasures."

"It's Hana."

"Hana," he breathed. "You will not believe it. Apparently, Will Kodaly's sister in Hungary has been put in charge of his estate. She reached out to American friends about someone to handle her brother's estate sale—she said the family doesn't want to look at any of it, aside from a few pieces she will itemize—it's too painful, she said. Anyway, the person she spoke to recommended me. She said I can make the first offer on any pieces I desire."

"Wow, that's amazing! Just his paintings are worth so much, Falken! Even though he was asking a pittance."

"Anyway, that's the situation. If you want to help me go through things before I open to the public, let me know."

"Yes, of course I do. Let me know the date, and I'll arrange to be there."

"Good. I'll be in touch."

I said good-bye and rang off. I could feel Thyra's gaze on the side of my face. "Was that a man's voice?" she said.

"Yes. My friend Falken. He owns Timeless Treasures—the little shop just outside the downtown area. Antiques."

"Ooooh," Runa said. "We love antique shops."

"He specializes in European things. So we have similar interests."

"Yes? Does Erik know about him?" Thyra asked.

I stared her down. "Erik has met him. He helped Erik choose a gift for me once."

Thyra laughed. "Oh, you are so adorable when you get all sparky. A hot-blooded girl. Runa and I have ice in our veins."

"Ain't that the truth," said Andy in an amiable tone.

"Here we are!" I said with obvious relief. "The tea house. You can just park in the lot there."

"No, let us off at the door, Andy," Runa said.

Andy did as she said, and I clambered out after Thyra, leaning in again to thank him for the ride.

"No problem. I'll be back later for these two." He lifted his chin at the twins, who now paced around the perimeter of the tea house like restless cats.

"They take some getting used to, huh?" I asked.

Andy turned to smile at me. "They do. But when you learn who they are, you love them."

"You love Runa?"

"I do. For my sins," he added with a little smile.

I waved and shut the door, and Andy drove off.

The sisters appeared on either side of me and marched me through the door. Thyra pointed at our Alpine train. "Look at the sweet little train, Ru. Oh, and what pretty hand-painted border on this entrance wall!"

At first, I thought they were patronizing me, but it was soon clear that they loved everything about the tea house. When my mother and grandmother appeared, their faces were surprised at seeing tall identical twins in their establishment. I said, "Mom, Grandma, this is Runa Wolf and Thyra Wolf. They're Erik's sisters."

My grandmother murmured something to my mother in Hungarian, and I heard the word *farkas*, which meant "wolf." Runa darted forward to shake Grandma's hand. "Mrs. Keller?"

"Mrs. Horvath," she said.

"Oh, I'm sorry. I'm so excited to meet you! Hana has told me about your psychic gifts. I would love to have you read my tea leaves at some point, if you can find the time."

My grandmother, like anyone, had her vulnerabilities, and she was susceptible to flattery. "Yah, I can make the time," she said. "We see what the leaves say for you."

Runa practically squealed. "Oh, you are a treasure! Look at this place! I just love the decor and the overall vibe."

My mother sent me an urgent glance, and I said, "Mom, I'll help you with that job in the back room." Before we could leave, though, François came in, all disheveled hair and French sexiness. Runa and Thyra looked at him like hawks who spied a distracted wren.

"Who's this?" asked Thyra, flipping her hair behind her shoulder.

François, the unflappable, stared up at the gorgeous twins with something like fear; he couldn't seem to look away. "François, these are Detective Wolf's sisters. They're my security detail today. Runa, Thyra, this is François, our pastry chef."

"French?" asked Runa.

"*Oui*," whispered François. He managed a stupid smile.

I poked him in the arm. "François has a girlfriend. Practically his fiancée. Her name is *Claire*." I said the last word loudly in his ear, and he came out of his trance slightly.

"*Oui*, Claire. She is my heart. Well, I must get to work."

He practically ran out of the dining hall, and the sisters looked after him with what seemed like predatory intent.

I followed François and my mother to the back room, where she spun around. "What are they *doing* here? They're a bit much, aren't they?"

"Yes. But there's something you should know. Do we have time to sit down for a minute? Or do we need to get right to work?"

She glanced at her watch. "Is this something Mama should hear?"

"Yes."

François was mashing hard-boiled eggs for his delicate little sandwiches. I could only see the back of him, but his ears seemed to have grown in the last thirty seconds. I said, "François, you should hear this, too."

He practically ran to the back table, where he plopped into a chair with an eager expression. My mother went to the door and said, "Mama? Can you come here, please?"

My grandmother appeared a minute later. "What's happening?" she asked.

"Have a seat."

"There's more? Even after the baby story?"

"Yes, more. Last night at the dance we were talking to all these people who knew Kodaly. And at dinner I got a bad feeling, like a sickness. Then it went away for a while. And then, when Erik and I were dancing in that gazebo—you know the one?—someone fired a shot through the window. Someone outside, I mean. And it hit me."

My mother gasped. "How—where?"

I pointed at my shoulder. "It just grazed me, but Erik's afraid the person was actually aiming. You know—to kill me." It was the first time I had said it aloud, and suddenly I wanted to cry.

"Oh my God," my mother said.

François stared at me, dazed. "You have been *shot*? By a bullet? Oh, my family warned me about America and its guns."

My grandmother studied my face. "Why would they shoot you? No motive."

"Well—Erik thinks it's because I talked to Cassandra at the library. I indicated that I was researching things about Will Kodaly and his background, and I took out a book about psychic phenomena."

"So?" my mother asked.

"So Erik thinks Cassandra might have gossiped about it. About us, our family being psychic. And if this guilty person heard, and here I was asking about the stolen painting—which I think has something to do with Will's death—and about Keszthely, and then the person heard, wrongly or not, that I had psychic power—well. He might have felt threatened."

"I see." My mother looked pale. Then she looked angry. "So your boyfriend thought that his *sisters* would be the best protection for you? Those mannequins out there? What if someone comes to the tea house?"

"That's why they're there, Mom. You don't understand. They—"

Suddenly we heard yelling in the outer room—Runa and Thyra calling to each other urgently.

"Oh no," my mother said. We got up in one movement, but François was the first one out the door. Thyra was on her cell phone; she held up a finger.

"What's going on?" my mother cried.

Thyra held the phone away from her head and said, "Intruder. Runa has it covered."

We all turned to look out the window, where Janos, our landscaper, was trudging past, placid as a shepherd, holding a trowel and looking like a man bent on weeding. Before we could ask whether this was the "intruder" Thyra spoke of, Runa appeared out of nowhere, flying—*flying* through the air, hair flowing, eyes bright, her mouth moving as if in a chant—and landed on Janos, taking him down in a spectacular tackle. She quickly pinioned his arms behind him, as though she had just wrestled a bull in a rodeo.

Janos opened his mouth, and even through the closed window we could hear the stream of Hungarian invective.

François bent double, and I feared he was going to be sick until I heard him laughing. In fact, I had never heard François do anything but chuckle, but now he was laughing so hard he couldn't breathe. "Merde," he said. "That's the funniest thing I've ever seen."

I turned to my grandmother, whose eyes were glowing with fascination. "Oh, my. Like the fairies, Hana! Like Szépasszony, singing as she flies! Did you see her?"

"Yes, we all saw her, Mama," my mother said dryly. "And we'll be lucky if Janos doesn't sue us. We need to go out there and talk to him." Even she seemed on the verge of some strong emotion, but whether it was laughter or anger, I wasn't sure.

Thyra appeared. "You know him? That old man? He looks like a vagrant."

I shook my head. "Those are just his gardening clothes. He's one of us, Thyra."

"Ah," she said. "I'll handle this." She marched to the door and outside, and we saw her approach Runa, who still rode on Janos's back like a lovely equestrian. The two women spoke; Runa stood up and reached out a hand to Janos, who took it, got up, and dusted himself off. The twins talked at him. They didn't seem particularly apologetic, but they did seem to be using their charm. There was a fair amount of hair flipping and arm touching.

I thought Janos, who was as expressive as an Easter Island head, would hold out against them, but within five minutes he had cracked a smile; and thirty seconds after that he was laughing, slapping his old knees. and pointing at them with a knobby finger.

"Good God," I said.

François was still laughing, but he clutched his stomach with a pained expression. "It hurts," he said, pointing at his abdomen. "But, ah, I could watch all day."

I turned to my mother. "That's why Erik sent them."

She nodded. "I take it back, what I said. They're perfect."

My grandmother was still beaming out the window. "Amazing," she said.

"Mama," said my mother with a no-nonsense clap. "We need to work."

೧ೂ

The family reunion happened to be half Hungarian, and my grandmother wandered around with her teapot, chattering in her native tongue to the friends she recognized. Runa and Thyra, as promised, had become as invisible as beautiful people can be, and mostly stayed in back with François or in the hallway that led to the exit. They had assessed each person who entered to determine whether or not they might be concealing a firearm and concluded that it was not likely that any of the visitors was in fact packing heat.

François had made a huge assortment of sandwiches—egg salad, turkey and pepper, ham and Swiss, cucumber and cream cheese—and the guests had consumed them all. When I marched out with the first dessert tray, filled with petit fours and tiny chocolate éclairs, the crowd said "ahhh."

When I went back for another tray, Thyra caught me in the doorway and whispered, "We have to hire this boy for some of our client events. He's a marvel."

"Better yet, have your client events here," I said. "People find us charming."

"An outstanding idea!" Thyra said. She looked down at her phone. "Your boyfriend is calling." She grinned at me with perfect white teeth and said, "Hello?"

I walked to the back room, where François was putting the final touches on his last cakes and Runa was staring at him as though he were a science experiment. Normally François would be dark as a thundercloud to be observed in this way, but since Runa was pretty and had provided him with (apparently) the best entertainment of his life, he was being patient.

"You can't do this quickly, or it will come out in a blob," he said, holding his frosting bag aloft. "It has to be slow, steady, careful."

"Lovely," Runa said. "They're like little works of art."

I waited for him to finish, then helped him load the

cakes onto my final tray. "These people eat like horses," I said.

François stretched. "Well, my part is done. I'm going to clean up." He went to the sink and began to fill it with hot water.

Runa looked at me. "I'm going outside. This is a time to be watchful, since the guests leave soon, right?"

"Yes. Another half hour, maybe."

"Okay. Back soon," she said, and glided out of the room.

At table three, Grandma was in a dialogue with someone, and I heard the name Kodaly. I stopped walking and inched closer to the conversation. "So he was born in Keszthely, then?" Grandma asked.

"Yes, I think so," said a woman with red curls who I didn't recognize. She had the standard old-Hungarian-lady look, with her flowered dress and flat shoes, but I didn't know her name. "I think his family moved when he was a boy, but Keszthely was always special to him. When he got a chance to go back to Hungary and paint for a few months, he decided to go there. That's what his sister told me."

"Ah." Grandma nodded, as though this made perfect sense. "And you said he met someone there?"

The woman sat up straighter, feeling the sense of importance that prime gossip can give to a person. "Oh yes. The talk among the Hungarians who knew him was that he met a woman there, and fell in love, and never forgot her."

I pretended to sort the teacups on my cart. Who was the Keszthely woman? Yet another name to put on the list of Kodaly's lovers? Did the guy have some sort of dating compulsion, or was he just lonely and looking for the right person?

Grandma and her friend kept talking, but they moved on to new topics that didn't interest me, and I wheeled my cart away from them.

Thyra appeared. "No one has entered your parking lot since the event started, and Runa has kept close tabs on the outer perimeter. And now she's got that old Janos working with her, as well. He claims that he always keeps an eye out for intruders."

I nodded. This was probably true; Janos had the look of an old knight. "Good to know. This group will be moving out soon, and then I do cleanup duty. Then what? Am I supposed to take you two home with me?"

Thyra shook her head. "No. Erik's picking you up, and Andy will come for us."

"Okay. Andy seems nice, by the way."

She shrugged. "I think he's good for Runa."

"What about you? Do you have a special man in your life?"

"Many." She grinned at me. "I like variety."

"Good for you. I'm more of a one man woman."

Her blue eyes were like lasers as they studied my face. "Good. That's good." Then she looked past me, to the people behind us. "We really do want to get a reading from your grandma, by the way. Will she do it?"

"Of course she will. She likes to read people. My mom has kept her on a leash for years, but now she's been set free, and she's having a good time."

It was true—my mother, fearful of whatever psychic power might be rooted into our DNA, had forced her mother to downplay her instincts for decades, partly because my mother was probably fearful of her own instinctive responses. Conditioned by the modern world to believe that psychics were charlatans, she had simply pretended the feelings weren't there. I understood, because I had done the same thing. A lifetime of subtle sensations, strong suspicions, and near visions had been corralled into categories like illness, melodrama, or stress. Now I knew better. I was Natalia's great-granddaughter. I, and two generations before me, had inherited Natalia's gift.

～

Runa and Thyra helped us clean up. Their energy was boundless. They zoomed around the tea house, wiping tables and sweeping crumbs. They laughed and chattered with each other, then got acquainted with my mother and grandmother by drying the teacups they washed.

By the time we seated Grandma at one of the tea tables and asked her to read their leaves, she was feeling happy: she had new friends.

Thyra went first; she scattered some loose leaves into her cup and poured in the hot water. She blew on it and drank it down quickly, flipped the cup upside down on the draining cloth, and then turned it a few times to dry the cup and allow the leaves to take their shape.

She handed the cup to my grandmother, who studied it and said, "Ah. Interesting."

Thyra leaned forward. "What?"

"See? *Sárkány*. The dragon. He is the beast within you. Means you need to make a decision."

Thyra nodded. "We have been pondering a lot of decisions about the store. Runa and I run a company of imported woolens, and we just started a new line of evening wear. We have to decide whether or not to open a new store."

Grandma found this interesting. "Be sure to consider the good and bad. Don't go only for shiny things, yes? Live inside both choices before you choose."

"That makes total sense. Thank you," Thyra said. She patted my grandma's hand with surprising affection.

Runa practically pushed her out of the way. "My turn," she said. She handed her cup to my grandma, who was half laughing at their antics. My mother stood against one wall, texting—probably to my father, with whom she kept in touch throughout the day.

Grandma peered into the cup. Her smile disappeared, and her eyes widened. She looked up at Runa, then touched her hand. Her face was tender, curious. Then she looked at the rest of us. "I need to be alone. You can all go pack up, yah? Let me talk to Runa."

This was unprecedented. I had never seen Grandma insist on a private reading, and like any normal human being I was now twice as curious about what she was going to say. So was Thyra, I could tell. Still, we weren't going to refuse her request. My mother, Thyra, and I went to the back room that François had vacated about an hour earlier. He had still been laughing a little when he left.

Now we stood in an awkward cluster, asking each other pointless questions. "Do you know what she saw? Did she seem upset? How did Runa react? What was Runa expecting?"

Finally, I opened the door a crack and peeked out. To my immense shock, my grandma was sitting forward in her chair, as was Runa, and their foreheads were touching. My grandmother murmured something softly, and Runa said something softly in return. Then they pulled apart and my grandmother took her hands. She spoke to her with a serious expression; Runa's eyes were riveted on Grandma's face. The scene was calm, almost surreal, but also intimate. I felt a stab of jealousy.

Then it was over, and Runa stood up, smoothing her sweater over her leggings. "Thank you," I heard her say. "Thank you very much, Juliana."

My grandmother practically bowed, and then they embraced. What in the world was going on?

Runa came to the back room. I had only known her for a few days and even I could tell that she had been deeply moved. Her ironic expression was gone. Her face was pale and grave.

"What in the world did she tell you?" Thyra asked.

Runa shook her head. "I can't talk about it yet."

She turned to me. "Erik is here. Thyra and I have to go."

We thanked the two of them for their help, and escorted them to the lobby, where we saw Andy pull into the lot a few minutes later. They waved and left, promising as they went to be in touch soon.

My mother and I turned to my grandma. "What the heck?" I said.

"Yeah, spill it, Mama."

Grandma stood tall. "No, I cannot. She will tell soon. But it's her life. It has to come from her." She nodded once at us, then went to get her coat.

⁓

Erik tucked me into his car as though I were a piece of glass. I laughed. "I'm fine. Your sisters were excellent guards, and it was quiet as could be here. Maybe we're wrong, Erik. Maybe there's nothing—"

His face was impassive as he drove. "We'll go on the assumption that we're not wrong. Meanwhile you are in my protective custody."

"You make that sound very sexy," I said.

His smile was wry. "Don't distract me. You look distracting enough, without saying things like that."

"Oh? Do I look distracting?" I pouted like a supermodel until he laughed.

"Well, not now," he joked. "Hey, I have your wolf for you. I know it has sad associations, but it's clean and intact, and you can put it on your shelf. Think of it as something that a great artist once owned."

"Yes, I guess so."

He decided to divert me. "Listen, when we get to this pumpkin patch, I'm going to want your initial read on John Banner. That's Kodaly's son—the mother raised him with her name, but she gave him the middle name of Kodaly. Fair enough, wouldn't you say?"

"Yeah. That way the boy won't feel deprived of his father's name, but the mom who raised him alone gets to have her own name carried on."

"Anyway, the boy and his dad had connected this year, as I told you. The mother implied it was a positive thing, but I want to know if you sense any negative vibes. If so, the kid would be a prime suspect."

I thought about this as we drove through Riverwood and saw troops of trick-or-treaters marching down the sidewalk, often with parents trudging right behind them. One mother pushed a stroller in which I glimpsed a little fuzzy bumblebee who was not even a year old.

The stroller made me think of the little Henrik Sipos. Was he afraid when the strange face appeared above his stroller?

"Hana?"

"Hmmm?"

"Are you okay?"

"Yeah. Just thinking. You know, my grandma had a weird interaction with Runa today."

"What do you mean?"

I told him about the private reading and the glimpse I had of the two of them, their heads pressed together.

Erik thought about this while we turned onto Route 4 and the landscape changed to green on either side of us. Eventually, the pastureland was dotted with orange, and Wolf turned into a gated driveway that led to a cute little house with a sign that read "Sherman's Pumpkin Patch." Erik kept driving past the house to a huge backyard filled with pumpkins, divided by size. The largest ones cost ten dollars, the medium seven, and the small five.

Even at this late date there were still a throng of people milling through the aisles, and some young people who wore red shirts emblazoned with "SPP" walked up and down, answering questions and wheeling pumpkins to cars.

I knew Kodaly's son right away because he had his father's head of wavy hair and his dark eyes. "That's got to be him," I whispered to Erik, indicating the young man with a tip of my head.

"I think you're right. Hang on a sec." Erik walked toward John Kodaly Banner and spoke to him in a low voice, then shook his hand. John turned to say something to a woman in a PCC T-shirt, then walked with Erik to the tree under which I was standing.

"Hana, this is John Banner. John, this is Hana Keller. She was actually the last person to—meet with your father."

Kodaly's son turned his dark gaze on me; his eyes were sad. "You talked to my dad—on that day? What was he— how was he doing?"

I understood what he felt; the pain of picturing his father's last moments, knowing his father had no idea of his limited time on earth. The bitter disappointment that he hadn't been able to talk to Kodaly himself; the misery of not having said good-bye. "He was fine. Relaxed, smiling. Just selling some things to raise money for art supplies, he said."

John nodded. "He was always painting. It's like the brushes were an extension of his body. He was teaching me, too."

"Oh? Are you an artist?"

"I didn't think so. But he did. He said he saw it in me. Now I—it's something I want to pursue. My dad said it's in my genes. It's my legacy, he said."

I thought instantly of Natalia, and the gift she passed down to us all . . .

"How does your mother feel about that?" Erik asked.

John turned to him. "Huh? My mom? She's cool with it. She always liked my art. She saved all those little baby pictures kids paint in grade school. She thought I had talent, too. My dad introduced me to all these artists in Riverwood that he was friends with. After he—" He turned away for a moment and wiped his eyes. Then he turned back. "Anyway, they've all been really cool to me. One of them offered to continue my painting classes for free. A couple of them, actually. I might take them both up on it—get two artistic perspectives."

"That's very kind of them," I said. "It also shows how much your father was loved and respected. That must make you feel good."

"I guess," he said. "It will. Right now it just feels bad."

Erik stepped closer. "How did you hear about your father?"

John's mouth tightened. "The last way anyone would want to hear. On the news. Normally they notify the family first, but no one knew my dad had family in the area. So I found out just like everyone else. It was like a punch in the stomach."

I touched his arm and understood: he was telling the truth. He felt pain. "I'm sorry," I said.

He shrugged. "I think even my mom is sad. She hasn't really talked to him in years, but she didn't hate him or anything."

"No—he seems not to have burned any bridges behind him," Erik said. "Do you mind if I ask—had your father said anything recently about a conflict he may have had, or someone he was in a dispute with?"

John thought about this, then shook his head. "Not that I remember. We always had fun when we got together. We would make lunch and watch YouTube videos and stuff. I showed him Bob Ross—he got a kick out of that—and he showed me this town he grew up in."

"Keszthely," I said.

"Yeah—wow, you said it just right."

"And what did he say about his town?"

John glanced at his watch. "It was kind of sad, really. He told me it was beautiful and charming and stuff. And he said he had fond memories of it, but that he went back a few years ago, and he met up with a woman there and fell in love with her. He said she was his one true love."

We all paused for a moment. A child sitting on an enormous pumpkin giggled and cried out for her father to take her picture. Birds chattered in the trees around us. "So if she was his one true love," Erik said, "where is she now? Were they together?"

John nodded. "Yeah, they were. Or they were about to be. I guess they had been lying low, but rumors were starting to spread, so they were going to go public. I think he was going to propose."

I thought of the Herend wolf, sitting in a bag in Erik's car. "Did your father ever show you a small wolf figurine? Or mention that somebody had given him one?"

John thought about this. "I don't know if he mentioned it, but I saw a wolf at his house. It was kind of weird, covered with diamonds, like it was caught in a net. It was actually pretty cool. I asked him where he got it a couple of weeks ago. I was joking around, asking if it was from one of his hundred girlfriends. That was a joke we had, because he always seemed to be dating someone new. Until this last lady, of course. Anyway, he got kind of irritated. He said supposedly it was from a girlfriend, but he didn't believe it. And he didn't want it, either. He said something like 'Never accept a wolf from a jackass.' I thought it was a Hungarian saying."

The miserable feeling had crept into my gut, and my eyes met Erik's. Whatever he saw there made him say, "Thank you very much, John, for all this information. If you think of anything . . ." and then Erik was giving Kodaly's son his card, and the boy returned to his pumpkins while Erik piloted me back down the rutted driveway to our car, parked against some cornstalks. The air was fragrant with the smells of grass, soil, and musty corn. The cold air and earthy smells rejuvenated me, and when we got to the car, I was feeling better.

"What's up?" Erik said.

"I just had a very strong feeling that the man who gave him the wolf is the man who killed him. Or at least the man who hated him."

"Let's not forget the man gave him a wolf with a tracker on it. Seems more likely he sent someone to kill Kodaly."

"So he had someone do his dirty work. But he's the murderer. He's the one behind it all."

Erik opened my door. "Possibly."

I climbed in, thinking. When he got in on his side, I

said, "John told us that Will said *supposedly* the wolf was from a former girlfriend. But that means that the girlfriend didn't give it to him directly, right? Otherwise he would know who it was from."

He thought about this. "So someone gave him the wolf, saying that a woman had asked him to deliver it."

"Which might be the only reason he took it at all. Especially if he thought the man was a 'jackass.'"

I could tell that the logic of this bothered Erik. "It's convoluted," he said. "And risky. Why not just come there and shoot him? Why have this whole weird plot that could go wrong?"

I shrugged. "Maybe we're missing something. Or maybe the wolf isn't important at all. Maybe Will Kodaly put the tracker there for some reason."

"Hmm," Erik said.

I sighed and stretched. "So who's my babysitter this evening?"

His green eyes met mine. "I am."

I smiled, but he shook his head. "No, not in a fun way. I have to go over my notes. But we'll be safely installed in your apartment, you won't have to worry about a stalker, and I won't have to worry about you."

"Unless my stalker poses as a trick-or-treater," I said lightly.

Detective Wolf frowned; I don't think this had occurred to him. "I'll be the one answering the door, then."

"What, with your gun out? Maybe we should just put a bowl of candy outside the building."

He nodded. "I think that's what we'll do. Iris might give me a hard time, but she'll be out getting candy herself, right?"

"If last year is any indicator, she will cover Riverwood from one edge to the other. She's a woman who wants her fair share."

He laughed, and I rolled down my window to breathe the fragrant air as our tires crunched down the long driveway.

Chapter 14

A DISTANT RUMBLING

When we arrived at my place, I flipped on my cozy orange lights; put out a little bowl of candy for my boyfriend, who sat at the kitchen table with his notes and his phone; and took my yellow legal pad into the living room. I lay on the floor and started making my own notes, trying to capture the latest information.

- Someone got Kodaly to take the wolf by saying it was from one of his girlfriends.

- —Why would Kodaly believe that? Why not just tell him the wolf was a gift?

- —Why was Kodaly even talking to someone he disliked?

- Someone told Grandma that Kodaly "fell in love" in Keszthely, and Will Kodaly's son said that the woman was his one true love. Who was this woman? Was she still in Hungary? Was he still in love with her, or was he a person who fell out of love easily? If he still loved her, did someone else resent it?

- Who stole the painting from the library? Why?

- Did the person who stole the painting somehow hear Cassandra Stone say that I was researching the painting and psychic things?

- Did Cassandra Stone herself steal the painting? She had access, and if she hired someone to shoot at me, it was clear where she got the information about my "abilities."

- At the dance we learned about the "interconnectedness" of the Riverwood dating life. The people at the center of one particular circle were Will Kodaly, Sofia Kálmar, her escort, Zane someone. Amber Derrien and her husband, Brad. Cassandra Stone and Richard Crenshaw. Were there more? If one of those men had become jealous of Kodaly's attentions to someone, had that man killed Kodaly?

- If the man who shot at me was worried about my potential psychic ability, what did he think I could "read" that would expose him?

I sighed and put my pen down. Antony and Cleopatra, who both wore elastic Shakespearean ruffs for the evening, and who had been sitting on either side of me like jailers, began to play with the pen, batting it back and forth to each other.

"Thanks for your help," I said to them. "I think it's dinnertime." I crept into the kitchen with my pad and set it down in front of Erik, who was on the phone.

"Yes," he said to the unknown caller. "I'll be here all night if you have questions."

When I had first met Detective Wolf, I'd been impressed by his tallness and his air of authority. I remained impressed, and now—the fact that he was seated at my kitchen table, that he had driven me here in his car, that he had *slept* with me the night before—made me feel something between smugness and euphoria.

Wolf clicked off his phone. "Can I help you?" he asked, trying not to smile.

"No. I just thought I'd share my notes. And ask what you'd like for dinner. And if you needed anyone to sit in your lap."

His sudden smile made him look ten years younger. "I absolutely need that. Let me just jot some things down before I forget."

"Okay. I'll feed my Shakespearean friends." I went to the sink, at the foot of which sat matching food bowls. I lifted the dishes and filled them with food. The cats had entered silently, dramatically (the ruffs made every movement seem an intentional thespian-like choice), and now they sat waiting for their meal.

I set the food down and filled their water bowls from my tap. I could hear voices murmuring in the parking lot; Paige's husband, Paul Gonzalez, had volunteered to sit outside the building and give candy to any children who wandered by. I think he saw it as a prime opportunity to smoke a rare cigar. Paige despised smoking, and Paul was too thoughtful to subject her to smoke, especially when she was pregnant. But sometimes, perhaps once a month or so, he liked to stand at the edge of the parking lot and watch the Riverwood grasses sway in the wind—and smoke a cigar.

I set the water down and stood up, so dizzy that I had to lean against the counter so that I didn't fall down. Something was wrong, wrong. I could hear the voices, getting louder, but I couldn't see.

I ran to the living room, still unsteady on my feet, and looked out the larger picture window. I could just see Paul's head; he was talking with a man whose voice was unfamiliar to me. I saw no children around this man. He was there alone, and now he was leaving. I caught a quick glimpse of his face before he turned toward his car.

"Erik," I called. He heard the weirdness in my voice and was at my side two seconds later. "That man with Paul—" I pointed, and Erik ran across the room and out my front door.

"Hurry, hurry," I said, but the car was already moving out of the lot. I tried to make out the license plate, but there seemed to be a glare on the spot where it should have been. I saw nothing.

But one thing had been very clear: the man in the parking lot was the man in Kodaly's painting *Dark Intentions*. And, in a chilling example of life imitating art, he had looked up at my window before he turned away.

⁓

We sat in Paul's kitchen: Erik, Paul, and me. Paige and Iris, Paul assured me, would be home soon. He had texted Paige and said he didn't want her out on the sidewalks while this potential murderer went free.

"What exactly did he tell you?" Erik asked.

"He said he needed to get in; he forgot his key. I told him I knew everyone in the building, and I didn't know him. He said he was dating someone in the building, but he couldn't say who—it was a secret."

Erik's eyes grew a darker shade of green. "Unbelievable."

"Yeah. I got out my phone and told him I was calling the cops, and he acted all bashful and said, 'Okay, I'll come clean. It's Hana Keller.'"

I gasped. "He said he was *dating* me?"

"Yeah. He wanted in the building real bad."

"Oh God. He knows where I live."

"You're going to be relocating," Erik said.

Paul looked regretful. "I tried to get his plate, but as you saw, he didn't have one. Like he purposely wanted to be under the radar."

Erik nodded. "We can still do a lot with make, model, and color. I've already called that in. Assuming he hasn't borrowed or stolen it, we might have a chance of finding him."

"Do I need to be worried—for Paige and Iris?" Paul asked.

"I don't think so," Erik said. "This guy is convinced Hana knows something about him. But every time he takes a stupid chance like this he brings us closer to him. We'll get him soon. Meanwhile, just lock things up tightly. Tell all the neighbors—admit *no one*."

Paul nodded. "I will."

Erik stuck out his hand, and Paul shook it. "Thanks for being there, Paul. We're going to pack up Hana and get her out of the building, so you don't need to stay on guard duty anymore."

Paul nodded. "I'll just finish my cigar," he said.

⌒

By seven o'clock we were piloting through the dark streets to Erik Wolf's apartment. I told him, once we were stowed in the car with my overnight bag, a litter box, and two Shakespearean cats in carriers, that the man in the parking lot was the man in the painting.

Erik was thinking hard about this, and he liked to think in silence. Finally, he said, "So Kodaly painted this image of a real man, watching a woman in her house, and titled it *Dark Intentions*. Who was he sending a message to with this piece? The woman? The man? Or was it an unconscious connection—maybe he didn't realize he had borrowed that face?"

I shook my head. "Too coincidental. This man is trouble. I felt it before I even went to the window. And he looked up at me; he saw me. There was—badness there. I think he fired the shot, Erik."

He shook his head as though he were shaking off water. "I don't know what to do when I'm trying to be a methodical policeman but I've got a psychic Hungarian girlfriend telling me to believe in her instincts."

I blinked at him. "Obviously, you should listen to me."

He barked out a laugh and pulled into a well-lit parking lot that I recognized as his. "Okay. Tonight you're here, and we'll work out a roster so that you always have somewhere to stay, and this jerk won't know where you are. Your parents might be too obvious, but we can use your brother's place, and Margie's, and Runa and Thyra's places."

"I'll just leave the cats with you, though. I don't want to disrupt their lives." I peeked back at Antony, who stared out of his carrier like a stern and wounded Hamlet. This reminded me of Amber Derrien asking me to cite a Shakespearean line. I had said, "'Something is rotten in the state of Denmark.'" It was true: something was rotten in this town, and, like Hamlet, I was able to smell the foul stench better than the people around me.

I reached through the bars of the carrier to touch Antony's nose. "You'll be out in a minute, buddy."

Erik parked the car and looked around his lot. "Okay.

I'll let you in first, then I'll come back for your cats and your things."

I took a deep breath, and he put a warm hand on my arm. "Are you all right?"

"Yeah. I am. I feel safe right now. I think if he were here, I'd feel kind of sick. That's how it's been so far. I get this nauseated feeling, and then I realize it's not physical."

Even in the dim car his eyes were discernibly green. "Really, they should study you—all of the women in your family. To see just what you can do."

"That sounds horrifying."

He grinned. "Let's go." He opened his door, jumped out, and jogged around to my side. I climbed out and he walked me to the entrance of his building, covering me with his tall frame. I thought of what Runa had said about eagles protecting a chick.

Soon enough we were established in his apartment and I was letting the cats out to roam the new terrain. I freed them from their ruffs (I had captured them in many a digital photo) and they ran out of the room, lynx footed and wide-eyed.

Erik switched on some lamps and said, "I never got to look at your notes. Do you mind if I look at those now?"

"Go ahead. We also never got to eat, so I'm going to explore your pantry. The most important question is, do you have paprika?"

He grinned. "I do. I bought it right after I ate at your house that first time."

"The day you kissed me, you mean?"

"Yeah. I was in the first stage of Hungarian fascination."

I lunged at him and gave him a resounding kiss. "You'll never escape. I am Vadleány, the Forest Girl, and you are under my spell."

"Truer words were never spoken. Now let me read."

I went into his kitchen. The Pálinka I had brought him was on the counter beside his refrigerator, and my printed fairy tale was stuck to the fridge with a magnet. I grinned.

I opened the stainless steel door and found some sausage, which I took out, as well as an onion, a cabbage (he really had bought Hungarian ingredients!), and some sour cream. Then I rooted around in his cabinets for some dry pasta. I would make sausage with a side of *háluska*.

Relieved to have a plan, I busied myself at his spare counter, chopping onion and cabbage and boiling water for noodles. As I worked, I thought of the man in the parking lot. He had said he was my boyfriend.

I thought of Will Kodaly, smiling at me with his handsome, crinkly face. He had been warning someone, perhaps warning everyone—maybe even me. The man had dark intentions, and Will Kodaly probably couldn't prove it, so he painted it. I couldn't prove it, but I felt it.

Erik Wolf, though, was different—he would find a way to the truth.

༄

Half an hour later, Wolf was digging into the food with his usual enthusiasm. "Delicious. Who knew noodles could taste like this?"

I shrugged. "I did. I grew up on that stuff."

He shoveled another forkful into his mouth. "These are good." He held up a finger and finished chewing. "Sorry. Didn't mean to talk with my mouth full." He pointed at the notes. "These are good. You have a very organized mind." This organization had won me points with him, clearly.

He jotted something on his own pad, and said, "Okay, logistics: do you have an event tomorrow?"

I shook my head. "No. Not for the next two days. Mom and Grandma like to go to mass on All Souls' Day, and then they just scheduled in a little free day before the holiday stuff begins."

"Good. That works out well. I already asked Runa if you can stay with her in the morning, and then Domo said he'll take you in the afternoon. Thyra will mind the store."

"You talked to Domo?" This was half irritating, half pleasing. My boyfriend and my brother, talking on the phone. "When did you do that?"

Erik shrugged. "Earlier today. He understands what's going on; he asked how he could help. He has the advantage of being able to work from home sometimes, and he's ready to make himself available indefinitely."

"Okay. Thanks. I hate to be shuttled around like a piece of furniture, but I know everyone is just trying to help."

"To keep you *alive*," he said. "Because they *love* you."

"They?" I stood up and moved closer to him. He stood up, too.

"Yes, they. They and I."

My arms slid over his shoulders. "You never told me what that Hungarian phrase meant. The one you said in the car before our ill-fated dance."

His lip curled. "I can't believe I know a Hungarian phrase that you don't."

"Say it again."

"*Te gyönyörű vagy.*"

"And that means?"

His hands slipped into my hair. "It means 'You are beautiful.'"

"Ah."

"Come, let me give you a tour of the apartment."

Laughter bubbled out of me. "I've already seen it."

"Just a tour of one room, then."

"Should we clean up the—?"

"We can come back. This is urgent." He took my hand and strode out of the kitchen, tugging me along behind him. For that moment, I forgot everything: Kodaly, the dance, the painting, the woman in Keszthely. I saw nothing but Erik Wolf, tall and blond, leading me into his bedroom.

Later that night I lay sleepless in his arms, listening to distant thunder and thinking of the dragon my grandmother had seen when she looked at Thyra's tea leaves. Like the fairies I had introduced to Erik a month earlier, the dragon had a certain duality in Hungarian lore. It was often the traditional reptilian beast found in many mythologies, but it could morph into a person, as well; and sometimes the dragon was a sign of change. In any case, people in the old myths knew that trouble was coming when they heard thunder, since this was understood to be dragons fighting above the clouds.

I rested my head against Erik's chest, soothed by his rhythmic breathing but fearful that the metaphorical thunder had already begun.

Right now we could only hear the rumbling, but that didn't change the reality of the *sárkány*.

The dragons were coming.

Chapter 15

....

A Tale of Two Spirits

Runa's apartment was a surprise. I had pictured a rather sterile elegance—white walls and carpet with silver accents—but what I found, when she swung wide the door and hugged her brother, was cozy and inviting. She had a view of the lake and wide windows that filled the room with sun. Her vaulted ceiling gave a sense of space, and the cream-colored walls added warmth beneath an impressive array of art, from framed originals to woven tapestries. In the center of her living room a blue sofa sat across from two blue chairs, and between them was an amazing multicolored throw rug that looked as though it was worth more than the contents of all my bank accounts.

Even more surprising were the two greyhounds who came wandering in like a pair of wayward deer; they thrust their thin noses into my hand and I bent to greet them. "That's Lucy and Desi," Runa said. "You don't have to pay attention to them."

"They're adorable," I said.

Erik touched my shoulder. "I have to go. I'll pick you up at Domo's tonight, okay?"

I stood up to kiss him, and Runa watched unabashedly. Erik waved and disappeared down the hall. She said, "He's my brother, and I've teased him all my life, but I know why the ladies love him."

"Ladies?" I asked.

She nodded. "He's had his fair share of interest. Since junior high."

"Ah." This didn't thrill me.

"Anyway." Runa looked distracted. "My home is your home. And help yourself to whatever you find to eat."

"I'm fine just now, thanks. I wouldn't have pegged you as a dog person."

"No? What sort of person did you think I was?"

That was a good question. How had I thought of her up until now? As one of a pair. As an exaggeration of beauty. As a cartoon. Then again, she had called me a Hungarian doll. "I don't know. I guess we probably made assumptions about each other, based on nothing."

She shrugged elegant shoulders. "I guess. Well, maybe we'll learn some things this morning."

I realized for the first time that she looked different. The other times I'd seen her, she was wearing makeup and fancy clothing. Today she wore a gray cotton shirt and jeans, along with a pair of colorful, patterned thick socks (Ulveflokk, I was guessing). She wore her hair in a simple braid, and her face was devoid of makeup. She looked about fifteen years old. She also looked vulnerable and sad.

"Are you okay, Runa?"

She plopped down on the blue couch, and the dogs jumped up to join her. "Oh, you know. Hanging in there."

I hesitated, not sure what to say. I walked to a stone fireplace built into the wall. Above it hung a medieval-looking tapestry, bold with red and blue.

She watched me. "Do you like it? An original Frida Hansen. I couldn't believe my luck, when I found that."

"You collect art?"

"Yeah. Since I was a kid in school taking art classes. I got my first original when I was eighteen. A Christmas present. Now I have a fair collection. I've got Andy interested, too. He loves Impressionism."

"That's cool. So that's how you ended up with a Kodaly, huh?"

"Yeah. One of my favorites. Andy got it for me, actually." Her face softened when she mentioned his name.

"He seems really nice. I enjoyed meeting him."

"He is nice." She picked up a blue and green pillow and fluffed it. "The first good man I've ever dated."

I sat down across from her on one of the blue chairs. It was outrageously comfortable. "You only dated bad men before him?" I was joking, but she didn't smile.

"Let's just say I was looking for the wrong things. I met Andy at a party on the Columbia College campus, an art thing hosted by one of his students. From the first time he started talking to me I realized that he was interested in what I had to say. Not because I was pretty or because I owned a business, but because he thought I was intelligent." She sniffed. "He still does. He sees inside me."

"That's great. You're a good couple, then."

She sighed. "I was planning to break up with him."

"What?"

"This is how stupid I am. I was thinking we were too boring, too predictable. No better reason than that."

"Does he—"

"No, he doesn't know, but I think he suspects something is up."

"Well—it sounds like you don't want to break up with him, Runa."

She was still holding the pillow in both arms, the way you would cradle a baby. "No, I really don't."

I stared her down. "Then don't. It's that simple."

She put the pillow down and grabbed the snout of Lucy or Desi, then worked on cleaning something out of his/her eye. When she freed the dog, it stayed where it was, as though she had never touched it. It sat regarding her with a quiet worshipfulness. She finally said, "It is simple. And it's not. Your grandma saw to that."

My eyes must have been huge. "My grandma? What—because of your reading? What did she say, anyway?"

Runa met my gaze. There were tears in her eyes. "You want to know? Here's what happened. She held my hand, and right away her eyes got big. She said, 'Maybe I shouldn't read the leaves today.' I said no, no, I want to do it. That's when she sent all of you away."

I thought of the way they had sat together, locked in conversation. "Was it something bad?" I asked, thinking of the dragon again. Of the dreadful, beating wings.

"She said she felt two spirits. Two hearts. She said it meant that I'm pregnant."

"Oh, Runa! Did you—verify?"

"Yes, as soon as I got home. The test says positive." She looked at me with something like wonder. "Your grandma knew that I was pregnant, from holding my hand." She wiped away a tear, and I moved across the carpet to sit by her side.

"Are you happy about it?"

She sighed. "I think so. I mean, I wasn't planning a baby,

but what she said—it just got me so excited. She said she feels a female spirit. A warrior, she said. A strong girl with hair flying out behind her. And I thought, *a daughter.*"

Impulsively, I pulled her into a hug. "Oh, Runa! Congratulations!"

To my surprise, she clung to me. "I don't know what to do. I'm afraid."

I leaned back and wiped away another tear from her porcelain cheek. "Afraid of what? Telling Andy?"

She shrugged. "That will be hard, too. We had agreed we didn't want children. He may want to leave me." She held up a hand. "I know I said I was going to break up with him, but I can't. I love him." She slumped back on the couch and shuddered out a sigh, as though this were terrible news.

"That's wonderful, Runa. He loves you, too. He told me so."

"What?"

"I asked if he loved you, and he said yes. He said, 'for my sins.'"

Runa was not insulted by this. It made her grin. "Oh, Andy," she said.

"Runa. It sounds to me like you're making problems where there are none. The pregnancy was a surprise, but you're obviously thrilled about it. Andy is not a problem, because you're in love with him. So why are you sad?"

She took my hands in hers and studied my fingers. "I wonder if you have her gift, too? Erik hinted that you might. So do you feel anything, holding my hands?"

I did, actually, but it was just a general tension flowing through her. Something was bothering her, had been bothering her since she spoke to my grandmother. "What's wrong?" I asked.

She was still looking at my hands. "Your grandma says this little girl in me will have to be a warrior, because she has a fight ahead of her. She says she—is sick."

"Oh no."

"I don't know what to do with this. You know what I learned, Hana? I learned when people start loving a child. It turns out it's the moment they know the child exists. That's when the love comes. I love her, and I'm afraid for her."

I gave her my no-nonsense look. "Runa. You haven't even gone to the doctor. You haven't even told Andy, or Thyra, I'm guessing." She shook her head. "Take this a step at a time. Call Andy—ask him to come over. Tell him about it. There's nothing you can't work out together, and don't you think he should have the chance to love the idea of her, too?"

She stared at me with watery blue eyes, shaking her head. "You Gypsy women, I'm telling you."

"Don't let my grandma hear you say Gypsy."

She giggled. Then she sighed. "I'm still sort of crying. You call Andy."

"What? No."

She grabbed her cell phone from a side table and handed it to me. "Speed dial one. Just ask him to come over. I'm afraid I'll start bawling."

"Runa. I've only known you a short time, but I know this: you can do anything. I watched you take down an old Hungarian man and truss him like a sheep, then get him to practically thank you afterward."

She giggled, but her giggles soon transformed into tears. She buried her face in one of the greyhounds.

I sighed and pressed speed dial one. "Professor Bell," said Andy's voice, sounding slightly bored.

"Um—Andy? This is Hana Keller. We met yesterday—"

"Yes, I know who you are, Hana. I'm glad to hear from you, although a bit surprised."

We both laughed awkwardly. I said, "Yes, well, I'm calling for Runa, actually."

Immediate concern. "Runa? Is she all right?"

"Yes. And no. She needs to talk with you. Is there any way you could come over to her place? Soon?"

He rustled some papers and tapped what sounded like a keyboard, perhaps checking a schedule. "I can be there in an hour. Will that be all right?"

"Yes, okay. She's fine, Andy, she's sitting right here, but she's had some really important news, and she needs you."

"Of course. I mean—is it her health?"

"She's fine. She's healthy. But she needs you."

"I'll be there in an hour. Hana?"

"Yes."

He cleared his throat. "Just tell me up front. Is she going to end things with me? I'd rather know in advance."

"Not even close. You're stuck with her."

His relief was so strong I could feel it like a wave through the phone. "Okay, then. Thanks. Bye, Hana." He ended the call, and I looked at Runa.

"Your knight is on his way."

"Thank you." Her face was dignified.

"Now, if I may butt into your life once more, when are you going to tell your sister and brothers?"

This ruffled her feathers. "Not before I tell my daughter's father, certainly!"

I patted her knee. "It sounds lovely, hearing you say 'my daughter.'"

The tears came again. "I know. I feel good, saying it out loud."

A troubling thought occurred to me. "Runa? They can't

tell the baby's gender until about five months. There's always the chance that my grandma is wrong. I mean, it's not science, what she feels."

She leaned closer, studying me. "Have you ever known her to be wrong?"

"No. But I only learned last month that she has an actual gift. We thought she was just eccentric. Or at least that's what I thought. My mother has always known, I think, but she pretended it was nothing. It scares her."

"No kidding. It scared me, too, having her eyes read my soul that way. I just wanted her to tell me what a big success Ulveflokk would be. Instead she told me this. About my little warrior girl. Now—everything is different."

I understood that. The last month had shifted my perspective in many ways, and I knew how that subtle shift could change a life. For one thing, I couldn't imagine my life without Erik Wolf in it.

I slapped my legs. "Have you eaten today?"

"Um, no. I don't tend to eat until afternoon."

"You have to change that, of course."

Her blue eyes were wide. "Why?"

"Because you're pregnant. You'll need to eat regular meals, and get prenatal vitamins from your doctor, and get lots and lots of rest."

"Oh no. How am I going to do that? I'm busy all the time."

"You'll find a way. Your sister will help you. You can hire someone to pick up the slack. Your priority is your baby and your health. I'm going to make you some food."

She stared at me, her mouth open slightly, and then nodded. "Okay." Then, after some thought, "Erik told me your Hungarian food is amazing."

"It is. I'll make some for you and Thyra. But right now,

I'm thinking an omelet? Maybe with a glass of milk for some calcium?"

"Yes, okay. You're making me hungry." She looked like a girl again, and I felt a strong urge to mother her, the way she and Thyra had mothered me when I cried in Erik's apartment.

"Great. I'll go check out your fancy kitchen." I started across the room and then said, "Oh no! What about your parents?"

Runa's face was wry. "You haven't met them yet, have you?" With a final pat on each of their heads, she gently pushed her dogs onto the floor. "We'll tell them last."

❧

After a cheese and chive omelet, two pieces of toast, and a glass of milk, Runa looked and sounded contented. She was still on the couch; I took away her plate and came back to tuck a pretty throw around her. She thanked me sweetly and told me that I would be a great sister-in-law.

"Let's not get ahead of ourselves," I said.

The sound of a key in the lock, and Andy burst through the door. "Runa? Hey. What's going on?" he asked, moving swiftly toward her. She lifted her face for his kiss, and he sat down beside her.

"She just had breakfast," I said. "Would you like some?"

Andy looked at me, his face confused. "Uh—no, thanks. I ate earlier. Maybe just tell me what's going on."

"Runa," I said. "Where should I go? Do you have a little office or library or something?"

She pointed at a hallway lined by built-in bookshelves. "Go down there, last room on the left. Lots of reading material in there and a computer, if you need it. I'm already signed in."

"Okay, sure."

I moved swiftly down the hall. I heard Andy's voice, before I shut the door, saying, "Babe, you scared me to death!"

I hoped Andy would be as happy about his daughter as Runa seemed to be. What a stressful day for Runa, pondering what Grandma had said, then taking a pregnancy test alone and finding out the truth. And wondering why her tiny child needed to be "a warrior."

Inside Runa's little office was a comfy mustard-colored chair, an antique desk, a small window with a view of her block, and a wall-to-ceiling bookshelf. Like the shelf in my bedroom, it was filled half with books and half with objets d'art. I walked along the length of it, admiring statuary and family photos. Unlike Erik, she had all sorts of family history on display: four blond children at the beach; the same children lined up at a professional shoot to the full family. I had seen Erik's parents before in one small picture in his bedroom, but Runa had their wedding photo in a silver frame, and I was struck not just by how much Mrs. Wolf looked like her daughters but by the resemblance between Erik and his father. Heredity was a funny thing . . .

There were other pictures of Runa and Thyra, Runa with her parents, Runa and Andy at some romantic-looking restaurant. Runa and Thyra cutting a grand-opening ribbon at Ulveflokk. Runa and Andy wearing T-shirts and competitor numbers at some Chicago 5K run. Runa at a familiar-looking table, posing with Amber Derrien. *Amber Derrien*. What in the world did she and Runa have in common?

The coincidence troubled me. It would be one thing if Runa lived in Riverwood, where everyone seemed to know everyone else. But Runa was a Chicago socialite and Amber was a schoolteacher. What would bring them together?

A stab of suspicion made me realize that I was feeling anxious, and a bit paranoid.

I went to Runa's desk and used her computer to sign in to Facebook, where I scrolled aimlessly for a while. Then I clicked into Gmail; Runa's e-mails were open on the screen. Determined not to look at them, I typed my address into the sign-in bar. I had seen the word "Ulveflokk" many times as my eyes sought the log out button, but I didn't read anything beyond that. For some reason, my eyes flicked back one more time and saw a word that stood out from the others: "Kodaly."

Too curious to resist, I clicked the e-mail and saw that it was from someone named Ron Sylvester. The subject line said "Kodaly art." He had written,

Dear Ms. Wolf,

I have been tracking down paintings by William Kodaly for several years; I am an avid collector of his work. I was able to trace an original work by him, entitled *True Love*, to an auction house in Chicago, and some determined questioning of art lovers led me to you. I know that must sound incredibly rude, but I tend to obsess over art that I love.

In any case, I am wondering if you had ever considered selling your painting. I would be willing to offer you twice what you paid for it, or to negotiate if need be.

Please let me know. It's a particularly striking piece, and I'd love to have it in my growing Kodaly collection.

He ended with the obligatory "Yours truly," etc. He had only sent it to her that morning. Feeling as guilty as a murderer, I clicked on her "sent" file and saw that she had already answered him.

Dear Mr. Sylvester,

I understand why you are looking to acquire the painting; it is beautiful, and a precious piece of my own collection. It was a gift to me from my lover, and I'm afraid I could never think of parting with it, for any price.

A shadow appeared in the hall; I looked up to find Runa in the doorway, smiling wryly at me. "Reading my e-mails, Hana?" she asked, seemingly unbothered by the idea.

"Oh my God, no! Except for one, because I saw the name Kodaly. I'm sorry. I just have Kodaly on the brain, and there it was."

She shrugged. "Whatever. So you saw that he wanted my painting, huh? I swear, these art collectors are obsessives!"

I understood that, on a small scale. Sometimes I'd glimpse a piece in Falken's store and be unable to stop thinking about it. On some occasions, I ended up going back to buy it. "He probably would have paid a lot."

"I wrote back to him," she said.

I clicked out of Gmail before she could see that I had viewed that, too. "Oh?"

"I told him no thanks. That it was a gift from Andy. That's true, but I wouldn't part with it anyway. Would you like to see it?"

"Yes! I'd love to." I stood up. "I'm sorry again for reading your e-mail."

Runa blushed a little. "I guess now we're sort of even."

"What?"

"Okay, confession time. When Thyra and I were at Erik's, we did the same thing on his computer. He saves all his passwords because, well, he lives alone. So we just clicked in for fun, and there was this long e-mail from you. We didn't even know who you were then. We felt guilty about halfway through, but it was very revealing."

My face grew hot. I wanted to feel indignant, but what could I say? You shouldn't read people's e-mails? "I guess we'll have to make a pledge: that neither one of us will snoop like that again. I know Erik would be unhappy about it."

She nodded. "But he knows we're nosy, so he probably halfway expects it. And his e-mail was always boring, before he met you."

I sighed. "Anyway. Did Andy leave?"

"Yes. He's conferencing with students today. He had to reschedule a couple to come here, but then he had to go."

"Is—did he—?"

She smiled hugely. "He was thrilled. Really happy—I would know if he was faking. He said that he only agreed to the no children idea because he thought I didn't want them. Apparently, he's always wanted a family. Now he has one."

"And what did he say—about the sick part?"

"He said it's silly to worry about what we don't know. That we'll go to a doctor and find out as much as we can, and until then we'll just withhold judgment. He's very practical."

"Practical is good. You two seem to balance each other nicely."

"I know." She was serene now, much happier than when I had arrived. "Now come and see my painting. It's a love story, so I have it hanging in my room."

She led me to her bedroom, a cool space dominated by white walls and blue and lavender accents. The painting hung above her dresser; it was surprisingly large. I walked close enough that I could focus on the details, and then two things happened over which I had no control: I moaned aloud, and my hands grew cold and began to shake.

The image presented the back of a man's head as he stood in a field, facing a woman who smiled at him as her dark hair blew in the wind like a sable cloud above her pretty face. A town was visible in the distance, with familiar sloped roofs and colorful houses—another view of Keszthely. The two lovers were alone, apart in space and time, and the wind seemed to wrap around them both and preserve this moment when they gazed at each other.

This, then, was the woman Will Kodaly loved, the woman who had stolen his heart in Keszthely—the woman he was rumored to have found again in recent days.

"Hana, are you all right?" Runa asked, touching my shoulder.

"I know that woman. He died because of her. I can feel it."

"What?" Runa looked from me to the painting, as though it would provide the answer.

I had not yet looked away from the sad, bright gaze of Sofia Kálmar, the girl from Keszthely, the woman in the painting, and William Kodaly's one true love.

Chapter 16

TRUTH AND DOUBT

R una made me some tea and watched me for a while. Then she said, "So you do have the gift, just like your grandma."

"There's something. It's only opened up recently, because I've been—experimenting. I don't really know what I have. But it's there."

"That's so interesting. I'm going to make you tell me my fortune all the time." She was starting to seem like the Runa I'd grown used to—confident, bold, and demanding.

"I think you've had enough of a fortune for a while," I said weakly, looking into my tea. "Anyway, I have to call Erik."

"You really think this woman killed him?"

"Oh no, not her. Someone who was jealous of what they had. He killed Kodaly."

"Well, that should be easy enough to figure out. Just find out who her boyfriend is."

"Yes. Erik can solve this today." I picked up my phone and dialed his number. Runa had put out a plate of granola, and she munched on this now and watched me as though I were a TV show.

"Erik Wolf," said his voice. I was too distracted to even notice how sexy it was.

"Erik."

"Hana? What's wrong?"

"I'm at Runa's. I just saw her Kodaly painting; it's called *True Love*. It's a tribute to the woman he was actually in love with—the title says that, but I can feel it too. He loved her."

"Okay, take a deep breath. We knew there was a woman he loved, in Keszthely, right?"

"Yes, but I *recognize* this woman."

"What?"

"It's Sofia."

There was a pause as Erik absorbed this information. "Okay . . . well, they dated a while back. So that doesn't necessarily mean anything. They fell in love in Keszthely, but then they broke up after they dated here."

"Erik, I know you're all about facts and evidence, and it's your job to be that way, but now is when you need to trust me. I had a reaction to the painting: a big reaction. It made me shake."

"Are you all right?"

"Yes, yes. The point is, he still loved her, and they were going to get back together. Like his son said, remember? That his dad had been keeping a relationship on the down low, but he was about to propose. And that people knew about it. Someone was jealous, murderous."

"This is what you felt? That the motive was jealousy and hatred?"

"Yes, exactly. And Sofia has a boyfriend right now, Erik! Maybe she told him that she was going to return to Will, and he wanted to make sure that wouldn't happen. But he couldn't implicate himself, so he gave Kodaly the wolf. Said, 'Sofia wanted you to have this.' Will would have taken it because it was given in the name of Sofia, but he felt suspicious, uncomfortable, and ended up putting it in his garage sale."

"Then the jealous guy hired some random murderer and said, 'Here's a tracking device. Go to the place indicated and murder the man who lives in that house'?" he asked, sounding skeptical.

"I know it seems bizarre. But this was the act of a fierce and possessive lover, Erik! A man who is not right in his soul."

"Don't assume. A woman can be a lover, too."

He was right. Could a woman have felt passionate dislike for Kodaly because *she* resented his love for Sofia?

Runa pointed at me. "When you're done, can I have the phone?"

I looked at her face, less worried now but still full of the emotions associated with her unexpected news. "Yes, of course. Erik—Runa wants to talk to you. Not about this, about something else."

"What?" he said.

"Hang on. Here she is."

"Hana, I don't have—" he started, but then Runa took the phone.

"Hallo, *lillebror*," she said softly. Like me, Runa seemed to know a smattering of her language of origin; also like me, she seemed particularly devoted to her roots.

She wandered out of the kitchen, talking softly. I went to her kettle and topped off my tepid tea with some boiling water. Then I drank it slowly, pondering the possibilities.

If we were right, then Will Kodaly and Sofia were about to commit to each other publicly. Perhaps they had already become engaged. I thought of Will's face, when I had brought him my painting of Keszthely. How soft and loving it had looked. And what had he said? "Some beautiful memories of that town—beautiful memories of beautiful people." I had thought he was talking about the natives, and perhaps he was. Or perhaps he was talking about Sofia, walking with him in the fields, her dark hair whipping in the wind, wrapping around the two of them like a lover's knot.

I finished my tea and rinsed out the cup at Runa's large sink. I set the mug in the drying rack and went back down the hall to Runa's bedroom, where the painting waited. I was prepared this time, so there was no shock when I looked at it.

Kodaly idealized love, or at least he did in this image. It was all color and motion and intensity. I could feel, with the man who gazed at her, the surprise, the sharp intake of breath, with the realization of what I felt. Is that what he had captured with his deft paintbrush? The very moment he had realized he loved her?

Runa found me standing there, staring at the small bit of Kodaly's life that was still preserved on the canvas. "Your brother is here," she said.

༄

Domo had paid Runa's doorman to let him leave the car at the front door. He marched me quickly out of the building and into his passenger seat, and then he sped away. "Erik has me pretty paranoid about this whole thing," he said. "I can't believe this guy came to your house! What are you, some kind of magnet for weirdos?"

He darted a concerned glance at me.

"No—I think it's the possibility of someone being psychic that creates problems. Don't forget this happened to Grandma, too. All because a woman was worried about detection. Now I think this stuff is happening for the same reason. Someone's guilt and fear manifesting as violence."

"Huh," Domo said. "Do Mom and Grandma know about this whole thing?"

"Yeah. Runa and Thyra were my guards at the tea house, so I had to explain. "

"Runa is that gorgeous blonde who let me in?"

I nodded.

"Who's Thyra?"

"Her identical twin. Erik's older sisters. They're black belts."

"Wow. That family has some genes, right?"

"They're pretty impressive. I can picture them all on some Viking ship in one thousand AD."

Domo's hands had been in motion since we got in the car; adjusting the heater, playing with the radio dial, punching his steering wheel to the beat of an Eagles' song.

"Are you nervous?" I asked.

"I don't know. I think it's just adrenaline. Erik made me a cop for the day, and I feel vigilant."

I scowled at him. "You are *not* supposed to be a cop. In *any* way. Just to provide your Domo hotel until Erik catches this horrible man, which hopefully will be today."

Domo's head swiveled to look at me. As usual he looked disheveled and more handsome because of it. "Why do you think it's today?"

I told him about the painting in Runa's apartment, and about my reaction to it.

Domo whistled. "Man, you and Grandma are a little too

spooky now. I think I'm going to keep my distance from you both and your weird juju. You know she claimed I was on the verge of getting a new job and getting married, right?"

"Yes. And Mom told me you've been interviewing."

He looked defensive. "That's just because I'm looking for a better salary. Computer knowledge is valuable."

"Yes. So you *will* get a new job, and it will turn out that Grandma was right."

Domo looked moody. "Whatever. God, the traffic is bad."

I agreed. I didn't like Chicago traffic; I far preferred the mellower pace of Riverwood, where polite drivers glided (for the most part) serenely around town like swans on water.

Thinking of Riverwood made me remember something; I found the number that Runa had programmed into my phone and called it. "Runa? It's Hana. Hey, I have a question about one of the pictures in your office. It looked really familiar. You're sitting with a woman at a large round table. Her name is Amber Derrien."

Runa laughed in my ear. "It should look familiar. It was taken at your tea house."

"What?"

"A couple years ago. Remember, I told you I went to two of those book discussion teas? I met Amber at one. We hit it off; we've had coffee a couple times since."

"Oh. Uh—okay. What a weird coincidence."

"Not that weird. What do you have—a hundred people at every event?"

"Not always. Somewhere between a couple dozen and a couple hundred, I suppose."

"So in a year, thousands of people come through. Thousands."

I thought about this, and it surprised me. "I guess so."

"I have to run. Call me later if you have more questions."

Runa hung up and Domo looked at me. "Did you say Amber Derrien? Her name comes up a lot these days."

"Right? How weird. Did you get the sense she had the hots for that guy who played peekaboo with her at the dance?"

Domo laughed. "Kind of. I figured it was her subtle revenge against her husband for going out of town instead of taking her to the dance."

"Yeah. I vaguely remember him from school days. Or at least I remember a figure named Brad." I grinned at him. "My memories become kind of ghostly after a while." I stared through the windshield at some yellow leaves pasted onto Domo's hood. "I'm glad to hear they're back together."

Domo sighed. "High school seems really far away. *Really* far." His face drooped slightly as he contemplated the relentless march of time. I patted his hand, reached in my pocket, and dug out a box of Halloween candy that I'd stolen from a bowl at Runa's apartment building.

"Want a Milk Dud?"

"Sure," Domo said, and we shared some chocolate.

It was fifteen more minutes before we reached Domo's place, which was just outside Riverwood, with a top-floor view of Hawk River and a ridiculously spacious apartment that he rented with his aforementioned computer-guy wealth.

"Is Margie here?" I asked.

"She will be later. She's working on some drawings that she has to send tonight." Margie was an architect who mostly worked out of her introvert's paradise of an apartment. "She's going to bring us some dinner when she comes. I told her I could just heat up the food Grandma gave me a couple days ago, but she likes to branch out to things beyond *paprikás* and *kolbász*."

"Okay. I just ate some granola at Runa's place, so I'm not that hungry."

"You will be. What do you want to do for now? Watch a movie? Play a board game?" He pulled into his parking lot and did a quick visual check. "Not a soul around; we're a little bit ahead of rush hour, so it's kind of deserted."

"Good. And, no, you don't have to feel you need to entertain me. I'm just going to jot down some notes, see if there's any way I can help Erik."

We marched into Domo's lobby together, then took the elevator to the fourth and highest floor. He had a corner unit with large windows on two walls. I did a quick survey of the parking lot and the grassy area across the street: no suspicious visitors. Domo's home was slightly cozier than it had been at my last visit. I assumed this meant that Margie was slowly domesticating him. There was an orange ball candle on a gray stone plate in the center of his dining room table; he actually had a piece of art hanging on one wall; and there were two framed photos on his sideboard. One was a picture of Domo and me, in Christmas finery, standing by a towering pine in our parents' living room. Another was a picture of Margie, sitting in front of the river on a picnic blanket and smiling. Like Runa, she had a girlish appearance but must have been at least twenty-five when the picture was taken.

Domo came to stand beside me; he grinned stupidly at the photo of his girlfriend, and I said, "Grandma was right about the other thing, too. You're going to get married soon."

He shrugged. "Whatever."

I punched his arm. "Not *whatever*. You want to marry Margie."

"Okay, don't say it like an accusation!"

"I'm not. I'm saying it like you never tell me anything."

My brother, who had teased me for most of my life, now stuck his face in front of mine and said, "I don't *need* to tell you anything. You're psychic."

"Mature, Domo."

Grinning now, he said, "I'm going to check in with work. There's some cheese on the board in the kitchen if you want some."

He disappeared into his bedroom to make his calls, and I strolled into the kitchen to see what sort of cheese was on offer. It was Brie. "Maybe just a little," I said, slicing off a piece and digging a cracker out of a nearby box.

Munching on my snack, I opened an iPad that sat on Domo's counter and signed in with his password (he did tell me some things). I began to Google all the people that Erik would be investigating. First came Zane. How many Zanes could there be in Riverwood?

I typed in just that name, Zane, and clicked enter. Sure enough, there was only one person who came up locally: Zane Talman, personal trainer. He had a website and an ad- dress in Riverwood. I clicked on the site but saw only con- nections to exercise routines and links to prices for various services. The site encouraged people to call or come in to the fitness center. There were no pictures of Zane.

Had Sofia decided to stay with him, now that Will was gone? Had that been Zane's motive all along? It was ridicu- lous, anyway, because killing a man wouldn't make a woman stop loving him or make her love the killer more.

I wondered how many men had loved Sofia. She was beautiful, and she probably had more than two decades of love affairs in her wake. She had been on and off with Will Kodaly. She had been (perhaps) about to leave Zane for Will again; had she ever been serious about Zane?

She had also dated other men, according to Cassandra. Amber Derrien's husband, for one thing. But he could be ruled out for two reasons: one, he had been in Indianapolis on the night of the shooting; two, he had dated Sofia as an act of revenge against Amber, but now was happily back with her again.

Where was the man who felt so passionate that he wanted to kill? Was I being misled by my instincts? Was I leading Erik down the wrong path?

On an impulse I Googled Amber Derrien's husband, Brad Derrien. Once again, I didn't find a photo, but I did get a newspaper article and a few business links that told me he worked in advertising. He had won an advertising award in 2016.

There was another man who was part of the "interconnectedness" of Riverwood; Cassandra's fiancé and Sofia's former husband, Richard Crenshaw. He couldn't still have feelings for Sofia, could he? And yet, he had been married to her. What if, despite his apparent devotion to Cassandra, he was secretly pining for Sofia? What if, when she told him she was going to marry Kodaly, he was suddenly filled with jealousy?

I turned off the iPad and drummed my fingers on the counter. What was I missing? And how did this all relate to the man who had been in my parking lot? But of course we were looking for two men: the one who had killed Will Kodaly, and the one who had directed him to do so. What was the link between those two men? Hopefully none of this mattered; I assumed that even now Erik had detained Zane Talman for questioning. By tonight this would all be over.

I went back into Domo's living room and flopped on the couch. He returned a few minutes later. "Margie just texted me; she's on her way, and she's picking up Chinese."

"Sounds good."

"I got a new video game. You want to play? There's not that much violence. You have to build your own town in order to survive."

"Well, I am partial to surviving. But I'm terrible at those. My avatar always just floats around helplessly while yours kills me."

"This isn't that kind of game," said Domo, handing me a joystick.

"Fine. I'll build my town and make it very happy and cozy."

"It's the Wild West," Domo said. "There is no cozy."

"Then what's the point?" I asked.

Domo laughed.

༄

He was still teaching me the game when Margie got there. As I had predicted, she looked far more subdued than she had at the dance; this was her recovery period. She and I spooned food into serving dishes while Domo set the table and lit the orange candle.

Then we sat down, and Margie said, "Are you okay? How's your shoulder?"

I shrugged. "It hurts a little, but I'll be fine. I took some Advil."

She looked shrewdly at me. "You're obsessing over this, right? It's like last month, when you were helping Erik solve that crime. Are you trying to work things out? Do you want us to help?"

This encouraged me. "Let's pretend it's kind of a board

game. I'll tell you all the suspects, and you tell me who you think did it. Like Clue."

"Oh, good," Margie said.

Even Domo looked interested. I began to lay out all the information: Kodaly's reputation. His former lovers (many of whom were missing puzzle pieces). The potentially jealous men. Kodaly's son and the ex-lover who had the child. The stolen painting. The man at my apartment. The shooting at the pavilion. The woman in Keszthely, who was most likely Sofia. Kodaly's surprising link to just about everyone: our mother, Henrik Sipos, Cassandra, Ms. Derrien, even Runa Wolf.

"Which reminds me," I said, pointing at Domo. "Remember I talked to Runa about a picture she had at her house, of her and Miss Derrien?"

"So?" He crunched into an eggroll, looking unimpressed.

"So it's odd that people from two very different segments of our lives are somehow connected to each other."

Domo raised his brows. "Did you actually think you were the center of the universe? Other people are allowed to know each other, Hana."

"Yes, but it's such an odd coincidence. Almost unnerving."

"I think you're taking this psychic stuff too far."

I shrugged.

Margie said, "Well, like you said, it's probably a jealous man. This Kodaly had a reputation."

Domo shook his head. "No, there's something weird here. All these women are just totally forgiving of a man who's had all these relationships? Does that sound real to you?"

I met Margie's eyes, and we both said, "No."

I said, "But it's all kind of strange. Like Kodaly is a character out of one of those Hungarian fairy tales rather than a real person. If I hadn't met him myself, I would have thought he was a fable."

"I think you should look at Cassandra," Domo said. "She admitted that her boyfriend cheated on her in Hungary. Then he left her. Hell hath no fury like a woman scorned."

He cheated on her in Hungary. That's what Cassandra had said. And then he had come home, quarreled with Cassandra, and ended up dating Sofia. But if Sofia had in fact *been* the woman in Hungary, then the two of them came home knowing that they needed to end their current relationships. It was underhanded, pretending that they were dissatisfied with their loves at the time, when in fact they were in love with other people and pretending to break up for some other reason. Why? Why not just admit there was someone else?

"I need to send some texts and make some calls," I said, and I went into the living room with my phone.

First, I texted Wolf my questions about Will and Sofia.

Second, I texted my grandfather, asking him if he had heard the story about Henrik Sipos. "If not, you and I need to have lunch soon," I wrote.

I called Katie. We were supposed to meet for lunch the next day, my second free day before the tea house got busy again.

"Sorry," I told her. "Erik's got me on lockdown until he nails this guy."

Katie paused, and I said, "Are you pouting?"

She laughed. "Sort of. We never get to see each other, and I was excited to have lunch outside the office for once."

"I'll commit to a new date."

"Or—hey, why not come see me at work? It's a secure building. No one knows your connection to me, so whoever this random madman is couldn't possibly know where you are. And we could have fun, without you being exposed."

"Hmm. Okay, I'll ask Erik. I think that would be okay. I mean, he let me go to Runa's apartment."

"Yay! Get back to me soon, so I can request a conference room for us to eat in. This will be fun."

"Okay. I'll call back within the hour," I said, and we said good-bye.

Finally, I called my grandmother. "Yah," she said softly. "Haniska?"

"Hi, Grandma. Sorry to call so late."

"We are watching Netflix."

I stifled a laugh. She and my grandpa had bought a new TV and a Roku, and now they spent their evenings enjoying home theater.

"Well, I won't keep you . . ."

"What's wrong?" she asked.

"Nothing. I mean, something, because there's a murderer out there, but also—I don't know. Why did you have to give me your genes? I don't like this second sight stuff. I want to give it back."

"Why?"

"It just complicates everything. And makes me second-guess everything. And then when I have these—insights— I have to worry that they're false. That I'm totally wrong, even though my instinct tells me otherwise."

"Ah," she said.

"Grandma. Since you were four years old, looking at that teddy bear in Békéscsaba, you've known things. My question is, have you ever been wrong? Have your instincts ever led you in the wrong direction?"

She sighed in my ear. "Hana, my little one. This voice

inside is not like the brain that can think something this
way or that way. It's not about—interpretations. The voice
inside tells you the truth. It does not have different sides, or
different layers. Just one truth, shining bright."

"So you never had to doubt what this *voice* told you?"

"No. But I never thought to doubt it. You have *only* doubts.
I don't know if this can affect things. Throw them off."

"Yeah. I guess that's the question. Thanks, Grandma.
Enjoy your show."

"Be safe, Hana *baba*. Let your wolf protect you."

⁓

"My wolf" drove me back to his place later that night. He
filled me in on the day's events, which had included calling
Zane in for questioning. Talman had come with a lawyer
and he had told them very little. He was not much interested in answering their questions.

"We checked his fingerprints; so far nothing we can
match to the scene. But something about his attitude, I
don't know. I think he's hiding something," Erik said.

"You need to talk to Sofia. She's the one that Will loved,
so she might be able to explain things about Will's final days."

He nodded, thinking about this. "I could. But I'd run the
danger of having her clam up under such an official questioning. She responded very strongly to you, when you
showed her sympathy at the dance. I might ask you to talk
to her first, Hana. See if she'll tell you anything casually
that she might not tell us at the station."

"Okay, I guess. But in the morning, I said I'd meet with
Falken to look at Kodaly's things. I guess you guys are
done with the house?"

"We finished processing the scene two days ago. Your
friend Falken is going to be itemizing everything in the

house for Kodaly's sister, and he's also going to share that
list with us. Our focus was on the basement, although initially the whole house was roped off. We got all that we
could get, so now I'll see if Falken can provide any additional clues, looking with the eye of a collector."

"So you'll go with me? And who's going to take me to
Katie's office at Imperius?"

He gave me a stern look. "You're only going there with
the understanding that you wait upstairs until Domo comes
to get you." He stifled a yawn. "I might have to ask an officer to drive you there and escort you upstairs. I'm a little
backed up at the office; I can't really even spare the time
with Falken Trisch, but frankly I need some clues. Talman
might be our man—he certainly acts guilty—but I have
nothing on him."

"And if he *is* the man, who was the guy at my apartment? Who is the man in the painting? And who was the
man I saw at Will Kodaly's house? The one who pulled
over just as I was leaving?"

Erik frowned. "All good questions," he said. "And I'm
going to get answers."

I didn't even have to touch his hand to know that this
was absolutely true.

Chapter 17

....

UNEXPECTED INQUIRIES

The next morning, I sat in Erik's kitchen, smearing jam on a piece of toast. Erik entered, wearing the Ulveflokk sweater I had bought him at Kodaly's sale. I stared for a moment, appreciating the sight.

"Katie was right. That does look amazing on you."

He shrugged. "It's warm."

Antony and Cleopatra, clearly feeling neglected in this new space, circled around his legs and made small sounds of protest. He swooped down and managed to pick them both up; they spent the next minute or so sniffing his face while he laughed.

"I made some eggs," I said. "Eat up, and then we should go. I want you to resolve everything today so I can go back to my apartment and my life."

He set the cats down and moved behind my chair, wrapping his arms around me. "Don't you like my apartment?"

"I love your apartment, but I don't like losing the freedom to come and go as I please."

He kissed my cheek, then buried his nose in my hair. "You smell amazing," he said softly. Desire fluttered inside me, but I pushed him gently away.

"No distractions," I said. "We need to get going."

He studied me with a serious expression. "Is something making you feel urgent? Some inner voice, I mean?"

"No, this is just regular anxiety."

He patted my hand and then went to the stove to get his breakfast. "I know it's rough. But we'll get through it, Hana. We did last month, and we will now."

"Okay. But I can't stop thinking—poor Will Kodaly didn't get through it. He should have had the chance."

He scooped some eggs onto a plate. "Toast is in the oven," I said. He claimed his warm toast, turned off the oven, and came back to the table, where he sat across from me.

"You're right: Will Kodaly should have had that chance. Someone in this world decided that they could deprive a man of his very life. That's evil. The work of the devils in the fairy tale you gave me." He gestured toward the refrigerator, where my Hana tale still hung under his dinosaur magnet, but his green eyes were on me when he said, "And that's why we send those people to jail."

⁓

It was strange to be back in William Kodaly's house, although not as dreadful as I had feared. The place had a sterile feel now, and the life of the man was no longer really in evidence, since Falken had turned the upstairs into a sort of warehouse, separating art from linens and tools from tableware. "How unfair, to have people rifling through your things," I said, listlessly touching a box labeled "Books and Magazines."

Falken shrugged. "Someone will go through all of our things in the end, Hana. It's what we guarantee by spending our lives accumulating possessions."

Erik agreed with a nod of his head. He wore a suit jacket over his sweater now. He looked around the living room, where Falken was doing most of the sorting and boxing, and said, "I know he had lots of papers and journals and things. Where did those go?"

Falken pointed to a large trunk under a window. "I've started accumulating them in there."

"Hana?" Erik said, looking at me. "Could you look at them? See if anything seems significant to you?" His phone rang, and he said, "Wolf. Greg! I'm glad you called. I'm at the Kodaly place now . . ." He walked out of the room, talking in low tones to his partner. When he came back a few minutes later, he said, "I've got to run. Check in with me if you find anything significant." He bent to kiss me, and then he was gone.

I turned my attention back to the room full of boxes. Falken was busy winding the cord of a Tiffany lamp that glowed, even when not illuminated, with shades of blue, green, and purple. He met my gaze and nodded. "You were right, Hana. The man's house is a treasure trove. He had the eye of a collector."

"Yes. And you saw his paintings?"

"Amazing."

"There's something ethereal about them, isn't there?"

"I can't even determine his technique. How he got the effect he did. But it's remarkable."

I sat down next to the trunk and flipped through some notebooks, letters, legal pads, sheet music. There was a lot to go through.

"I suppose the police catalogued all this?"

"My understanding is that they took photographs of everything. But I don't know how they would process those. How would anyone know if something was a clue, or even if *anything* was?"

I shrugged. I started going through the stack of letters in the trunk. Several of them were written in Hungarian and bore the postmark of Keszthely. Not surprising—Kodaly's family had once been there. I set them aside and looked at the postmarks of the other letters. Some were from art organizations or universities—a quick glance in some envelopes told me that they referenced either awards Kodaly had won or requests for him to visit campuses as a speaker or an artist in residence. One notified him of an honorary degree that had been bestowed upon him. Kodaly really had been well-known; how had I never heard of him?

Time passed. After half an hour I was nearing the end of the pile. I noted bits and pieces of personal correspondence, although these were few; no one wrote letters anymore. My eye caught on a plain white envelope labeled "Békéscsaba." What connection did Kodaly have to that town?

I lifted the envelope, and my hand grew hot. "Oh no," I whispered, half fearful to see what was inside. The envelope contained a printed e-mail, dated about a year earlier. It was written in English, on professional stationery that bore a centered company name: *Portnoy Investigations*.

Dear Mr. Kodaly,

Thank you for your business. We have been unable to find out anything else about Natalia Kedves beyond our initial report about the child's abduction and return.

We did determine several things about her personal life, which I will enumerate here. Her husband, Imre,

died in the Hungarian Uprising in November of 1956.
She had one daughter, Juliana, whom she raised alone.
She did not remarry. She lived in Békéscsaba until 1978,
when she and her daughter moved to Budapest. In that
city, the daughter met a young man named Andras Horvath and married him two years later. They had three
children: Zoltan, Magdalena, and Luca. Eventually the
whole family emigrated to the United States. We could
find no one in Békéscsaba who remembered Natalia or
had heard the rumors about her. We did find the old policeman, Joseph Rohaly, in Budapest. He verified the
story and spoke highly of Mrs. Kedves, saying that she
was the most astounding person he had ever met.

We plan now to close our investigation in Hungary.
Please let us know if you would like us to extend the
search or if we should send you the final invoice.

                         Sincerely,
                         Alexander Portnoy,
                         Portnoy Investigations

I lowered the letter; Falken appeared at my side, touching my arm with a warm hand. "Hana, you're very pale.
Are you all right? Are you going to faint?"

Wordlessly, I handed him the letter. He read it, saying,
"Oh, my," every few seconds. Then he gave it back to me.
"He was investigating your family."

"My great-grandmother in particular. She was psychic.
I'm guessing that's what he wanted to know more about,
but why?"

Falken shrugged, nonplussed.

I looked back at the letter. "It's so weird to see my family written about in this—scientific tone. Like they're in an

encyclopedia. My grandpa! No one calls him Andras. His friends on the railroad called him 'Drosh,' which got shortened to 'Dosh.' Then everyone called him that." My eyes scanned the page again. "And they even investigated my uncle Zoltan and my aunt Luca! It's crazy."

Falken nodded. "It is odd. This man was a stranger to you, right?"

"Yes, but not to my mother and grandmother. He knew them . . ." I thought of the painting called *Magdalena's Eyes*. Had I been wrong all along? Was Kodaly in love with my *mother*? Or had he been fascinated with my family for some other reason? I thought of the moment that he had shaken my hand and introduced himself. There had been a momentary burst of light, just as there seemed to be light around many of his paintings. He had said something about my family, and that he'd like to discuss them over coffee. What had he wanted to say?

I set the letter down and took out my phone. "Falken, give me a second, I want to make a call."

I moved into an empty hallway of Kodaly's sad house and looked for a number, then pressed call.

"Riverwood Chamber of Commerce," chirped a woman's voice.

"Henrik Sipos, please."

"I'll see if Henrik is in. Just one moment!" She disappeared, and I was treated to a Muzak version of Adele's "Hello."

"Good morning. This is Henrik Sipos," said Henrik in a formal tone. He sounded once again like a Hungarian ambassador.

"Henrik, this is Hana Keller."

"Oh, hello, my dear! How are you this morning? I am sorry to hear there was this event of vandalism at the dance.

I hope you were having a nice time before then?" His voice was full of warmth and affection.

"I—it was lovely, thank you again, Henrik. I wonder if I could ask you a question."

"Of course."

"It's about Will Kodaly, and his painting of your reunion with your mother."

"Yes."

"Did he—ask questions about that reunion? And about my great-grandmother Natalia?"

"Oh yes! He was most curious about it. Like many people, he seemed to have a fascination with the idea of the second sight, you know. And he wanted to know everything: how did the police find her? How did she work? Did she have a crystal ball or those fortune-telling cards? I laughed a good deal at this idea."

"He wanted to know her methods? Why?"

"He could not imagine how this works. To simply know something. To see something. Like the blue barn. He decided he wanted to paint the barn, too, after he finished the reunion painting. All based on what he imagined, of course. I was at first surprised, but then I realized—it is a special story. Anyone would think so."

"Yes. And—did he ask you anything else?"

There was silence for a moment. Then Henrik said, "He did ask something. He said, 'Did it make her happy, this gift?' I said I did not know."

"Thank you, Henrik. I appreciate it."

"Anytime you would like to call, dear Hana."

We said good-bye, and I walked to Kodaly's empty kitchen, where a lonely chair sat in the middle of the room. I slumped onto this and tried to gather my thoughts. Why had Kodaly wanted to know about Natalia? Was he in fact just fascinated by psychic phenomena? But would a general fascination extend to hiring a private investigator? And why had he wanted to know if she was happy?

I sighed, then picked up my phone to text Erik: Kodaly hired a private investigator to go to Békéscsaba and learn more about Natalia and her whole family!!!!!!!

He wrote back: That's weird. I'm on it. About to question Talman again; then I'll talk to Sofia and ask her about that. I know you didn't talk to her yet, but this can't wait.

With a sigh, I put my phone away and looked around Kodaly's kitchen, from the lonely whisk on his counter to the postcard held onto his refrigerator with a magnet (just as Erik's held my Hungarian fairy tale).

I got up and went to the refrigerator. The postcard was an art print of a Van Gogh field of waving wheat, a sensory blend of beauty, color, and feeling. I slid it from behind the magnet and looked at the back. It bore no return address, and only one scrawled word beyond Kodaly's own address: "SOON."

The police had most likely seen this, but I took a photo and sent it to Erik.

Then I went back to Falken and the task of looking through the possessions of a dead man.

Chapter 18

THE FOREST WITH MANY PATHS

Officer Tate picked me up in a police cruiser; it was a sort of intentional déjà vu, climbing into the same car from the same location. I gave him the address of Katie's building. "You can just let me off at the entrance," I assured him.

He shook his head and looked at me in his rearview mirror. "Detective Wolf gave me very specific instructions. I'll be walking you in, and upstairs."

"Oh—okay, thanks."

"You two are an item, huh?" It was an inappropriate question, especially because Erik was his superior officer, but his face was friendly and eager, and I was guessing everyone at the station knew by now.

"Yes."

"That's cool. I saw a picture of you on his desk once."

I felt an unexpected flood of warmth, then a ridiculous smile that I covered with my hand in a pretend yawn.

I decided to change the subject. "Who's that little person on your visor? The little fireman sitting on a fire truck?"

He laughed. "That's Aaron. He's two, and he's a real handful. We're expecting another one."

"Oh, congratulations!"

He said, "My wife gets all the credit. She's great. I don't know how she does all that she does, but she manages to do it all."

"The miraculous modern woman," I said. Then I thought of Natalia, and said, "But I guess women were always miraculous."

"No argument from me," he said with a smile.

We chatted about his son until the Chicago skyline loomed large and Officer Tate found his way to Superior Street. "It's that giant building there," I said. "Imperius is on the fifth floor."

"Got it," he said. He pulled into a slot that said "No Parking Any Time."

"The perks of being the police?" I asked lightly.

He laughed, then said, "Look at this guy. We really need to address the homeless problem. Not just in Chicago, but everywhere."

I looked where he pointed and saw a man slumped against a light pole, his long hair hanging around his face. He held a sloppily scrawled sign that said "They Are Coming." This made me think of the *sárkány*, their giant wings beating. My heart started up the same rhythm as the dragons in my mind.

"You okay?" Tate asked.

"That man seems familiar," I said.

"Him?" Tate dismissed him with a sniff. "Not the kind of guy you'd run into, I don't think. Okay, I'm gonna do a quick look around, then we'll move into the building."

He got out. I texted Katie: I'm here. I looked back at the

man who slumped against the pole. He wore faded brown corduroys and a flannel shirt, along with large, nondescript boots that seemed ill fitting. I couldn't tell if he were awake or asleep or even unconscious.

My door opened and I jumped. Tate said, "We're all set."

I climbed out of the car, and he stood close by my side as we walked briskly to the entrance. We moved into the large marble-floored lobby with Art Deco light fixtures just as Katie was emerging from a central elevator. She ran over. "Perfect timing! I just took my lunch. Ed went out to get us some food; isn't he sweet?"

"He's very sweet. This is Officer Tate. He was nice enough to escort me here today."

Tate's eyes were flicking around the room, cop style. Katie shook his hand, and he said, "And I'll be escorting you both up to your floor. The sooner we're out of this open area, the better."

It wasn't fun to think of myself as a giant target for some random marksman. Katie led the way back to the elevator, and we climbed aboard with Officer Tate, who refused to let other passengers on with us. "Take the next one," he said in a no-nonsense voice.

We stepped off the elevator on the fifth floor and into the impressive lobby of the Imperius Advertising Agency. The space was dominated by a long gray reception desk with the word "IMPERIUS" on the front in large white letters. A tasteful vase of autumnal blooms sat on one end of the counter, and a clipboard sat in the middle.

An attractive receptionist looked up at us from her desk behind the counter, where she had been typing something rapidly on her keyboard. "These your guests, Katie?"

Katie pointed at me. "Just this one. The police officer is her escort. She gets special treatment."

The receptionist, whose name tag said "Persephone," raised her elegant, sculpted eyebrows but said nothing as she stood up and moved to the counter. She pointed at the clipboard and said, "Sign in here, please. I'll get your visitor badge."

I thanked Officer Tate, who shook my hand and moved back to the elevator. When the doors closed, he was texting on his phone, and I imagined I knew who he was notifying. Persephone handed me a badge; I peeled off the backing and affixed it to my blouse.

Katie straightened her long silky ponytail and said, "Come on. We don't have to squeeze into my cubicle; I did manage to sign out a conference room." I followed her slender form down a blue-carpeted hallway, peeking now and then into offices where I saw people writing on computers and, in another room, exchanging lively dialogue while clustered around a whiteboard.

"This space I reserved is right by all the bigwigs," she said with a mischievous grin. "I think they might want to see two cute girls eat sandwiches."

I laughed and followed her into a narrow room with a gleaming walnut conference table. "Grab a chair," Katie said. "They're really comfortable."

The chair *was* comfortable, I noted. Moments after I settled in and spun myself around a few times, Eduardo appeared, looking handsome in a white button-down shirt and gray cardigan with black work pants. He sent a smoldering look to Katie, who blushed, and set a bag in front of me. "Sub sandwiches in there, and I grabbed a couple waters and Diet Cokes. I have a meeting in five, so sorry to miss you, Hana. Have a nice lunch."

"See you around," said Katie, her face still red.

His face was serious; only his eyes betrayed him. "Yeah, I think we have a conference together at three."

"Got it," Katie said.

Eduardo waved and left the room. She turned to me and said, "We're keeping our relationship quiet for now."

I nodded. "Very professional of you. But it won't take a body language expert to see what you two have. I think the temperature went up a full two degrees when he walked in here."

Katie's eyes widened. "It's so weird. Here, have a sandwich." She handed me a Styrofoam plate and a wrapped sandwich. "Before, we could pretend to be platonic. I don't know what's different, but it's different."

I shrugged, unwrapping my lunch. "It's because you both realized what you could lose, and it flipped a switch. Now you feel more desire."

She smiled at me, a secret, happy smile. "No comment."

"So what else is new at Imperius? What project are you working on?"

She rolled her eyes. "We are currently trying to find a way to make dandruff shampoo alluring."

"That *is* a hard sell. But if anyone can do it, you can." I took a big bite of the sandwich.

"Thanks for your confidence," Katie said. "I'm having a water. Do you want one?"

"I'll have a Diet Coke. Erik is getting me hooked." I took another bite. "This is really good."

"Ed knows all the good places. And somehow he gets there and back really fast. I think he runs." Her face reddened again; I couldn't imagine what she was thinking.

"You are a whole new Katie. Look what some good romancing can do."

"You should know, with your giant Thor of a boyfriend. I'll bet he knows how to *romance*."

Now I was sure it was my face that turned red. I changed the subject. "Hey, there was this guy outside your building, holding a sign that said—"

"'They are coming'?"

"Yes!"

"He's there all the time. He's the one who was hassling me, and Ed came out of nowhere and told the guy to lay off. Remember?"

I nodded.

"I know our bosses have called the cops on that guy, and they've come out and even taken him away sometimes, but he always comes back. Something special about this corner, I guess."

"But he talked to you? He warned you about something?"

"Just weird stuff. Similar to his poster there, about something coming, or someone. I assumed he was worried about aliens or monsters or something."

"Huh. Officer Tate said that we need a better plan in the city for guys like him. Guys who need help."

"Well, duh," Katie said, picking an onion off her sandwich. "I forgot to tell Ed no onions. Anyway, when you're finished, I'll give you a little tour." She watched me for a moment, then said, "Is Erik going to give you bodyguards until he catches that guy's killer?"

I nodded. "I think so. It's weird, but I also appreciate it. I feel safe. And I'm making friends," I joked.

Katie laughed, then sighed. "We have to make more time to get together like this. Otherwise we can go a month without seeing each other."

"I know! And this is fun. Your bosses don't care that you have me in here?"

She shook her head. "People have their friends and families in here all the time. They just have to stick to their lunch hour."

"Great. It's a really cool building."

"Yeah, I love it. It's one of the older office buildings in the city. Goes back to the 1920s, hence all the Art Deco stuff you can see in the lobby and the elevators. It makes me think about time travel. I prefer the stairs to the elevators, actually. They're huge, and they echo, and they go all the way down to the parking garage. One time when Ed and I were here late, we played hide-and-seek. It was *terrifying*." She sounded exhilarated, though.

"I'm really happy for you, Katie."

She looked at me out of the corner of her eye. "I know you said something to Ed. Did you call him?"

"What? No! I would never do that."

She regarded me with a sardonic expression.

I said, "He called *me*."

"Seriously? When?"

"Almost a week before the dance. He wanted to know why you broke things off with him. I said I couldn't get involved, but he was so distraught. I just told him he should try to be romantic."

She sighed. "Well, he is. He might have been faking it at first, but now he's gotten really good at it. He's a natural. I think he's finding things out about himself."

"He does seem different. I have to say, the new Eduardo is very sexy."

Her bright eyes found mine. "Right? It's like I never saw him before."

I brushed crumbs from my hands, surprised at the speed with which I'd eaten. "I'm finished. That was delicious. Where should I put this plate?"

"There's a garbage can by the door. Are you ready for the tour? Let me just clean this up."

We tidied and wiped the table. She left some of the drinks on a sideboard with a note that said "Help yourself!"

Then she led me back into the blue-carpeted hall and started showing me the place where she spent all her time—and her boundless creativity. We peered into a common area, open, with a vaulted ceiling and many desks with large computer monitors on them. People toiled away here, and it looked like a newsroom. Then we passed some glassed-in offices where important-looking people talked on phones. Katie told me about projects they were working on, about crazy time constraints, about office feuds. She pointed down one long hallway and said, "We can't go there right now. Tom's creative team is pitching to a client."

"Well, I wouldn't want to get on Tom's bad side, whoever he is," I joked.

"Let's head this way; I can show you my cubicle and the sort of hub of our agency."

She took me down an elegant gray-walled hallway and I had a thought. "Hey, how well do people at one agency know people at another ad agency? I heard someone's name the other day and that he was in advertising, and I just wondered if you know him."

"Yeah? Who's that? That's our little cafeteria, by the way," she said, pointing into a large room on her right.

"His name is Brad Derrien," I said.

She turned to me, laughing. "Ha ha. Good one."

"What is? I'm serious. Have you ever met Brad Derrien?"

She jogged down the hall and spun around to face me. "Are you for real?"

I stared at her blankly. And then the misery came, rushing up from somewhere below my feet and flowing into my body. I opened my mouth to try to express what I was feeling, but Katie was laughing.

"Brad is one of our VPs. Take about ten steps"—she did so—"and you're in front of his office!" I held out my hand to stop her, but she was already knocking on his door. "Brad, do you have a second? I wanted you to meet my friend Hana."

She looked at me expectantly, and I dragged my feet forward. They felt thick and waterlogged; somehow Katie didn't seem to notice the dread that hung around me. I reached the door and looked inside at the man who had stood up behind his desk, and I made eye contact with the man from Will Kodaly's painting.

The man from my parking lot.

The man who had probably shot me.

It felt like a bullet even now, an actual impact into my soft middle, and I fell against the doorway.

"Oops, Hana, did you trip?" Katie said, helping me stand upright.

"Yes," I croaked.

I realized the truth then, that I had been right: Kodaly died because a man couldn't bear to give up on Sofia, but it wasn't Sofia's boyfriend, Zane, who had wanted poor Will dead—it was the married man who was still in love with Sofia.

"How nice to meet you," said Brad Derrien, showing his teeth. I did not recognize him as the man who had once visited Ms. Derrien at our high school. He was tall and brown haired, with a craggy face and an expensive-looking suit. Everything about him felt predatory. In that instant of connection, though, when we locked eyes and understood the truth about each other, I realized that he was not just a danger to me, but to Katie, and that I had to pretend for her sake until I could run away.

"You, too," I said. "You have a nice agency here." I could barely hear what I was saying because of the ringing in my ears.

"Yes, we're proud of it." His eyes flicked to Katie. "Do you need to get back to work? I could entertain Hana for you—tell her some war stories."

Katie looked surprised. "No, it's cool. I still have twenty minutes of lunch and I want to show her my cubicle."

"Well, I won't keep you then," he said. "Nice meeting you, Hana." He was walking toward his desk, going for a drawer.

"Yes," I managed, and I followed Katie down the hall.

"Listen," I told her. "I just got a text from Erik. He wants me to meet him downstairs right away. He found something out about the case and I have to go."

She stared, uncomprehending. "What? When did you even check your phone?"

"I'm so sorry, but I have to run," I said. "Go back to your office and call Erik."

"What? I thought you just said—" She stopped because I was running away from her, as fast as I could. "Hana?" she said, sounding afraid.

I kept going. I couldn't have stopped if I wanted to. Fight or flight had kicked in, and my instinct was flight. I saw the elevator, but I remembered what Katie had said about the stairs: they went all the way down to the basement garage. I could go there and ask the valet to call me a car, or I could stay in the shadows until I was able to slip undetected onto Superior Street, where cabs were readily available. At the time, this seemed like the best plan. Derrien had been desperate enough to show up at my apartment; that meant he was desperate enough to hurt someone if he had to. I didn't want him near people that he might perceive as witnesses.

I flew down the stairs, wide and well lit, and when I had almost reached the first level I heard the door slam at the top of the stairs and heavy footfalls running down.

The poor lost soul in front of the building had been right, as had my subconscious.

He was coming.

I would face the *sárkány* after all.

∽

As my feet ran, barely touching the concrete stairs, I heard Katie's words in my head: "We played hide-and-seek. It was terrifying."

Terror. I was terrified, and my brain wasn't forming logical connections.

I reached the bottom and faced a gray door that said "Garage." I pushed on this and did a quick survey of the dim, open area on the other side. I had three choices: dart into the line of cars and use them as cover as I made my way to the garage entrance and eventually the street; make a run for the rickety-looking elevator across the garage and to my right, where I could ride back up into the building; or find a hiding place, text Erik, and wait for help.

I opted for the third one. Derrien's steps were growing louder, pounding, pounding down the stairs as he desperately sought to silence me. Didn't he realize it was all over? That even if I disappeared or died, Katie would tell the police that I had been here (and Erik knew anyway), so what really would he accomplish by hurting me?

I dove to my left, where a large pillar sat in front of a row of cars. Distantly, I could see sunlight, and motion, as the gray shapes of cars went back and forth outside the open garage door. I stood behind the pillar and scanned the parked cars; one of them was a giant square thing, black and ugly, but beautiful to me now because it would provide shelter and a vantage point from which to spy. I ran on silent feet to this vehicle, flying around to the driver's side window. I crouched there but was able to peer through the glass at Brad Derrien, who burst out of the stairway door like a bull, his face sweating and afraid.

To my relief, he went first to the elevator, in the direction opposite me. I took my phone from my pocket and turned it on. I attempted to sign in with my digital fingerprint and saw the message "No Signal."

A scream threatened to escape, to explode out of me in a wave of fear and tension. I bit my lip and forced a deep breath. Where was everyone? Why was no one coming or going? All I needed was a distraction.

He had turned and was coming back. His eyes scanned the cars, methodical, disturbing. "Hana," he said in a low but audible voice. "Come out, for goodness' sake. I just want to talk to you."

I crouched lower, wondering what I would do when he reached my row.

Then, to my relief, he stopped walking. His head swiveled around; he seemed to be assessing his options, as I had done. "I know that you know things, okay? I just want to ask you some questions. I'm fascinated by psychic phenomena. If you thought it was anything else, you're way off track. Just come out. We'll go back up to my office and chat. I can't have you leaving here thinking that I'm chasing you!" He attempted a laugh—a paltry, ugly sound. The guilty can't remember joy; my grandmother had told me that once.

Why did he think I would believe anything he said when he had chased me down the stairs, sweating with the effort of it? Had he hurt Katie before he left? She must have known, must have seen something in his face. Had I deserted my friend when I should have stayed to protect her? Why, why did he even think he could get away with this?

In a flash I understood that guilt has its own logic, and that fear of detection will make a person do stupid things. Perhaps because he was a murderer he feared the idea of a psychic person most of all, because that person could look down (he might think) into his dark, dark intentions.

Dark Intentions. Kodaly had known, had seen them in this man. Had he seen it consciously? Or had Derrien's face in that painting been only an unconsciously derived resemblance?

I pressed my hands into the cold metal of the car's side panel. Soon I would have to run.

"Hana," he said again, his voice less friendly this time. "Come out."

I hesitated, and then froze: he was lowering himself to the ground. He was going to lie down and look for my feet. I would be exposed.

I turned and ran silently, hunching low, trying to stay out of his sightline. I made it to another huge white pillar and dove behind it. The open garage door was closer now, but still too far to make a run for it. "Hana," he said. My name became something horrible on his tongue. "Come out, hon. I'm going to find you either way. You can't make it out of here without me seeing you; you haven't had enough time."

The pillar was cold against my back; I stood, agonized by indecision.

Brad Derrien's voice said, "And besides . . . I think I know where you are." He laughed.

He had either seen me or realized that I was in the only place not visible to him.

Terror is debilitating. I could only summon random

snatches of images, no concrete plan. I saw Erik Wolf's green eyes, regretful and sad. I saw my brother and Margie, holding hands. I saw Katie's brown silky ponytail and Eduardo's crimson suit. I saw my grandmother's lined face, and then I saw her as a four-year-old girl, kissing a teddy bear.

And her mother, summoning up answers from her own mind.

Natalia. What had she said about life? She had told it to the old policeman, who had told Henrik Sipos.

"The mind is a forest with many paths . . . when you are lost, one will be illuminated." Something like that.

I closed my eyes. Brad Derrien had gotten to his feet, and his footfalls came closer, step by step, as he peered between rows.

I kept my eyes closed and focused on my inner vision. The inner eye. I saw a forest full of trees, autumnal, beautiful. A wind chasing leaves around and three dirt paths, all awaiting me. Time slowed now: something opened in me, and each path became an idea, swirling leaves into a visible word. One said "Taxi." Another said "Phone." And a third, in a great, busy swirl of color, said "Ulveflokk." This one was far brighter than the others, bright even through my closed eyes.

My lids flew open. Ulveflokk. What had Katie told me, at Kodaly's garage sale? "It's right down the street from me." But which direction? Would I be better off running to Runa and Thyra than trying to hail a cab in front of the building and potentially having Brad Derrien shoot me down or swoop in and carry me back into the garage?

People might intervene, or they might not. I had seen the stories about poor victims who cried for help and got no response, even when people were near. Onlookers tended to assume others would take an active role, and they themselves did not. Or sometimes they misunderstood the situation . . .

"Hana," Derrien said. He was closer, and his voice was almost seductive now. He was getting excited by the hunt.

My stomach turned; I tasted bile.

A car rattled over the speed bump under the garage entrance. An attendant moseyed out of a glass box to say something through the person's window. To shout it, actually. "That's not the right ticket! Are you sure you have the right garage? I think this is for one on Clark. Did you try the one on Clark?"

The car's motor was loud, and the attendant was yelling over this. My footsteps would not be heard.

I ran.

Whether he saw me or not, I cannot say. I thought I heard a yell behind me, something surprised or outraged. I had never run so fast in my life, nor did I know that I could fly that way, barely touching the ground, hearing only my own blood pounding, pounding with the rhythm of my feet.

A burst of light and air, and I was on the sidewalk. I heard yelling behind me; was he calling to me or to the attendant?

A scan of the street: I saw no cabs, and I had no idea which way to run. "Natalia, help me," I yelled into the city noise; it sounded like a sob.

My feet turned and ran right. To this day I don't remember making a conscious decision; I simply ran, my eyes scanning buildings, storefronts, signs. I knew I had found Ulveflokk before I saw the word, because of their symbol: four wolves howling at a full moon.

The power of advertising, Katie would tell me later.

I dove through the doors, and some women at the front racks looked at me with stunned expressions. I tried to say something to them, but my throat was so dry I couldn't even croak. A young couple walked past, clutching matching sweaters. They didn't notice me at all.

I scanned the store. A young man sat behind the checkout counter, staring at his phone. Behind him and to the left was a sign that said "Employees Only." I ran toward it, bumping gracelessly into racks and displays. I vaguely registered some sort of music playing, flutes and fiddles and some sort of folksy chant over the top.

The doorway loomed in front of me; I stole a glance over my shoulder at the sidewalk outside. I didn't see him . . . had he not followed me? Was I safe?

I turned back and burst through the door. Runa and Thyra were both there, on either side of a long clothing rack, flicking expertly through clothes. They looked up in twin surprise. "Hana?" Thyra said.

Runa was two seconds more alert. She threw down the dress in her hand and moved to me, lithe as a cat. "What is it?"

"He's chasing me," I managed. I pointed to my throat. Thyra walked forward with a water bottle, and I drank. Then I said, "Killer. Kodaly's killer."

"Come and sit down," Runa said. "I'll call Erik."

She had her phone out; she poked it, and then it was at her ear. "Erik," she said, and Brad Derrien burst through the door, shutting it behind him.

He was out of breath, too, and sweating. He took out a gun, obscene and black, and pointed it at us.

"Hello, ladies," he said with a terrible smile.

Chapter 19

TO THE WOLVES

He pointed at Runa. "I'll have to ask you to give me that phone."

She did so. Her hand wasn't shaking, and her face was expressionless. "This is your man, Hana?"

"Yes. He killed William Kodaly."

"Wrong," said Brad Derrien. He motioned for Thyra's phone and mine, and we gave them to him. "I did not kill him. I have an alibi."

"Then why are you here? Why did you come to my apartment?" The proximity of others had made me bold.

His eyes widened. "You knew about that, huh? Like I said, I just want to talk to you."

"Then put the gun down," Thyra said.

Derrien shrugged. "Can't do that. Where does that door there go?"

"To the alley," Thyra said. "Why don't you head out there, and we won't chase you?"

He laughed. "Chase me? I'm the one with the gun, lady. If anyone's going to run, it will be you."

"I thought you said you only wanted to talk," I said. I was trembling, half with fear and half with anger. I was worried about the anger, and what it might make me do. I was on the verge of some terrible explosion.

Runa took a step backward, her hands in the air. "Okay, so let's talk. What do you want to talk about?" she said. Her blue eyes were cold and trained on him.

He pointed. "We should go in the alley. I don't want anyone to hear us."

Thyra did not like this; I could tell she was thinking through her options. "The alley is not contained. All sorts of people go up and down. You'll want to stay here until you've said your piece."

Derrien scowled. He obviously wanted us to act more afraid than we were acting. The funny thing was that I could feel the fear in the room, almost taste it, and it came from all four of us. But Runa and Thyra looked as calm as statues.

Derrien pointed at me. "Here's what you need to know. I didn't kill Kodaly. Someone else did that."

My mouth hung open. "Why in the world do you want me to know that?"

"Because I know you suspect me!"

"How would you know that? You don't know me. You've never met me. Maybe you chatted with Cassandra Stone and heard about my family? Heard the rumor that we have abilities? And then you decided to shoot at me while I was at the autumn ball? That you weren't out of town at all, the way you told Amber?"

His face darkened. "I didn't do that." He was lying though; his eyes told me that.

"The only reason you would have found me threatening

is that you feared I would know the truth. Know it, through some other means than the police have, and this possibility made you nervous. Is that pretty close? Because otherwise I can't explain why you and I are standing here now." My hands were on my hips; I leaned forward with aggression born of adrenaline. Runa caught my eye and shook her head. She wanted me to tone it down.

I took a step back and let my hands fall to my sides.

Derrien said, "How about if you just shut up for a minute?"

We all stared at him, a trio of coldness that was lowering the temperature in the room.

He wiped his forehead with the hand that wasn't holding the gun. "Let me think."

Runa and Thyra exchanged a glance; I didn't know what it meant, but I felt a certain power in them. It thrilled me—but this, too, might have been born of adrenaline.

"I know why you killed him," I said. "Because you loved Sofia, and she told you that she was going to go back to him. That she loved him. And he suspected you; he put your face on the man in his *Dark Intentions* painting. A painting I'm guessing you stole because you feared people would recognize you."

Derrien's brows rose, and then he got defensive. "Sofia was not in love with him. She loves me," he said.

"Then why kill him?" I asked.

"Because—I didn't kill him!" Derrien shouted.

Someone knocked at the door. "Ms. Wolf, is everything all right back there?"

Derrien lifted his gun and pointed it directly at me.

Runa said, "Everything's fine, thanks," in a voice both calm and dismissive. The person outside said, "Okay, let me know if you need anything."

"Thanks, Finola," Runa said, her eyes on Derrien's gun.

I had the sense that the distractions were helping. Derrien was confused, afraid, wondering about his next move. The dialogue was keeping him from working it out.

"Why did you put the tracker on the wolf? And why did you tell Will Kodaly that Sofia gave it to him?"

His eyes widened, but he tried to lie. "What makes you think there was a—?"

"The police found the tracker on the very first day. They know that someone used it to find Kodaly's house and kill him. And now it's clear that if you wanted Sofia to take you back, you'd have to produce an alibi. She would hate you if she knew you killed her lover. So you hired someone to do your dirty work, right?"

Panic flitted through his eyes. "Is that just *your* theory?" he asked.

"No. The police know all this. They also know that I came to Imperius today. I arrived with a police escort because you made so many clumsy attempts to kill me."

"This is ridiculous," he said. His sweat was visible now. "We need to clear all this up. I didn't kill Kodaly, but I think I know who did."

"I do, too. The man you gave the tracker to. The man you told to drive out to Kodaly's house and kill him. What I can't imagine is who would possibly—" A horrible image appeared in my brain. "Oh no," I said. "You didn't."

Derrien winced slightly as my eyes locked on his.

"You used that poor man in front of Imperius. The paranoid man who fears that some unknown predator is coming. You fed his fears and told him to kill Kodaly."

Runa and Thyra looked indignant. "Chester? The man at the light pole?"

I nodded, watching Derrien's face. "You had the means and the opportunity. All the police have to do is find out where you bought the surveillance equipment and the other things will fall into place. And of course they'll know that you showed up here with a gun and threatened three women."

Derrien's eyes were dangerous now—the eyes of a cornered animal. "I'm tired of listening to all of you. You think you're better than me?"

"Yes," Thyra said. "And smarter, too."

Derrien aimed his gun at her. "How smart do you feel now?" he asked. With a mighty lunge, Runa heaved the clothing rack at Derrien; it hit him in his midsection just as the gun fired. I dove to the ground.

Someone screamed: was it him? Was it one of the twins? Had it been me? My heartbeat thudded in my ears and drowned out most of what was happening. I couldn't see anyone on my side of the clothing rack. I heard a punch, another scream, more punches.

"No!" wailed Runa's voice.

Horrified, I struggled to get up. What had I done? I had led him here. I had put their lives in danger—Thyra's and Runa's and Runa's baby! With a sob I inched forward, moving through clothing that lay on the floor. Someone was pounding on the door outside. "Ms. Wolf? Ms. Wolf? What's happening?"

"The police will be here soon!" Runa cried. As if in answer, sirens sounded distantly.

I peered around the corner and saw Brad Derrien curled into a fetal position on the floor; Thyra stood above him, her face bloody and the skin around her eye growing red. She held his gun in her hand.

Runa stood beside her, looking perfectly fine. I pointed at her with a shaking finger. "You cried out! You said, 'No!'"

Runa smoothed her blonde hair. This time her hands were shaking. "Because he tore my blouse. It's real silk."

My sigh of relief seemed to last for a long time.

I said, "Thank you. Both of you."

They smiled at me.

By the time the Chicago police arrived, the twins had already tied Derrien's hands with some packing tape, and when Erik Wolf and Greg Benson burst in ten minutes later, my blonde saviors were already holding different outfits against me, deciding what I should wear for the photo shoot. "You thought you got out of it, Hana, but you didn't," Thyra said, grinning like a Viking after battle, her gory eye turning redder by the minute.

"It's the least I can do," I said. "I'll pose in the *nude* if you want me to."

Runa considered this. "It might be good—maybe riding that fake reindeer we used last year. Maybe a tastefully placed Ulveflokk sign."

Erik had finished talking to the other police officers by then and had moved to my side, holding me against him. My trembling had almost ceased. He said, "Maybe not, Runa."

Her eyes were defiant. "It's Hana's decision! If she wants to be nude for a photo shoot, she can."

"I *don't* want to," I said. "I was using hyperbole."

Erik was studying his sisters. "Are you guys okay?"

"Yes," Thyra said, laughing a bit too much.

"No," Runa said, winding a Nordic-patterned scarf around my neck, and she began to cry.

❧

Derrien was led away moments later. I hugged both of the women who had saved me, clinging to them more than they probably wanted. Then Andy appeared, his face pale. "What the heck is going on?" he asked.

Erik said, "Everyone's fine. But you should take Runa home."

He did. To my surprise, someone named Rolf also appeared, a big shaggy-looking man with long blond hair and an unshaven look. He examined Thyra's eye and her cheekbone; Erik murmured that he was her boyfriend, and a doctor. My mouth hung open in surprise, and Thyra winked at me, then said, "Ow."

Rolf hustled her out of the room, murmuring about X-rays.

Then somehow, I was there alone with Erik Wolf, amid a jumble of clothes and a stack of Ulveflokk packing boxes, on which four wolves howled at a lonely moon.

"You scared me," he said. "All of you. Katie called, and then Runa called, and I heard a man yelling in the background. I cannot tell you, Hana—"

"I know just how afraid you were. I felt the same when I was flying down the stairs of Imperius, terrified that any minute he would catch me. Then I was playing hide-and-seek in the parking garage."

"Oh God. Oh, Hana!" He squeezed me against him. "We were looking at Derrien already; Talman didn't pan out. I had just talked to Sofia, asking her if she'd mentioned to anyone that she planned to go back to Kodaly. There was just a short list of people, and that's when Greg and I knew. A minute later we got Katie's call."

"It was scary. But I knew to come here, that it was my best bet. Your sisters were amazing. They never looked scared, even though I knew they were."

"They've always been brave. I'm proud of them, and I'm proud of you, Hana."

"For what? Running?"

"No. For figuring this all out. And facing down a madman."

I shook my head, trying to clear the cobwebs. "How am

I going to tell my family about this? How am I going to tell my grandma that a man held a gun in my face?"

Erik looked down at me with the hint of a smile. "And how are you going to tell her that when you were in danger you ran to the wolves?"

"Oh boy," I said.

"Maybe don't tell her that part," Erik said.

Chapter 20

....

THE WOLVES TO COME

The story came out over the next several days. I got information from Erik, from television news; from Sofia, who called me in tears; from my grandmother, who was on the Hungarian grapevine; and from stories printed in the Riverwood press. Derrien was in jail; Chester, the man he had manipulated into committing murder, had been declared unfit for trial and was being cared for in a psychiatric facility. Wolf and Benton had found evidence of Brad's purchase of the surveillance equipment, along with e-mails he had written to Sofia, begging her to take him back. They had matched the footprint outside the window at the Riverwood Pavilion to Brad Derrien's shoe in Derrien's basement, and they had found the gun used to kill Kodaly and the one used in an attempt to kill me.

Dark Intentions, Sofia told me, had been painted by Kodaly after they had an argument about her ex-lovers. He said that she had terrible taste in men, and that Derrien in particular was disturbing. She dismissed him, saying that jealousy was not flattering. "He told me in just those words: 'The man has dark intentions.' But I wouldn't listen to him," she said, wiping at tears. "He tried to warn me again, with the painting. But Brad was back with Amber, and I assured William that everything was fine."

"But, Sofia," I said, "how did Will *know* that Brad had this dark side?"

Sofia sniffled in my ear. "He told me that he had psychic ability. That it informed his art, lifted it to a higher level. I'm afraid I sniffed at that, too. I called him silly and vain. Now of course I know it's true."

❦

"He thought he was *psychic*," I said to Erik that night as we ate in my apartment. "And that explains so much! When I met him, he shook my hand, and there was this burst of light—just for a second—and he looked at me like he knew me. He said my family fascinated him."

"Wow," Erik said.

"And when we were talking about my grandmother, he asked if I had anything in common with her besides my brown eyes. He wanted to know if I was psychic, too. He wanted to find—his own kind, I guess."

"And he did," Erik assured me.

"Yeah. I mean, the fact that he had my family investigated . . . he really wanted to know something, but what? If he really had a psychic ability? Or how his life would turn out if he did?"

"Didn't you say he asked Sipos if Natalia was happy?"

"Yes. Wow. Did he just want to know whether his gift was a positive in his life? Did it torment him in some way?"

"It was probably a two-sided coin." He reached out to touch my hand. "Isn't it?"

I nodded. "It is. But look at what it did for his art! Falken told me that since the press has made a big deal of Kodaly's paintings, the demand for them has gone up. One of them just earned five hundred thousand at auction, and the prices will go up from there."

Erik's green eyes were solemn. "Would you sell either of your Kodaly paintings to make half a million dollars?"

I shook my head. "No. It would be like selling a holy relic. I can feel his power, his life, on those canvases. And they're beautiful. You know how I feel about beautiful things."

"I do. I notice you put your wolf on display."

I had done so, the night before. My bedroom held an amazing shelf, made by my father and my grandparents. It held my favorite books and my growing collection of porcelain. Erik had removed the tracker from Kodaly's ill-fated wolf, but I chose to see the porcelain figure for what it was—a thing of beauty, a work of art, and a gift that Kodaly had given me because he saw that it made me happy. In this way, I could look at it and not feel sad or ashamed. It had lost its terrible stigma.

"Yeah. It looks good by that gold teacup."

He smiled into his coffee cup. "I'll never have to worry about what to buy you on special occasions. I have you figured out."

"Not entirely, Detective Wolf. You'll still need some skills to solve my mysteries."

His gaze moved upward and met mine. "Then I'd better start investigating."

❧

Right before Thanksgiving, my mother and grandmother hosted a tea event called Friends of Kodaly, along with many of Kodaly's old friends and old flames. Sofia came alone, her eyes more sad than ever. Amber Derrien came, too, accompanied by the man she had met at the dance. His obvious devotion seemed to be helping her deal with the horror of knowing that her husband had killed Kodaly.

Falken had allowed us to temporarily display some of Kodaly's art in the tea house, and people milled around looking at canvas after canvas, invigorated by the man's talent.

I rushed between tables, filling cups with tea and replenishing sandwiches and cakes. François had outdone himself. I snuck into the back room to tell him so, and I found him standing irresolute, his face flushed.

"François? Are you all right?"

He looked at me, his eyes blurry with feeling. "I have looked at these paintings, all of them. This man was a genius. This man's gift—I cannot explain it. It is sublime. I want to own one of those paintings, Hana. The man on the mountain, did you see it?"

I had—it was one that had been in Kodaly's basement and offered at twenty-five dollars. "Yes. It's beautiful." The painting was deceptively simple: a man stood at the top of a mountain and lifted his face to view the open sky. Kodaly's gift for creating light, however, made it a subtly layered piece, the light graduating from dark shadows up to almost blinding sun and pure white clouds. It was a painting of triumphant freedom.

"I want to look at it every day," he whispered. "It speaks to me. It shouts to me!" His eyes were miserable now. "But this man's art sells now for hundreds of thousands. That's what they tell me."

Who could possibly appreciate Kodaly's art more than this young man who was almost in tears over a painting's beauty?

"Let me talk to Falken," I said. "See what I can do."

François shrugged. "Yes. Ask him if I can pay a dollar a year for five hundred thousand years."

I patted his shoulder and went back out, forgetting the compliment I had gone in to give. I found Falken in conversation with some women in one corner. I waited until he finished, then said, "You know who's the most moved by this art today? My French chef. You know Francois, right?"

"Yes. Good for him," Falken said with his gentle smile.

"There's a painting he really wants, Falken. I'd like to give him the chance to buy it. Can you do that for me?"

He shrugged. "You recall what the man was asking, back at his garage sale. No one else here needs to know that, but I suppose we can offer your François the original price. The art gallery in town is going to make me an offer on any that you don't want to buy. And they'll provide certificates of authenticity for all of the art that came out of his house."

"Beautiful. François wants the one called *Morning Sun*. Take it back to him, before someone else claims to want it."

"Will do." He touched my shoulder, then loped over to one of the easels that held Kodaly's paintings. He took down the amazing man-on-the-mountain painting, with its backdrop of light and sky, and he moved into the kitchen. I followed at a distance and peered into the room just in time to see François, dignified but tearful, pulling Falken into a heartfelt embrace.

⁓

After the food and tea had been served, my grandmother sat at a table with Henrik Sipos and an old woman I didn't recognize. The three of them talked for a long time. They laughed often, and at one point I saw my grandmother wipe away some tears. I knew, without going closer, that they were talking about her mother. No matter how many years go by, the loss of a mother is a wound that never quite heals.

At one point, Henrik caught my eye and indicated with a gentle wave that I should join them. I did so, smiling at him and my grandmother. "Hello, Hana. Thank you for hosting this nice event. I am glad to be able to honor my friend William," Henrik said in his formal way.

"Of course. We wanted to honor him, too."

He gestured to the old woman, whose white hair was bright as a halo. "I would like to introduce my mother, Stefania Sipos."

My eyes wide with surprise, I moved swiftly to her and took her hands in mine. "Mrs. Sipos, it's so lovely to meet you."

Her voice was flute-like and quiet but firm. "You look so much like her. So much like the woman who saved my life. Let me kiss your cheek."

I bent down and received her soft kiss, then kissed her cheek in return.

Henrik beamed. "Your grandmother and my mother and I have many happy memories of Békéscsaba. We have built a friendship on these shared remembrances."

"That's wonderful. You're always welcome here at the tea house," I said.

He acknowledged this with a bow of his head. "And now I have a surprise. Do you remember, I promised that I would bring you something?"

"I can't recall," I said.

"I told you I had pictures of Natalia when she was young and still living in Békéscsaba. I have brought one today, to show to you and your family. In fact, I have made a copy, so this one is for you to keep."

He reached into a little briefcase that sat on the floor by

his chair and pulled out an envelope. "Juliana, this is your mother. The photo was taken in 1964."

My grandmother opened the envelope and smiled. "I recall," she said. "I recall." She handed the picture to me.

There was Natalia, in a black-and-white photograph that didn't reveal the color of her hair, and yet I knew it was very much like mine. She was not looking at the camera, but smiling at something off to the side—perhaps her daughter—and folding her arms casually against herself.

She looked like me. I opened my mouth, then shut it. There was nothing to say.

"You keep it, Haniska. Put it in a frame on your pretty shelf," my grandmother said.

"Thank you, Grandma. And thank you, Henrik." I lunged forward and kissed his cheek. He turned slightly red and chuckled.

"Of course, of course. For your family, anything."

Stefania smiled at him proudly. Time did not change some things: Henrik was still her baby.

~

Runa and Andy stopped by at the end of the event. Runa pulled me aside and said, "I was going to ask your grandma—did she think maybe that madman with his gun was the danger she had foreseen for my baby? But I'm afraid to ask. I hope that's what it was. I hope that she's fine now."

"Me, too, Runa. What did the doctor say?"

"Things look good so far. I'm about two months along. Andy's already picking names." She smiled at her boyfriend, who was chatting with Domo.

"Where's Thyra today?"

"She's at the store. She has some flyers from your photo

shoot. Wait until you see them. Erik will be fighting off the men."

"I doubt that."

I pointed at my grandmother. "Juliana is hosting a big Hungarian Thanksgiving. She wants you Wolf girls to come, and Andy and whoever Thyra brings. Can you attend?"

She pursed her lips. "My mom does a traditional thing, too. You'll probably be invited to that. So we might have to pick two different days."

"Grandma will be okay with that. As long as she gets to ply you with Hungarian food."

Runa smiled. "I'm looking forward to it."

Erik approached, and Runa waved. "Talk to you later, Hana."

Erik slid an arm around me. "Was it something I said?"

"She wants to go be with Andy. They're really excited."

"Yeah." He kissed my hair. "My sisters like you. That is a rarity, I assure you. They tend not to like anyone. And weirdly enough, they like you even more since you almost got them killed."

"Don't remind me."

Now he was playing with my hair, weighing it in his hands. "Come out in the lobby for a minute."

"Okay." I followed him out of the loud dining hall and into the quiet of the foyer.

He said, "Your grandma took me to the back room about an hour ago."

"Oh? To force-feed you Pálinka?"

"No—she read my tea leaves."

"Oh my God. What did she tell you?"

He smiled. "She said I am a shepherd, and that many other wolves were coming, but that I am strong and resolute and can keep the wolves at bay."

"But *you* are a wolf. That's been her fear all along."

"She has resolved that by saying that I am a shepherd named Wolf rather than a wolf itself. And that this is how I am able to catch wolves—by posing as one."

"Wow."

"She has a complex mind."

"In a crazy sort of way."

"I like your grandmother, and your great-grandmother, and your mom and dad and brother."

"And do you like me?"

"Haniska," Erik Wolf said, lowering his lips to mine, "you have no idea."

But I had a pretty good idea. And the more he kissed me, the more sure I was.

I relaxed into his arms, and into the gentle green-gold light that shimmered around us.

Acknowledgments

···

Thank you to all who read *Death in a Budapest Butterfly*, especially my new Hungarian friends Violet Markioly Barreto, Caroline Petercsák Booth, and April Grainey. Thanks also to book supporter Jill Wicklein and readers Elizabeth Laumas, Kate Kalas, Melanie Lievre Lorenscheit, Stephanie Ludwig, Taylor R. Williams, Elizabeth Holt Glazer, Holly Pirtle, Julie Carithers Overstreet, Kavita Nauth, Nicole Garafolo, Bonnie Shadrake, Lynell Ahlstrom, and Deb Murphy for their support of the Hungarian series. *Köszönöm!*

Big thanks to book launch supporters and friends Mark Andersen and Ann Marie Andersen; David Chaudoir; the entire Tan family—Jerica, Shira, Kian, Lit-Jen and Lara Pullen; Catherine Lawry, Cynthia Quam, Mia Manansala, Kimberly Cornwell, Michael Black, Alli Bax, Lori McGreal, Molly Klowden, Diane Cummings, Patti Williams, Rachel Meiner, Mary Beth Lavezzorio, Pam Costello, Susie Bedell, Terri Hanrahan; my dear neighbors Lisa and Burt Blanchard, and my sisters Linda Rohaly and Claudia Rohaly.

Also to the delightful Margaret Jane Bedell, Haddie Bedell, Quinley Costello, and Olive Costello. I am always thrilled to see young readers who love books.

Thanks to reading group friends Nubia Durazo, Midge Cogan, Bonnie Shadrake, Lynell Ahlstrom, and Linda Henson, and to the proprietors of Centuries and Sleuths, Augie and Tracy Aleksy.

To my father, William, for his love and support, and his fascinating memories.

A big and long-overdue thank-you to Jim Goulding, who has been supportive of my writing efforts from Day One!

Thanks as always to Michelle Vega and Kim Lionetti, for your gracious help and wisdom over many years.

Thank you to both Joe Rohaly my grandfather, and Joe Rohaly my nephew, for letting me borrow their lovely name for this story.

Thank you to Jeff Buckley, who helps me with every book event without complaining.

From Hana's Recipe Box

....

HANA'S HALUSKA
(pronounced HOLL-ooshka)

This is a side dish that takes about 40 minutes to prepare and serves 4–6.

    1 medium white onion
    1 medium head of cabbage
    1 half stick of butter
    1 tsp salt
    ½ tsp pepper
    1 box or bag of egg noodles (16 oz)
    1 pint of sour cream

Dice onion and chop cabbage; sauté both in butter until tender. Add salt and pepper. Simmer for about fifteen minutes.

Cook and drain egg noodles; add them to the softened onion and cabbage.

Add more salt to taste. Fold in some sour cream just before serving. Reserve some sour cream and serve on the side with the finished dish.

Juliana's Palacsinta
(pronounced pahla-cheenta)

You can fill these delicious crepes with jam or with the cheese filling described below.

2 cups flour
1 tsp salt
1 tsp sugar
4 eggs
2 cups milk
Butter as needed
Powdered sugar

Heat oven to 350. Mix the flour, salt, and sugar. Beat eggs and mix in milk. Gradually add to the dry flour mixture until you have a thin pancake batter. Melt butter in a pan and pour a thin layer of the batter mixture and brown on both sides. This will take less than a minute.

Put the thin pancake on a plate and add your chosen filling. Roll up and place in a buttered baking dish. Repeat until the batter is finished. Sprinkle powdered sugar on the rolled crepes. Bake 10-12 minutes. Serve warm; top with sour cream, fresh strawberries, or strawberry jam. (Apricot jam is also a popular choice.)

Cheese filling

> 1 lb dry curd (Dry cottage cheese—sometimes this is
>   hard to find at the grocery store, but you can find it
>   if you search!)
> 1 egg
> ½ cup sugar
> Vanilla to taste

Mix all of the ingredients, adding sugar and vanilla to the
desired level of sweetness. Add to the recipe as indicated
above.

Ready to find
your next great read?

Let us help.

Visit prh.com/nextread